THE CHUPACABRA CATASTROPHE

A CHARLIE RHODES COZY MYSTERY BOOK TWO

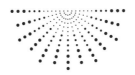

AMANDA M. LEE

WINCHESTERSHAW PUBLICATIONS

ONE

"There has to be something."

I looked Millie Watson in the eye and folded my arms over my chest, resolute. Millie, who looked like a fifty-five-year-old extra for an off-Broadway showing of *Grease* – pink satin coat and liquid eyeliner included – clearly didn't find my enthusiasm endearing.

"Charlie, has anyone ever told you that you're annoying?" Millie wasn't one to mince words and she opted to refrain from pulling verbal punches here.

"If you think you're the first one to say something like that to me, you're not." I refused to back down. She didn't so much hurt my feelings as pique my interest. Millie was one of the few people at The Legacy Foundation – that's where I drew my paycheck while looking for the fantastical – who always seemed excited to see me. Even now, when I knew Millie had a hangover and would probably rather be napping in the break room, I believed she would hear me out before completely dismissing me.

That's right, Charlotte "Charlie" Rhodes (that's me, in case you're wondering), had a few questions for one of the more seasoned members of the group. Millie just happened to be handy when I decided to ask them.

"You have to know something, Millie," I wheedled, adopting a whiny voice that got me more than a few random toys when I was younger and working my father. "I'm dying here."

"You are far from dying." Millie flicked me between the eyebrows, causing me to rear back and glower. "Do you want to know what your problem is, Charlie?"

This was so not how I saw this conversation going. I was used to whining my way to answers, occasionally blundering my way to them or even outright annoying someone until they blurted out what I wanted to hear. Millie wasn't like most people, though, and she refused to simply roll over and give me what I wanted simply because I asked for it.

"I really don't want to know what you think my problem is." I lowered my gaze to the floor and rubbed the back of my neck. It was time to regroup and approach Millie from a different direction. I was determined to get answers, but Millie was equally determined to hold me off. I wasn't in the mood to play that game.

"Your problem is that you have no patience," Millie said, barreling forward. "I get it, girl. You're young and you have so much energy you think it might burst right out of your chest – kind of like the creature in that movie *Alien*. It's kind of cute sometimes. It's not always cute, though. You need to remember that."

"What's not always cute?" Jack Hanson, the Legacy Foundation's head of security, meandered over to where we sat and flopped in a chair as he stared at some contraption in his hand.

"What's that?" I switched my attention to Jack, which wasn't hard because he's all lean muscles, chiseled cheekbones and shoulder-length hair that makes him look like a male model rather than a security chief. Before you get too excited about my hormones going out of whack, he's also dismissive and often treats me like a child. Quite frankly, that eradicates all the other stuff. No, really it does.

Jack arched an eyebrow as he slid a cool look in my direction. I'd been with the Legacy Foundation for only a little more than a month, but I had a suspicion that it felt longer to him. "What is what?"

"That thing in your hand."

"This is something I'm working on for a new radio device Chris is convinced would've helped us on the last job," Jack replied, referring to our boss, Chris Biggs. He was the nephew of the company owner Myron Biggs (who also happened to be Millie's ex-husband, but that's a long story I haven't quite heard all the details on yet). Chris was enthusiastic, handsome and never talked down to me. He also spends all his time in the lab mooning over one of the other scientists, Hannah Silver, so I very rarely saw him.

"Are we talking about the lake monster dinosaur here?" Millie asked, sipping her coffee. Her hair, which was shot through with silver, didn't look to have been washed today. That was nothing new. Millie was known to frequent biker bars when we were close to home – no joke – and sometimes she rolled from whatever dive she spent the night entertaining herself in right to work. It clearly drove her ex-husband crazy, which I was pretty sure was the point of the little exercise.

"That would be the one." Jack, his expression flat, used a small screwdriver to work on his toy. He was a gadget guy, which gave him something to do with his hands, and he preferred focusing on work rather than people. It was an annoying trait. In fact, I'd decided everything about Jack was outright annoying these days.

"I think that case could've gone either way," I offered to no one in particular. "I happen to believe that the Colorado locals saw something that could be the Loch Ness Monster's cousin and we simply missed it because it was too smart to let us get a glimpse of it."

Jack arched a dubious eyebrow as he flicked his dark eyes to me. They were almost always impossible to read and went almost completely black when angry. How did I know? Well, in my brief weeks with the group, I'd had occasion to make Jack angry a few times. I was starting to turn it into a game and really enjoy it.

"Charlie, there was a dinosaur in the lake." Jack's tone was even and cool. "It just so happens it was a fake dinosaur and the local miniature golf course decided it didn't want to pay to dispose of it as much as they wanted to make it disappear, so they dropped it in the lake because they thought no one would notice."

"See ... that story doesn't make any sense." I wagged a finger for emphasis. "The locals said they saw the dinosaur above water. Cement sinks."

"It wasn't made from cement," Jack shot back. "It was made from plaster or something. It bobbed along the top of the water until it got saturated and sank. That's what people saw."

"I happen to disagree." I stared at my fingernails, which were gnawed rather than pretty and pink, and ran my tongue over my teeth as I waited for Jack to explode. Instead of getting my wish, he merely shook his head and went back to his work.

Millie, who fancied herself something of a fix-up artist, watched the exchange with something akin to glee. I knew what she was thinking, and I didn't like it one bit. She kept trying to play matchmaker between Jack and me – something I dissuaded at every turn – and she was determined to get her way.

For his part, Jack remained focused on his repair and refused to engage in Millie's games. He was calm, cool and often kind of a douche. I wished I could be more like him when it came to Millie's shenanigans. Other than the douche thing, of course.

"Do you want to know what I think?" Millie interjected, drawing two sets of eyes in her direction.

"Not even remotely," Jack answered.

I bobbed my head. "I always want to know what you think."

Millie smirked. "You want to stay on my good side because you're convinced I have power over Myron and Chris, which means I can pick and choose assignments," she said. "I don't have that sort of power."

"You're working for a company owned by your ex-husband and you get away with whatever you want," I argued. "That seems to suggest you have some sort of power."

"Not as much as I would like," Millie said dryly. "As for the lake monster, I agree with Jack. It was a putt-putt throwaway."

I wrinkled my nose, my anticipation dropping. "It could've been both," I muttered.

Millie wagged her head as she eyed Jack. He looked smug, which I really hated. Millie seemed to enjoy agreeing with him and often took his side during arguments, which only served to make his ego even more unbearable. "I still think it was a putt-putt monster, no matter how much you feel like pouting," she challenged. "That doesn't mean the next monster we go looking for won't be real, though, so keep your shoulders square and emotions high."

"You sound like a demented self-help guru," Jack drawled, furrowing his brow as he stared closer at the contraption. "You should have your own television show."

"I've been telling people that for years," Millie said. "What is that thing? I don't see how any radio doodad could've helped us with a plaster dinosaur."

"I don't either, but Chris is convinced that our inability to talk to each other while we monitored the lake from multiple points – that storm really screwed us up that one night and caused a bunch of mayhem – is the reason we're not writing the plot for the next *Jurassic Park* movie right now," Jack said. "He wants me to boost the signal on these things."

"Can you do it?" I asked, tilting my head to the side. Jack was handy and enjoyed toiling over electronics and weapons. I didn't get it, but I respected the trait. It was one of the few things I liked about him ... other than his looks, body, hair, smile and gravelly voice, of course. What? I told you that I'm not interested in him that way. He might look like a wicked angel, but he talks down to me like a terrible babysitter. It's not an attractive combination.

"I don't know," Jack replied. "I'm still working on it. A lot will depend on if we get a new job and take off or if we stick close to home for a bit."

"I hope we stick close to home," Millie volunteered. "The Rowdy Roadhouse is having a wet T-shirt contest this weekend and I want to participate. I think there's a good chance I can take home the title. The winner gets free drinks for a year."

My mouth fell open as I conjured a picture of Millie in a wet T-shirt contest. She wasn't ancient by any stretch of the imagination, but she was old enough to know that wet T-shirt contests weren't a good idea. "You can't be serious."

"Oh, but I am." Millie pressed her lips together as she locked gazes with me. "Do you have something to say about that?"

I risked a glance at Jack and found his shoulders shaking with silent laughter. He was clearly having a good time. "You're messing with me," I said after a beat. "I should've realized that."

"You're too literal sometimes," Millie agreed. "As for the wet T-shirt contest, it's real. I'm simply a judge. I don't want to miss it, though. There's nothing I like better than messing with stupid girls who want to show their breasts off in public."

"You should tell me when that's happening," Jack suggested. "I might actually stop in – to offer you support, of course. Although, the Rowdy Roadhouse is a bit much for me. Whenever I go there I end up having to wrestle some loud moron to the ground and threatening him because public drunkenness is never attractive."

"You just haven't been drunk enough with me in public," Millie teased. "But I'm not sure the girls who hang out at the roadhouse are your type. They lack … um … substance."

"I'm fine with that." Jack was blasé as he removed a screw and rested it on the table next to his chair. "Sometimes the best women have zero substance."

The statement grated even though I pretended otherwise, and focused my attention on the wall behind Jack's head, allowing myself to stew even though I told myself I was simply annoyed on behalf of my gender.

"I think you're having a hard time trying to convince yourself of that," Millie countered. "If we had a nice quiet week here, though, I certainly wouldn't complain."

"Well, you totally jinxed us by saying that," Jack said. "Now that you've put it out there for the universe to hear, odds are we'll have a case within the next twenty minutes."

"Do you want to bet on that?" Millie challenged.

Jack smiled. "I bet you fifty bucks we're out of here in twenty minutes."

It seemed like an easy bet, but Millie was nobody's sucker.

"What do you know?" Millie asked, her eyes lit with interest as she leaned forward.

"What makes you think I know anything?"

"Because you're refusing to make eye contact and you're not exactly what I would call a good liar," Millie replied without hesitation. "You know something."

I followed Millie's gaze, doing my best to study Jack with the cool detachment he managed so well when looking at me. He looked the same as always, intent on his task and otherwise only mildly engaged in the conversation. Perhaps that was an act. Millie would obviously know better.

"Where is Chris?" Millie lifted her head and studied the room. The Legacy Foundation maintained its offices in the basement of a large business complex. The Biggs family had its fingers in a whole lot of pies, and the foundation seemed to be the red-headed stepchild of the bunch. That didn't mean we weren't well funded – because we were – but we were also shuttered away in the basement so people wouldn't ask too many questions. Even though it was his family doing the shuttering, Chris didn't seem to be bothered by it. He was far too interested in the work to care.

"Last time I saw Chris he was in the lab with Hannah," I offered helpfully. "That was about an hour ago. They were looking at some sort of bloodwork on Hannah's new microscope. I didn't understand what they were looking at, but they seemed excited."

"They were looking at each other but didn't realize it," Millie supplied. "They're both hot to trot for each other but can't quite seem to admit it to themselves. It's getting frustrating. I'm considering locking them in that lab and turning the heat way up so they have no choice but to strip naked. Maybe then they'll finally get somewhere."

Jack snorted, amused. "Why not let them do things on their own timetable?"

"You act like you just met me," Millie complained. "I'm not known for my patience."

"I never would've guessed," Jack teased. He always lit up around Millie. It wasn't a romantic attachment, but he appeared to genuinely enjoy her company. It was the only time he loosened up and allowed himself to have a good time. "I thought you were the queen of patience."

"Ha, ha." Millie wagged a warning finger. "You think you're a funny guy, but you're not. Chris is my nephew. I might be divorced from Myron, but Chris is still family. The boy has always been dedicated to his work above all else. I would like him to look around and notice that there're more than monsters in this world."

"I don't think he likes it when we call them monsters," I offered, rolling my neck. "He prefers we use the scientific terms."

"I am. They're monsters." Millie made a clucking sound with her tongue. "Is it so wrong that I want the boy to get some?"

I almost choked on my soda as I sipped. People say I'm the blunt one, but Millie often puts me to shame. When I first landed at the Legacy Foundation I harbored a crush on Chris for exactly two minutes. That's how long it took me to realize that he was over the moon for Hannah, even though she didn't notice. I backed off right away, because even though there's no harm in a little work crush there's no sense engaging when the other party doesn't even know you're alive.

"I think we should talk about something else," I suggested.

"I agree," Jack said. "The last thing I want to talk about is Chris getting some."

"That's because you need to get some, too, and you're determined to live like a monk rather than a twenty-seven-year-old man with viable options close by," Millie said, her gaze briefly resting on me. The simple stare was enough to make me feel uncomfortable, so I squirmed in my chair and went back to staring at the wall.

"I'm perfectly fine being a monk," Jack argued. "We've had this discussion, Millie, so there's no reason to have it again." His tone was weighted, his gaze pointed. "Knock it off."

8

Most people would pull back in the face of Jack's obvious anger. Millie wasn't most people.

"I'm good," Millie said, her eyes flicking toward the door as Chris bustled through it. His face was flushed, his hair windswept and he looked excited.

"What's going on?" I asked, my stomach clenching at the thought we might have another case. We'd had three since I joined the group. One turned out to be a human (although I got to meet real-life witches in the process, so that was exciting), one turned out to be a plaster dinosaur in a lake and the third turned out to be a mutant strain of fireflies that people were convinced were pixies. I was ready for something real, something I could sink my teeth and brain into.

"We have a case," Chris announced, brushing back his hair as he regarded us. "We need to pack up."

"Where are we going?" Millie asked, casting a suspicious look in Jack's direction. "I knew you knew something, by the way."

"I have no idea what you're talking about." Jack adopted an air of innocence. "I'm simply sitting here minding my own business."

"We're going to Texas," Chris replied, ignoring the exchange. "There are multiple Chupacabra sightings. We're finally going to be able to see it."

The Chupacabra? Huh, that *was* exciting. "Do you think it's real?"

Chris' smile was benevolent. "I always think our cases are real, Charlie."

He meant it, and that was one of the reasons I like him. "So let's mount up." I hopped to my feet. "The Chupacabra isn't going to wait forever."

"Oh, geez." Jack rubbed his forehead. "We have two of them now."

Millie snickered. "I think it's cute."

"I think it means I need to pack some aspirin." Jack rolled to his feet and avoided my steady gaze. "I can be ready in twenty minutes. Make the call to the airport. Let's go find the Chupacabra, shall we?"

That was the best idea I'd heard all day.

2

TWO

The foundation has its own jet, so we could talk about the case on the ride down. It was a cozy atmosphere, comfortable, and Chris was so excited his enthusiasm was somewhat catchy.

Not everyone was susceptible, though.

"What do we know?" Jack asked from the seat next to me.

"We know that we have a body – although I don't have the specifics on that yet – and numerous people have seen a dog-like animal that has spines along its back," Chris replied. "I don't know about you, but that sounds like the Chupacabra to me."

Jack kept his world-famous patience in place as he flashed a tightlipped smile. "I guess I'm not familiar with the Chupacabra, so I have trouble coming to the same conclusion."

"I can take that." Hannah Silver, her flaxen hair so light it almost looked gray, dug in the bag at her feet and came out with a notebook. "The Chupacabra is also known as the goat sucker."

"The goat sucker?" Millie made a face. "I guess it's good Myron isn't going with us. He'd either end up dead or orgasming."

Chris shot his aunt a quelling look. While he was genuinely fond of her, he was also beholden to his uncle. That often put him in a tough spot when Millie got going – and she was almost always going on one topic or another. Myron happened to be one of her favorite topics.

"The Chupacabra legend is relatively new when you compare it to other creatures of its ilk," Hannah continued, apparently oblivious to the snark flying around her. "The first reported attack was in 1995. It happened in Puerto Rico, when eight sheep were found dead with puncture wounds in their chests."

"And what's to say a human didn't do that?" Jack challenged. "While I'm not big on killing animals for no reason, I think that male teenagers have been responsible for similar attacks throughout the years purely out of boredom."

"I guess that's a possibility, but a local saw the creature a few months after the first attack," Hannah replied. She was the no-nonsense sort, dedicated to the job and the science associated with it. She wasn't as enthusiastic as Chris, who couldn't hide his emotions, but it was clear she was keen to find tangible proof. "Her account was largely discredited because the creature she described was identical to one in the movie *Species*, and she admitted to having seen the film recently."

"Great," Jack intoned, leaning back in his chair. "We're chasing a movie monster. This should be fun."

I flicked his ear, frustration getting the better of me. "I'm trying to listen."

Jack stared long and hard before shrugging. "Sorry. I didn't mean to interrupt movie critique time."

I rolled my eyes. "Go on, Hannah. Some of us aren't rude jerks who want to act superior."

Jack pressed the tip of his tongue to the back of his teeth as he narrowed his eyes. Wisely for him – I was in that bad of a mood – he kept his acerbic thoughts to himself.

"Go on, Hannah," Chris prodded. "We're listening." He wasn't one to admonish his crew, but I could tell that Jack's dismissive words ate at him. Perhaps Jack could tell, too, because he turned his attention to staring at his fingernails rather than interrupting.

"Most of the stories have been discounted, but that hasn't stopped the sightings," Hannah supplied. "In 2010, for example, a University of Michigan biologist concluded that all Chupacabra attacks in the United States were actually the result of coyotes with mange."

"That sounds lovely," said Laura Chapman, an auburn-haired siren who thought a little too much of herself for a woman who got the job because her father was an accountant with the company. She made a face. "Can humans catch mange? I would really rather not catch mange."

"It probably wouldn't go well with the syphilis you're already carrying," I muttered under my breath. Thankfully I said it low enough that only Jack could hear, and when I darted a look in his direction I found his lips curving. "What?"

Jack shook his head and turned back to the group. "If all the Chupacabra sightings have been discredited, why do we think we're dealing with the real thing here? It sounds to me like we're dealing with a mass hoax, kind of like the Fiji mermaid."

"Just because we haven't caught an actual Chupacabra doesn't mean they don't exist," Chris argued. "We haven't caught a sasquatch either, but we know they exist."

Jack looked as if he was going to argue the point, but thought better of it. "Right. What else do we know about the Chupacabra, other than that it has spines growing from its back and it likes to attack goats, I mean?"

"The most important thing to remember is that the Chupacabra is more leathery looking than fur-covered," Chris offered. "They stand about three to four feet high and have a pronounced spinal ridge and eye sockets. They also have fangs and claws. The injuries they leave behind are most often in a downward facing triangle. That's how we know we're dealing with a Chupacabra."

"That's how we know, huh?" Jack inhaled heavily, his chest heaving. I didn't know him well, but I'd come to recognize the reaction as a calming mechanism. He had a short fuse and was a nonbeliever. I still hadn't figured out why he was part of the group if he didn't believe in the supernatural.

As for me, I wasn't sure I believed in the Chupacabra. It sounded a bit fantastical. Because I experienced psychic flashes when I touched someone or when I was lost in a dream, and could move things with my mind, I tended to err on the side of the supernatural. Oh, did I not mention that? I'm exactly the type of person – or thing, depending how you define it – the Legacy Foundation seeks. I've opted to keep that to myself for obvious reasons.

"Since the first event in Puerto Rico, which was more than twenty years ago now, Chupacabras have been sighted in almost every state, even as far north as Maine," Hannah said. "The sightings are much more prevalent in warmer areas, though, which is where we're going."

"That brings me to my next question," Jack said, shifting on his seat. "Where are we going?"

"Texas," Laura answered, smirking. "I believe we've already gone over this."

Laura is one of those women who think every man in the world is after her. Her assumption included Chris and Jack, although they largely ignored her for very different reasons. I was fairly certain Chris didn't ignore her out of malice. He was simply so caught up in what he did that he couldn't be bothered to drag his attention away from the task – or Hannah. He was clearly besotted with Hannah, although he didn't admit it to anyone, including her.

Jack's disdain for Laura was something else entirely, and I was still trying to figure it out. Part of me wondered if they'd been involved – had a fling or perhaps a short romance – because his dislike was overt. Given the way Millie teased him about being a monk, though, I had my doubts. Jack seemed far too pragmatic and stubborn to get involved in a relationship with a co-worker. In fact, weeks earlier we accidentally ended up snuggled together in a tent while looking for Bigfoot, and he was horrified to the point that he threatened to turn himself in for inadvertent sexual harassment. We moved past it, but only after I told him he was being a ninny. Since then we'd been treading lightly around one another. I wasn't sure why he reacted the way he did.

13

"We're going to a place called Hooper's Mill," Chris supplied. "It's in the middle of nowhere."

The way he said it caused me to snap my head in his direction. "We're going to be out in the middle of nowhere hunting for the Chupacabra? That doesn't sound safe."

"Don't worry," Laura sneered, looking to Jack. "I'm sure your knight in shining armor will be around to protect you."

What was that supposed to mean?

"I need to hear more about the setup," Jack prodded, ignoring Laura's dig. Whatever his feelings toward the woman – and they weren't pleasant – he was good at getting under her skin. All he had to do was ignore her. Sooner or later she melted down in fantastic fashion because she didn't believe anyone was capable of ignoring her over the long haul.

"Hooper's Mill is a former turn-of-the-century silver rush town," Chris explained, oblivious to the potential discord flying around the jet cabin. He wasn't always good with human emotions, so he often missed what was right in front of him. "It's one of those places that sprung up out of nowhere and died just as quickly."

"By 'turn of the century' you mean 1900, not 2000, right?" I asked.

Instead of shooting me a "you're an idiot" look, Chris chuckled. "Yes. I mean 1900, not 2000."

"Ugh. You guys make me feel old," Millie lamented. "I need a drink."

"Here." Bernard Hill, our version of Mr. Fix-It, handed Millie a bottle of water and grinned. He was three years older than her, but flirted nonstop. Sometimes I wondered if they had a little something going on the side when they thought no one was looking. I hadn't asked – yet. I figured it was only a matter of time before my mouth ran away from me, though. It always happened eventually.

"Hooper's Mill had one boom, and then it busted quickly," Chris explained. "It's a very small location, kind of like those haunted old west towns you see on television and movies. It's only ten buildings, and it's been abandoned for the better part of a century."

"And we're staying there?" I was excited. "Does that mean we're picking up supplies and camping in a ghost town?"

"Oh, geez." Jack rubbed his forehead. "We'd better not be staying in an abandoned mining town."

"We're not," Chris said, causing me to deflate a bit. "The town doesn't have running water and it's only thirty minutes from the border. It's not safe or convenient to stay there. We'll be lodging in a small town about twenty minutes away. The amenities there aren't great – I believe they have only one hotel and one restaurant – but at least we'll have running water and beds."

"That's a relief. But just one restaurant, eh," Laura asked. "I guess that means no mall?"

"Definitely no mall," Chris confirmed. "We'll meet a local outdoor enthusiast by the name of Zach Corrigan at the hotel this afternoon. Once we land, we'll pick up our rentals at the airport and head straight to the hotel. After that, we'll make some decisions."

"And you don't know anything about the body that was found?" Jack probed. "Don't you think we should have more information before heading out to a purportedly haunted town?"

"I didn't say the town was haunted," Chris clarified. "I said that it reminded me of haunted ghost towns in movies. I've seen a few photos from the real estate ads."

"Real estate ads?" I perked up. "Is the town for sale?"

"Yes." Chris bobbed his head. "The deceased's name was Dominic Sully, and per the message that just came through from the main office he was considering buying the property to turn it into an amusement park of sorts."

"Amusement park?" Jack cocked an eyebrow. "What kind of amusement park can you make in the middle of nowhere?"

"There's a lot of nostalgia associated with certain times in history," Chris explained. "Apparently Sully was thinking of turning it into a western theme park, a place where people would get dressed up in costumes and find themselves part of a story.

"There would be fake gunslingers, horses and updated hotels so people could stay right in town," he continued. "I don't know that he filed any plans with the state, which I believe would be necessary given the historic nature of the town, but that's what he told the real estate developer. Uncle Myron emailed me the update a few minutes ago."

"And he died?" I asked. "How?"

"That's a good question," Jack said. "How did a real estate developer die in the middle of nowhere? I think it's far more likely that the town's proximity to the border played into this rather than the Chupacabra."

"Except that people in the small town where we're staying have seen the Chupacabra multiple times over the past few months," Chris said. "Some livestock has been taken out, the particular wound pattern we're looking for left behind. And now we have a body with the same wound pattern."

"Which could be intentional." Jack didn't back down, despite Chris' insistence. "Maybe someone wanted to use the legend of the Chupacabra to cover up for a murder."

"That's one of the reasons they called for us," Chris confirmed. "Listen, Jack, I know you're prone to steering our investigations away from the supernatural because that's how you're wired – and I'm generally glad for that because you're good at your job and a voice of reason – but we can't know anything until we land and look over the area."

"Chris is right," Millie said, catching Jack's gaze and giving him a dark look. "We don't know what we're dealing with yet, so there's no reason to argue either side of this. Once we know more, then we can start arguing."

Jack opened his mouth as if he was going to push the argument further, and then snapped it shut. He held his hands palms up and shrugged. "Okay. You have a point. I just don't want anyone assuming that we're going to land in the middle of a ghost town and stare down a Chupacabra."

"I don't think anyone believes that," Hannah said. "We can't know more until we get the lay of the land and look around. With that in mind, even though I would love to see Hooper's Mill right away, I think it's probably best if I go to the medical examiner's office and take a look at the body."

"Do you think they'll let you see it?" Laura asked. "Texas doesn't strike me as the sort of state that will simply allow you to wander in and invite yourself to an autopsy."

"No," Hannah agreed. "But I have a few contacts with the state licensing board. I'm hopeful I can call in a few favors. Even if they won't allow me to participate in the autopsy, they might let me observe. That could put us ahead on this one."

"That's a good idea," Chris said. "As for the rest of us, we'll head straight to the hotel and drop off our things. Then we'll meet this Zach Corrigan, get a feel for him, and decide if we want to head out to Hooper's Mill this afternoon or wait until tomorrow."

"Why would we want to wait until tomorrow?" I asked. "Wouldn't it make more sense to go out there right away?"

"I'm with you. I want to see everything as soon as possible." Chris flashed a warm smile. We didn't spend much time together, but he'd been open and amiable since I arrived. I had a feeling he simply liked having another enthusiastic sort in the group. With Jack constantly naysaying, Laura doing whatever it is she does and Millie shifting with the wind, Chris didn't always have many group members taking his side.

"I still want to talk to an expert," he continued. "My guess is he'll say that we don't want to get caught in Hooper's Mill after dark."

"Isn't that when the Chupacabra is most likely to come out to play?"

"Yes, but there are no streetlights in that town," Chris reminded me. "There are no building lights. It will be completely dark except for the moon and our flashlights. We need time to go over the buildings to make sure there aren't any hidden dangers. We need daylight for that."

"Believe it or not," Jack added. "Safety is our top priority."

I shot him an annoyed look. "I get it. I was just asking."

"For now, we're going to meet up with Zach Corrigan and get some information." Chris was firm. "We'll decide what comes next after that. Either way, we'll see Hooper's Mill within the next twenty-four hours. You can look forward to that, Charlie."

I was definitely looking forward to that. We might finally be able to see the absurd and strange up close and personal. That was the reason I joined the group.

3
THREE

Zach Corrigan wasn't what I expected. He was young – under thirty – with windswept brown hair that was finger combed away from his face, chiseled cheekbones and blue eyes that seemed to stare right through to my soul. He had broad shoulders, a narrow waist and a set of powerful arms that were on display thanks to his tight T-shirt.

"It's nice to meet you."

Zach greeted Chris first, the two men exchanging an enthusiastic handshake.

"I saw him first," Laura hissed, moving up behind Jack and me.

I glanced over my shoulder, surprised. "Why are you telling me?"

"Just so you know that he's going to be mine and there's no sense making a play for him," Laura replied, smoothing her hair. "A town without a stoplight doesn't have a lot of options when it comes to men. In fact, I'll wager he's the only option, and he's mine."

"I'm not here to pick up a date," I reminded her.

Laura momentarily flicked her eyes to Jack and offered up a dubious smile. "Yeah. You keep telling yourself that." She pushed her way between Jack and me and made sure she was the second one to meet Zach.

For his part, the man never changed his expression, keeping his smile in place as his gaze bounced from face to face.

"I'm so happy to meet you," Laura drawled, extending her hand. "You look like you know exactly what you're doing. I hope we have a lot of occasion to ... explore ... Hooper's Mill together."

"Can you believe her?" I tilted my head to the side. "I swear it's as if she's in heat or something."

"That's just the way she is," Jack said. "She gets her self-worth from her looks. When she doesn't have them to fall back on, she's going to have a very rude awakening."

"And what's that?"

"Just that she needs something internal to back up the external," Jack replied. "Don't worry about it. You don't have that problem."

He probably thought that because Laura looked like a model and I resembled the model's assistant. Oh, well. It's not as if I could change it.

"And you are?" Zach was smooth as he slid in front of me, grinning as he took in my loose-fitting cargo pants and T-shirt.

"This is Charlie," Chris offered. "She's the newest member of our team."

"Ah, that must be why you look so shiny." Zach winked, showing off a dimple in his left cheek. "I do love a shiny woman."

Jack took me by surprise when he shoved out his hand and gripped Zach's without warning. "I'm Jack Hanson. Head of security. What can you tell me about Hooper's Mill?"

"Sheesh, Jack," Laura complained, fanning her face. It was unbearably hot in the hotel lobby. The ancient air conditioning unit in the window toiled hard, but it didn't offer up much relief. "Let's get settled before you start the inquisition."

Jack ignored the admonishment. "I'm head of security. I want to know what we're dealing with."

"That's smart." Zach's amiable countenance never slipped. "I thought you guys might want to drop your stuff off in your rooms, and then we could share a light lunch in the dining room. It's not much, but the sandwiches are good. And you're going to want to keep hydrated in this heat."

"Yeah, I noticed the heat." Laura wiped her hand over her brow. "Does it ever cool down?"

"It cools down at night, but it never gets cold," Zach replied. "We can talk about all of that over lunch. Why don't I help you get your stuff upstairs?" Instead of waiting for an answer, Zach grabbed my bag and slung it over his shoulder. "Which room is yours?"

"Charlie has room eighteen on the second floor," Chris answered automatically, handing over an old-fashioned key rather than a card. It seemed the hotel was behind the times when it came to technology. "I think Zach is right. Everyone has twenty minutes to drop off their things and freshen up. Then we'll meet in the dining room and talk strategy."

"That sounds like a plan." Zach winked again. "How about I help you up the stairs, little lady?"

"Oh, well … ." I wasn't sure how to answer. Laura's glare made me uncomfortable enough that I shifted from one foot to the other.

"I'll help her with her bag," Jack announced, grabbing the duffel from Zach before the man could put up a fight. "Charlie's bag is easy. Why don't you help Laura? She has three bags and could clearly use the help."

Laura beamed as if Jack had given her the best gift ever. "That's a great idea!"

"Okey-dokey." Zach kept his smile in place and shifted to Laura. "I guess I'll help you."

Jack kept a firm hold on my bag until he was sure Zach was otherwise engaged, and then he flung the bag at my chest. "It's not heavy. You can carry it up yourself."

I tried to hide my glower, but it didn't work. "You're a real peach. Has anyone ever told you that?"

Jack was more interested in watching Zach than interacting with me. He put his hand at the small of my back and prodded me toward the stairs. "Your room is on the second floor. Get moving."

"Oh, I was wrong," I drawled. "You're not a peach. You're a rotten apple."

Jack was blasé when he finally met my gaze. "You'll live."

MY ROOM WAS DEPRESSING, in a horror movie kind of way. The bed was small, barely a double, and the comforter was so old I was certain it came from Annie Oakley's talented sewing sister herself. One look at my reflection told me that the heat wasn't going to be my friend. I splashed cold water on my face until all my streaky makeup rinsed away, and then pulled my long dark hair back in a ponytail to get it out of my face before changing my T-shirt.

I met Jack in the hallway as I was heading down and noticed he'd secured his long hair back at the nape of his neck. "How could you be a Marine with that hair? I thought Marines had short hair." I never think before I speak. I simply blurted out the question and stared.

If Jack was surprised by my forcefulness, he didn't show it. "I let it grow when I got back to the States. I happen to like it."

"I didn't say there was nothing to like. It's just ... you're so military except for the hair. I don't get it."

"And what's 'military' about me?"

"The way you carry yourself. The way you crouch low when you sense danger. The way you're always looking over your shoulder. Drug dealers do that, too, but I'm guessing you're not a drug dealer on the side."

Jack lifted an eyebrow, amused. "Has anyone ever told you that you might benefit from a muzzle?"

"Because I talk so much?"

"Amongst other things." Jack ushered me toward the stairs. "I see you washed your face."

Was that a dig? "It was hot and I was sweaty. My makeup ran. Excuse me for living."

Jack cleared his throat. "I think that came out wrong," he said. "I just meant that you took off the makeup. That's good. You don't need it – especially around here."

"Oh, well … ." That was kind of a compliment. Almost. I wasn't sure what to say. "I don't mind your hair," I offered finally. "I think it's cool. It makes you look like one of those bad boys on the covers of popular romance novels these days."

Jack snorted, his face lighting up. "You read a lot of romance novels?"

"I like it when the romance is mixed with a ghost story or mystery. That way I don't feel dorky for reading a romance novel."

"Good to know." Jack scanned the lobby when we arrived at the bottom of the stairs. It was quiet, signifying that we were probably the first to return from our room visits. "What do you make of Mr. Corrigan?"

The question caught me off guard. "What do you mean?"

"I'm asking what you think of him."

"Oh, well … I don't know." I honestly didn't know how to answer. "He seems nice enough, charming in a way. He winks so often I kind of want to ask him if he's got a hair on his contact lens or something."

Jack snickered. "I noticed the winking thing."

"He's extremely handsome," I added, wrinkling my forehead when a muscle in Jack's jaw worked. "I think he and Laura are probably going to spend a lot of time flirting over the next few days."

"What about you?" Jack's eyes were devoid of emotion when he flicked them to me. "Are you going to flirt with him?"

"I know you think I'm boy crazy or something, but I'm not. I'm here because I want to learn something, see different things. I'm not here to flirt with whatever guy crosses my path."

"I didn't say you were." Jack chose his words carefully. "I was asking a simple question."

"Well, then I'll give you a simple answer. I'm more interested in seeing the Chupacabra."

"Glad to hear it."

"If I was interested in Zach, though, I wouldn't tell you."

Jack narrowed his eyes. "And why is that?"

"Because it's none of your business."

"I'm the head of security. Everything you do when we're on an investigation is my business."

"Oh, really?" I wasn't in the mood to play games. "Well, if that's the case I also changed my bra and shirt when I was in my room. My bra was wet with sweat and kind of gross. I don't know if you keep a journal or anything, but I don't want you to fall behind."

Jack scowled. "Why do you have to be such a pain?"

That was a good question. "Perhaps you simply bring it out in me."

"You wouldn't be the first woman I deranged." Jack gestured toward the dining room. "Let's get a table ... and a drink."

"I thought we weren't supposed to drink on the job," I challenged.

"You heard Zach the magnificent. We need to keep hydrated. I'm debating keeping hydrated with whiskey."

"Perhaps I'm the one deranging you," I suggested. "Have you ever considered that?"

"Only every day since I've met you."

Jack pulled out a chair so I could sit, taking the one to my left and smiling at the approaching waitress as she bustled in our direction. Jack ordered two iced teas without asking and passed me a menu as the waitress slipped into the back to get our drinks.

"What if I didn't want iced tea?" I challenged.

"You always drink iced tea."

"I ... well ... that's beside the point. Maybe I wanted something else."

"Oh, it's like you're trying to give me a headache," Jack muttered, rubbing his forehead.

Thankfully for both of us the rest of the crew picked that moment to swoop into the dining room, excited chatter cutting off whatever snarky thing I planned to say next. Zach's smile was still firmly affixed to his handsome features, and he sat to my right – Laura quickly snagging the spot on the other side of him – while everyone else dispersed evenly around the table.

After the waitress delivered our drinks, she took sandwich orders from everyone, and then we got down to business.

"What can you tell us about Hooper's Mill?" Chris asked as he mopped at the condensation his iced tea glass left on the table. The hotel was stifling even though it had air conditioning units in almost every window.

"It's earned something of a reputation around these parts," Zach replied. "Every kid in the area – and that's not a lot of kids, as you can probably tell – grew up with the idea that the place was haunted.

"I grew up about three towns over, and I knew all the stories," he continued. "When I was a kid, I wanted to visit because of the ghosts. As a teenager, I wanted to visit because of the parties."

"Parties?" Jack sipped his iced tea and lifted an eyebrow. "What kind of parties?"

"The normal kind that teenagers have," Zach replied. "Everyone knows everyone in this area, so it's hard to put one over on law enforcement when it comes to underage drinking. What the kids in these parts used to do is lie about spending the night at a friend's place and then meet out at Hooper's Mill and spend the weekend camping and screwing around."

"Sounds like normal behavior," Jack said. "Do they still do that? Could they be responsible for what happened to Dominic Sully?"

"I guess, in theory, that's possible," Zach conceded. "But I don't think that's what happened. Sully caused a lot of waves when he made his interest in the property public. It really was the best thing that could've happened to this area, because there's not much of an industrial base and the park Sully had planned would produce some jobs.

"I'm sure you've taken a good look at this town now that you've landed – and it probably only took you thirty seconds – but very little sustains this place," he continued. "The residents wanted Sully to come through on his promises."

"Did all the residents feel that way?" I asked, something niggling at the back of my brain. "I'm guessing there are a lot of natives in this area who don't want their land going to a theme park."

"Natives?" Laura wrinkled her nose. "Do you mean Indians?"

"I believe she means natives, as in indigenous natives," Jack corrected. "She's got a good point. Given the proximity to the border, there's probably a heavy Hispanic influence in the area."

"Not as much as you might think," Zach countered. "This area is mostly made up of white folks, not to be derogatory or anything." Zach sent an apologetic smile to Bernard, the only person of color at the table.

"I think I'll survive being around white folks," Bernard said dryly, earning a throaty chuckle from Millie.

"This area is small, remote and set in its ways," Zach said. "There is a Hispanic population, but they don't really concern themselves with Hooper's Mill. Like I said, most people I know were happy about what Sully had planned."

"And what do you know about his death?" Hannah asked. "I plan to go to the medical examiner's office, which I believe is one town over, once I'm done here. I'm curious about what people are saying about the death."

"People are used to Chupacabra sightings, so that's naturally what they jumped to," Zach replied. "We've been losing livestock for months, and a lot of people have claimed to see shadowy animals in the hills."

"That's not really a Chupacabra sighting," Jack pointed out. "That's an unidentified animal sighting."

"Yes, but other people have seen the beasts up close."

"Beasts? As in plural?" I couldn't help being intrigued. "You think there's more than one Chupacabra here?"

"I believe that's pretty much a foregone conclusion," Zach replied. "I saw some weird prints when I was out at Hooper's Mill last week. They were right in the middle of the street."

"What were you doing out there?" Jack asked.

"I run a tour company," Zach replied, seemingly unbothered by the question. "I give tours of the desert. The biggest draw is Hooper's Mill. Ghost enthusiasts want to see the town and I know it well because I've been out there so many times. Believe it or not, I make a decent living giving tours."

"I believe it." Laura smiled at him, her expression dreamy. "Do you ever consider leaving the area, though? There are other places you could work as a tour guide."

"I've considered it, but my family is close by. For now, at least, this is my home."

"Well, we're happy to have you," Chris said. "After lunch, I thought we'd split up. Charlie, Millie and Bernard can go with Hannah to the medical examiner's office. Laura, Jack and I will go with Zach to Hooper's Mill."

I immediately balked. "Why can't I go with you guys?"

"You can tomorrow," Chris said. "Today is just a quick scouting mission."

"But ... ."

Jack took me by surprise when he interjected himself into the conversation. "I think Charlie should come with us and Laura should go to the medical examiner's office."

Chris arched an eyebrow but otherwise kept his face neutral. "Why?"

"Yeah, why?" Laura challenged, her hackles raised.

"Because Charlie is quick on her feet and wants to do the work," Jack answered without hesitation. "Laura is more worried about impressing our guide. We won't have a lot of time to mess around tonight."

"You listen here," Laura hissed, lowering her voice.

Chris cut her off with a shake of his head. "Jack is head of security. If he thinks Charlie and you should switch places, I'll agree with him."

"That's not fair." Laura adopted a petulant whine.

"Life isn't fair," Jack shot back, his eyes momentarily snagging with mine before he turned back to his iced tea. "Everyone will get a chance at Hooper's Mill. For this afternoon, Charlie will be more helpful. That's simply the way it's going to be."

"I won't forget this," Laura warned.

"I don't doubt that."

I stared at Jack a long time, dumbfounded. He helped me. I had no idea why, but he did. I wasn't sure what to make of it, but I was determined to get to the bottom of his vehemence once we were alone.

There was no way I could let that go.

4
FOUR

*T*he surprises kept coming when, after lunch, Jack handed the keys to the rental to Zach and climbed in the backseat with me. I studied him a moment, brows knit and hundreds of questions flitting through my brain, but ultimately I forced myself to refrain from making a big deal regarding the turn of events.

At least for now. Later, when no one was around to hear me hammer him, would be an entirely different story.

"The road is rutted," Chris noted from the passenger seat, his eyes keen as they scanned the desert on either side. "The pavement just stopped in the middle of nowhere a few miles back and turned to dirt. It doesn't look like you get a lot of rain out here."

"That's not entirely true," Zach countered. He occasionally caught my gaze in the rearview mirror and he winked each and every time. I was starting to think it was a nervous tic or something. "We get deluges of rain, but they come after long stretches of heat. When we get a storm, it's generally a big deal. People head for cover when the sky starts darkening."

"The road isn't paved," I noted as I pressed my forehead to the window. "It's almost like a two-track."

"What's a two-track?"

"Pathways in the woods," Jack replied. "I get what she's saying. This road is rough. Not many people use it."

"There's no reason for a lot of people to use it. There's nothing out here that interests locals. I mentioned the kids, but they don't come out here during the week."

"And there's no way that the body was out here over the weekend, right?" Jack asked. "There's no way Sully stumbled upon the kids while they were partying and they panicked or anything, is there?"

Zach shook his head. "No. From what I understand, he'd been dead only about twelve hours or so when they found him. I should caution that he hasn't been formally identified yet because of the condition of the body, which no one would expand on when I asked about it. If he'd been out here longer, the scavengers would've got to him even more than they apparently did."

"Yes, but we're supposed to believe the Chupacabra got to him first," Jack pointed out. "It seems to me that's a scavenger of sorts."

"I guess you have a point." Zach smiled into the mirror. "You don't seem excited to look for the Chupacabra, Jack. Why is that?"

"I have no idea what you mean," Jack replied, suddenly finding something fascinating to stare at through his window.

"I mean that everyone else seems excited at the prospect of seeing something strange," Zach said. "Charlie, who is just as cute as an umbrella in a mixed drink, can barely sit still. You, on the other hand, are kind of sour and morose."

"Sour." I snorted under my breath. "That's a good word for you."

Jack scalded me with a dark look before cracking his neck. "I am determined to keep the members of my team safe. I'm sorry if you find my questions off-putting. They go with the job."

"Jack is good at his job," Chris added. "He's not a natural believer like the rest of us. I think that's good. He anchors us to reality when some of us might fly away. Isn't that right, Charlie?"

I was surprised to be addressed in such a manner. "It's good that he's protective," I agreed, meaning every word. "If he could occasionally be protective without being a douche, that would be great."

Zach barked out a laugh. When I risked a glance at Jack I found him watching me with glittering eyes.

"That was a joke," I offered lamely.

"Very funny." Jack's tone was dry. "Very, very funny."

Yeah, I would pay for that one later. For now, I had more important things to focus on. "Have you ever seen the Chupacabra, Zach?"

"Now that there is an interesting question." Zach beamed as he talked, although his tone bothered me. He was about the same age as Jack, who also found it necessary to talk down to me, but Zach did so in a manner that suggested I was stupid. When Jack did it, he acted as if I needed constant supervision and he was the one who needed to provide it. Zach's tone was completely different, yet somehow I didn't like it.

"I guess I can't say with any certainty that I saw the Chupacabra, but I did see something when I was out here one day," Zach started. "It was after a tour and, for once, I had my own vehicle and I was the only one left. Most of the time I drive people out to the town, but this was a bigger group and they wanted their own vehicle, so I met them at Hooper's Mill.

"Anyway, they left and I was about to go myself when I heard something in the saloon and I decided to check it out," he continued. "That was probably a mistake, but since I spend so much time in Hooper's Mill I couldn't stop myself."

"They have a saloon?" For some reason that part of the story snagged my interest. "Maybe you can get your drink there, Jack."

"Keep talking and I might find a way to make that happen," Jack warned.

Zach barreled on as if he didn't hear us snarking at one another. "The saloon was empty, but I could've sworn there was a moment where I saw something in the mirror behind me," he said. "I know that sounds odd – I tend to be more of a ghost fanatic than a Chupacabra fan – but I swear I saw something in that mirror.

"So, I pretty much scared the bejesus out of myself and hurried back to the truck," he continued. "It was almost dark. There's a reason

I won't stay in Hooper's Mill after dark, and it was only reinforced when I got in my truck.

"I flicked on the headlights, and there, right in front of me, was the strangest creature I'd ever seen." Zach's voice hopped a little as his excitement grew. "So there I am, sitting behind the wheel of my truck, my palms are sweating something fierce. The creature – I don't know what else to call it – had eyes that glowed red. Now, I'm willing to admit that part might've been my imagination, but it didn't feel that way in the moment."

"I'm sure it was your imagination," Jack said, rolling his eyes.

Zach ignored him. "So the thing is spitting and growling, and all I can think is that it's some weird iguana or lizard monster, because it had spikes along its back. Well, I have to tell you, my heart was going something fierce and I thought I might pass out. All I could think to do was get away, so I spun out of there so fast I wasn't even thinking when I pulled onto the highway."

"You didn't think to take a photo?" Chris was understandably disappointed.

"No, but I wish had," Zach replied. "When I got back to town I was worked up and people asked what happened. I told them, and they laughed at me, of course."

"Of course," Jack echoed. I elbowed him in the stomach to silence him, but all he did was smirk when he caught my arm before I could do any real damage.

"I'm not sure I saw the Chupacabra," Zach hedged. "Whatever it was, I don't know how else to describe it."

"Well, I'm hopeful we'll see it, too." Chris happily patted his knees in excitement. "I can't wait to see this place. It sounds like it's going to be a lot of fun."

"Yeah," Jack muttered. "It's going to be a real barrel of ghosts and Chupacabras."

HOOPER'S MILL WAS PRETTY much exactly what I'd imagined. I couldn't stop my head from swiveling back and forth as Zach pulled to a stop in front of a ramshackle building. I unfastened my seatbelt and hopped out before Chris had a chance to utter instructions.

"Hey!" Jack grabbed my arm when I moved toward the saloon, his grip tight and his eyes icy when he stopped my forward momentum. "Let's come up with a plan before you run off half-cocked, okay?"

I knew he was only doing his job, but he was such a wet blanket I couldn't help being disappointed. "We're in a ghost town, Jack."

"No, we're in an abandoned town that just had a possible murder," Jack corrected, causing me to deflate a bit. "Chill for a second and let us talk."

My inner snark goddess came out to play before I could stop her. "You mean let the adults talk?"

Jack refused to be backed into a corner. "If that's how you want to look at it. Let's come up with a plan first. Okay?"

His expression was almost pleading, so I relented. "Okay. I didn't mean to run off like a ninny. I just ... it's exciting."

"Yes, well, at least you called yourself a ninny this time." Jack led me to the spot at the front of the truck where Chris and Zach waited. "I think we should stick close together for this first inspection, Chris. We don't know the area, and we need to get the lay of the land before we start running around willy-nilly."

Chris, his expression blank, shrugged. "You guys can stick together as much as you want, but I intend to get a full rendering of the street and as many of the buildings as I can with the camera. I want to take it back tonight and make a plan for a much bigger excursion tomorrow."

"Then we'll all do that," Jack offered.

"I want to look in the saloon," I argued.

"She wants to look in the saloon," Zach repeated, grinning. "How about I take Charlie to the saloon and you guys film the street? We're not going to have a lot of time to waste because the light is limited. We only have an hour before we should turn back."

"See, you heard him," Chris pressed. "We don't have a lot of time. I have to get the video."

"And you should watch him, Jack," Zach added. "I'll keep an eye on Charlie."

Jack looked as if that was the last thing he wanted. "Let's switch that around." Jack ordered, catching Zach off guard before he could wander into the saloon with me. "You know the town's layout better. You go with Chris. I'll stick with Charlie."

"Oh, now, as much as I like Chris, I think Charlie will be more fun." Zach adopted a mock grin that probably made most women go weak in the knees. I wasn't most women.

"I like Jack's idea." I wasn't saying that merely because Zach irked me. I wanted to talk to Jack in private. "We'll check out the saloon. You guys handle the filming."

"Oh, well ... ." Zach looked as if he was going to put up an argument, but I didn't give him the option. I grabbed Jack's arm and jerked him toward the saloon. Both swinging doors were intact, but just barely.

"We'll see you guys at the truck in an hour," I called out.

"We'll see you," Jack sneered as he followed me. He kept a triumphant look on his face until we were out of Zach's line of sight and then let it drop. "Why are we checking out the saloon again?"

"Because it's the saloon and that's where all the cool things happened in old west towns," I replied, as I released his arm and scanned the room. It was dark and dry, termite-infested furniture making ghostly heaps in corners. Time had ravaged the furniture to such a degree it was impossible to figure out what items used to litter the room. The floor was uneven and warped and webs drifted from the low ceiling. The chandelier, which must've been beautiful and shiny at one point, looked as if it was one stiff breeze away from falling.

The bar remained standing, although the planks sagged in places. The shelves behind the bar were long gone. The mirror that remained was splintered, making my reflection look like something straight out of a funhouse.

I was delighted. "Wow," I murmured. "Is this place the coolest or what?"

"Or what," Jack replied dryly, scuffing his foot against the floor as he tested his weight in various spots. "This floor won't hold much longer. This place isn't safe."

"I'm starting to think you don't think anything is safe."

"That's my job."

"Yeah?" I cocked an eyebrow as I tilted my head. "Can I ask you something?"

"If I say no, will that stop you?"

I shook my head, causing Jack to heave out a sigh.

"Ask away," Jack supplied, running his hands over the bar as I debated how best to broach the subject.

"If you hate me so much, why did you step in and suggest that I come out here with you guys instead of Laura?" I asked finally.

Jack jerked his gaze over his shoulder and met my eyes. "I don't hate you, Charlie. Why do you think that?"

"Because you act like I'm the little sister you never wanted and I'm insisting on tagging along on your great adventure, which you're convinced will ruin everything."

Jack ran his tongue over his lips, considering. "I don't mean to be Captain Killjoy. I take my responsibilities seriously. You're gung-ho, and there are times I worry that's going to get you in trouble."

"Fair enough." I meant it. "Still, you had a prime opportunity to leave me behind at the hotel and you fought to include me. Why?"

"Because even though you're a righteous pain in the behind – and that's exactly what you are some of the time – you're also eager to learn and willing to put in the work," Jack replied. "Laura's lazy. She only has this job because of her father. You deserve the opportunity to prove yourself."

"So even though you hate me ... ."

"I don't hate you." Jack cut me off with a curt headshake. "Stop saying that. I feel the need to protect you. If that comes off as surly or morose, that's not my intention."

"Okay." I accepted his apology without any lingering doubts. I could tell he meant it. "I'm sorry."

"What are you sorry for?"

"All of the mean things I've been thinking about you. I thought you were obnoxious, but now I'm starting to think that's simply your personality."

Instead of being offended, Jack barked out a laugh. "I guess we're even. Neither one of us can run from who we truly are."

"I guess so." I turned back to the saloon. "We should look around. If Zach's tall tales are to be believed, we need to be far away from this place when darkness falls."

"Do you believe his tall tales?"

"I don't know." I saw no reason to lie. Even though Jack irritated me at times, I knew him to be trustworthy. "There's something about him I don't like. I wish I could say that I don't trust him to do his job, but it's something else."

"Something how?" Jack was intrigued. "Something ... sexual?"

I was almost relieved to hear him bring it up first, and I let loose a weighted sigh. "Thank you. I didn't want to say something and look like an idiot if I was reading him wrong."

"If it's any consolation, I don't think you're reading him wrong," Jack offered. "But I don't think you're reading him entirely right. He's clearly a player. He probably doesn't have many options in a scarcely-populated area like this. That's why when he sees pretty single women his age he jumps all over them."

"That explains why he's been flirting with Laura," I clarified. "I think he's been acting weird with me, too."

Jack's expression was hard to read. "What did I just say?"

"You explained why Zach has been hitting on Laura. I'm talking about me."

"You don't have a rock-solid image of yourself, do you?" Jack made a tsking sound and shook his head. "Trust me, Charlie, he's more than willing to take a tumble with both of you."

I didn't consider myself a prude, but I was horrified. "Together?"

Jack's chuckle was so warm and unexpected I couldn't stop myself from smiling. "I'm sure he would love that, but I think he'd take you on separately, too. If he makes you uncomfortable, stay away from him."

"Okay, well ... thank you for arranging for me to come."

"Don't make me regret it," Jack warned, assuming his stalwart Marine persona. "Stick close to me while we go through the building. No wandering off."

I clicked my heels together as I mock saluted. "Sir, yes, sir."

"Oh, and my headache is back."

"You need to get used to that."

"I'm starting to figure that out on my own."

5

FIVE

"*L*ook at this."

Jack and I spent five minutes searching the room before something caught my eye on the floor toward the back wall. Jack eased around the counter and knelt, his eyes dark as they scanned the rotting planks.

"What is that?"

I held my hands palms up and shrugged. "Chupacabra tracks?"

Jack rubbed the back of his neck as he stared at the spot in question before lifting the camera around his neck and snapping a few photos. I watched him, intrigued by his focus, and waited until he was done to ask the obvious question.

"Do you think they were left by a Chupacabra?"

Jack met my gaze and pursed his lips. "I'm going to be honest with you because I think you've earned it. I don't believe in the Chupacabra."

"I'm pretty sure I already knew that."

"There are other types of animals out here." Jack adopted a pragmatic tone. "It could be a coyote … or maybe a feral hog … or … um …."

"The Chupacabra," I finished, grinning.

"Fine. It could be the Chupacabra."

Even though he'd conceded, I decided to tell him what I was really thinking. He'd been open and amiable since we'd talked things out, so I hoped I wasn't risking our new-found peace. "I'm not sure I believe in the Chupacabra either."

Jack's eyes flashed with something I couldn't quite identify. "I thought you believed in everything."

"I believe in some things," I corrected. "I believe in Bigfoot. I still think that's what I saw in my tent that night in Hemlock Cove."

"Fair enough."

"I also believe in paranormal abilities ... and psychics ... and ghosts ... and witches." I had no idea why I threw that last one in. It was pushing things, but I also knew witches were real because I'd met a few when we were searching for Bigfoot. Of course, Jack didn't know that. I kept it from him because I was hiding my own magical secret and was desperate to keep everyone from finding out.

"Witches, huh?" Instead of reacting with disbelief, Jack merely smirked. "I guess I can get behind some of that."

"Not all of it?"

"I saw a lot of things when I was overseas. A few of them couldn't be explained. I think I'm with you on the ghosts."

"Because ghosts can be internal and external?" I had no idea why I asked the question. It wasn't the first time the word "haunted" jumped to the forefront of my brain when I thought about Jack. Whatever happened to him when he was in the military, it wasn't something he was over. Heck, perhaps it was something he'd never get over. But he clearly didn't want to talk about it.

"Exactly." Jack snagged my gaze. "Aren't you haunted by certain things from your childhood?"

That was an annoying question. One he already knew the answer to. My adoptive parents died when I was eighteen. I still didn't know my birth parents ... or how I inherited an ability I was still learning to control and always desperate to hide.

"I guess I am," I conceded, glancing around. "I still think the Chupacabra would be more fun than internal ghosts."

Jack grinned as he stood. "You have a point." He flicked his eyes to the dark area down the hallway before clearing his throat. "I'm going to check down there. I want you to stay here."

That sounded like absolutely no fun at all. "Why? There's nothing in here."

"We don't think there's anything in here," Jack corrected. "That doesn't mean there isn't. It's dark down there. There could be a snake or something."

"Like a trouser snake?"

Jack stilled. "What's a trouser snake? I've never heard of that. In fact … ." Realization dawned. "Holy crap. Did you just make a dirty joke?"

My cheeks burned. "Actually, do you remember the inn we stayed at in Hemlock Cove? It was something Tillie Winchester said, and it stuck with me."

"Sounds just like her." Jack squared his shoulders. "I'm still checking out the hallway alone. The floor might be ready to give way or something. You stay here."

"Sir, yes, sir."

"Ha, ha." Jack rolled his eyes before swiveling, flicking on his flash-light and shuffling down the hallway. His path was exacting as he extended his toe to check the strength of every floorboard. I soon lost interest in watching his progress. My inner danger alarm wasn't dinging – something that often happened when bad things were about to happen – and instead I turned my full attention to the mirror.

I didn't know what to make of it. The glass was old enough that it had a warped appearance. It was covered in dirt and grime, although portions of the room behind me were visible despite the splintering. In a weird way, the broken mirror almost looked like a piece of art.

I focused on one of the corners – an area that seemed to be missing pieces – and when I moved my eyes back to the center I did a double take as I registered a hint of movement behind me. Like a complete idiot, I remained rooted to my spot as fear overtook me. The movement continued, kind of like the leading edge of a ghost I couldn't quite see, and the fluttering moved closer to me as my heart skipped a beat and I suddenly lost the ability to swallow.

My heart pounded in my chest, blood rushed past my ears, and still the movement grew closer. It was almost on top of me when my fear response kicked in and I lashed out with my mind, using my telekinesis to launch one of the fallen lumps of garbage from the floor in the direction of the swirling energy matter.

I ducked my head and regained the ability to move, swiveling as I gasped out a breath and came face to face ... with Jack.

"What the holy hell was that?" Jack stood a good fifteen feet away, his dark eyes wide as he scanned the room.

How much had he seen? Did he realize I moved the pile of refuse? Did he see the thing I registered in the mirror? I couldn't make my tongue work.

"You're pale." Jack strode closer, and I thought for a moment he would hug me. The idea settled me, caused my extremities to warm a bit, until instead he grabbed my chin so he could stare into my eyes. "Charlie, what did you see?"

"W-what do you mean?"

"I saw you in the mirror." Jack was decidedly calm. "You were frozen in your spot as if you saw something, and then the hunk of crap – which I think used to be a chair – moved."

Crud! He'd seen. How was I supposed to explain what happened? "I ...."

"You didn't see the Chupacabra, did you?"

I shook my head. "I don't know that I saw anything," I said finally, unsure how to proceed. "It's more that I felt something. I don't know how else to explain it."

"Okay." Jack's voice was even. That only served to agitate me.

"You don't believe me."

"I didn't say that," Jack countered. "I thought for a second I might've seen something, too. It was right behind you. I was going to yell for you to move, and then suddenly the chair flew across the room."

Uh-oh. "Yeah, that freaked me out a bit, too." That was a total lie, but odds were he wouldn't believe I was responsible for the chair. That was for the better. "Maybe we're dealing with a ghost rather than the Chupacabra."

"We're definitely dealing with something," Jack said. "I found more of those tracks toward the back. I took photos. It's getting dark, though." He pointed toward the broken-out front window for emphasis. "We need to get out of here. We'll go back to the hotel and talk about a plan of action for tomorrow."

I nodded without hesitation. "Sounds good."

Jack's expression was sympathetic as he rested his hand on my shoulder. "Are you okay?"

"I'm fine. I honestly feel a little foolish because I did that kid thing where you freeze and can't move when I thought I saw the swirling … whatever it was."

"Don't feel foolish for that." Jack prodded me toward the door. "Your body has a fear response for a reason. Listen to it."

"What if I'm just a coward?"

Jack chuckled lightly. "I don't think that's the case, but I guess we'll find out eventually, huh? Come on. Let's find Chris and Zach. I'm ready to call it a night."

JACK KEPT ME CLOSE for the ride home, handing Chris his camera so the man could study the footprints from the saloon. That kept Chris busy for the duration of the ride back to town. Zach was another story.

"You look as if you've seen a ghost." Zach made sympathetic clucking sounds as he stared at me in the rearview mirror. "Are you feeling okay?"

"She's fine," Jack answered for me, his eyes flashing. "It was a creepy setting. We're both … fine."

"Well, I'm sure she'll feel even better after she has some dinner," Zach said. "The restaurant down the way – the only decent restaurant in town – has wonderfully authentic regional food. I'm sure that will make her feel better."

"Regional food?" I scratched an imaginary itch on the side of my nose. "Is that like ... Mexican food?"

"More like barbecue," Zach replied. "Ribs, burgers, steaks. I hope you're not a vegetarian, because I'm pretty sure the restaurant has nothing to offer if you are."

"Oh. Barbecue sounds good."

"It definitely does," Jack agreed.

Once we hit the hotel, Chris instructed everyone to freshen up before meeting back in the lobby so we could walk to the restaurant together. Jack's eyes were probing as he dropped me at my room, and I wasn't surprised to find him waiting in the hallway after I splashed water on my face and ran a brush through my hair.

"You don't have to hover," I chided as we descended the stairs. "I'm okay."

"Maybe I like hovering," Jack suggested. "Have you ever considered that?"

"Not really."

"Well ... you're still pale." Jack put his hand to the back of my neck as he directed me toward the front door. "You're a little clammy, too."

"I splashed cold water on my face."

"Don't argue with your doctor." Jack mustered a smile, which stayed in place until Zach stepped out of the shadows and intercepted us on the front porch.

"Milady?" Zach offered his arm for me to take, but I instinctively avoided him by cutting in front of Jack and positioning myself between the security chief and a distracted Chris, who seemed much more interested in the camera he carried than the weird testosterone display between our temporary guide and permanent security chief.

"Let's get some dinner," Jack said pointedly, his gaze hard as it held Zach in place. "I think Charlie could use the energy boost."

"I think we all could," Zach said, grinning. If he was bothered by my rather obvious snub he didn't show it. He kept up a running commentary as we headed toward the restaurant.

The rest of our team was already seated – Millie and Bernard munching on bread while Hannah and Laura had their heads bent together, chatting about something. Once everyone reunited, the information started flying fast and furious.

"All the blood was exsanguinated from the body," Hannah supplied, her features calm and placid despite the heavy topic. "That doesn't necessarily mean the Chupacabra did it, but it's definitely interesting."

"And has he definitely been identified as Dominic Sully?" Jack asked, handing me a warm slice of bread. He seemed keen to make sure I ate so I could bolster my shaky reserves.

"Actually, no," Millie replied, causing several sets of eyes to drift in her direction. "The body is too beat up for a proper identification right now."

Jack stilled. "What do you mean?"

"The body is ... different looking," Hannah replied after a beat. "With all the blood gone and several little nibblers taking bites while it was out at Hooper's Mill, no one has been able to make a proper identification."

"So it's not Sully?" I asked, leaning forward.

"We're not sure," Millie replied. "Sully hasn't been seen, but he's something of a loner and his secretary says that's not abnormal. He tends to go wherever he wants, whenever he wants, and he doesn't call or check in for days at a time. His people are trying to track him down."

"If it's not Sully, who is it?" Jack asked. "Surely if someone was missing from this area the authorities would know. It shouldn't be hard to track down an identity in an area with such sparse population."

"There are a lot of undocumented workers passing through," Zach interjected. "This is an area where people don't always check in with one another. If someone took off ... we might not know for a long time."

"So what does that mean?" I asked.

"It means we need to identify that body," Chris answered. "We can't go forward until we're absolutely sure who we're dealing with. There could be multiple motives assigned to the death of a particular individual."

"Chris is right," Jack said. "It's better if we know what – or rather who – we're dealing with."

"All we can say with any certainty is that it's a man in his fifties," Laura said. "He didn't have any identification on him – which is weird however you look at it because I don't think the Chupacabra is out to participate in identity theft – but the medical examiner hopes to have more information tomorrow."

"I hope to have more information tomorrow, too," Chris said. "We didn't get as much time to look around Hooper's Mill as I would've liked. It's a fascinating little place. You could practically feel it come to life as darkness fell."

That was an interesting way to put it. Is that what happened in the saloon? Did something come to life? As if reading my mind, Jack handed me another hunk of bread. It was as if he was trying to soothe me with carbohydrates.

"Eat," Jack prodded, keeping his voice low.

I thought about arguing, but there didn't seem to be a point, so I bit into the hunk of bread and briefly pressed my eyes shut. When I opened them again, I found Jack leaning close. I almost jolted at his proximity, but I figured that would send the wrong message. Of course, I had no idea what the right message was, so I was lost in a quagmire of questions.

"Don't mention what you think you saw in the mirror right away," Jack whispered. "I don't want Chris getting all worked up."

"You want me to lie?" I spared a quick glance around the table, but no one was paying attention to us.

"Not lie," Jack clarified. "Just ... hold onto the information for now. Chris is looking for the Chupacabra. What happened in that saloon is different."

"I still think he'd want to know."

"I'm not saying to keep it to yourself forever. Just keep it quiet until our new friend isn't around."

Whatever was going on, Jack really didn't like Zach. He wasn't the only one. "Okay. I'll keep it to myself."

"Thank you."

"What are you two talking about over there?" Millie asked, her eyes lit with mirth. "Are you whispering dirty ideas to one another?"

Jack scowled. "Can you keep your mind out of the gutter for five minutes?"

Millie shook her head. "It's impossible."

"We were talking about having people stay at Hooper's Mill overnight," I interjected, ignoring Jack's furious look when I unveiled the lie. "I think it might be worth the risk. There's potential to see an entirely different world there after dark."

"I don't think that's a good idea at all," Zach said.

"I hate to agree with Zach – I mean … really hate it – but I don't think that's a good idea either," Jack said. "We have no idea what's out there."

"That's why we should stay," I argued. "We should find out."

"No." Jack emphatically shook his head. "I'm head of security. It's a stupid idea."

"And I'm head of the team and I'm not ruling anything out," Chris overruled Jack, much to my delight and Jack's chagrin. "I want to consider it."

Jack wasn't ready to give up. "But … ."

"We'll talk more about it tomorrow." Chris' tone was no nonsense. "Tonight, let's have some dinner and get a good night's sleep. I agree it's not wise to go out there tonight. Tomorrow is another day."

6

SIX

I was tired after dinner, the adrenalin rush from what happened in Hooper's Mill quickly fading, but taking its toll. The only thing I could think about was crawling into bed and checking out for eight solid hours. Even though the mattress sagged in the middle and the room left a lot to be desired, sleep was all I could think about.

That idea lasted exactly fifteen minutes, until I climbed into my fuzzy sleep bottoms and T-shirt, and groaned at the knock on my door.

It took everything I had to fumble my way out of bed, and when I opened the door Millie stood on the other side. I immediately wished I'd pulled the covers over my head and pretended to be asleep.

"Whatever you have planned, I'm not doing it." I blurted out the words before Millie could mention whatever idea took over her very busy brain. I hadn't known Millie long, but I was convinced she lived by a set of rules the rest of us didn't, and she wasn't good at taking "no" for an answer.

"I haven't even told you what I have planned yet," Millie complained, making a face.

"Yes, but I remember the last time you came to my door when I should've been sleeping and I can still hear Jack yelling."

"You're such a whiner." Millie didn't bother hiding her eye roll. "We barely got in trouble for that. You're exaggerating."

"How would you know?" I challenged. "You were passed out. I got in trouble while you slept it off."

"Hey, I had a terrible hangover the next morning. That was punishment enough."

I'd seen her the next morning and I could hardly argue. "I'm not going on whatever crazy mission you've dreamed up." I crossed my arms over my chest to let her know I meant business. "It's not going to happen."

"Come on," Millie prodded. "I have a great idea."

Despite myself, I was intrigued. "A great idea to do what? If we steal one of the rentals and head out to Hooper's Mill, Jack will track us down and he very well might kill us."

Millie arched an eyebrow, surprised. "I have no intention of stealing a vehicle and heading to Hooper's Mill. It's good to know where your mind is, though."

I balked. "That's not what I meant."

"Oh, don't take it back now. You're starting to get more interesting." Millie wagged a finger near the tip of my nose, her lips curving. "As much as I'd like to steal a vehicle and head out to Hooper's Mill – and that does sound mildly interesting from a scientific perspective – that would be virtually impossible because Jack and Chris locked up the keys to both vehicles."

"Oh." I deflated a bit. "So what do you have in mind?"

"Well … there's this bar."

"Absolutely not," I barked, vehemently shaking my head. "I am not going to a bar with you."

"Shh!" Millie's eyes flashed as she pressed a finger to her lips and looked up and down the hallway to make sure no one heard our argument. "You are like the queen of the meltdown. Has anyone ever told you that? When you're about to break the rules you don't announce it for everyone to hear."

"I have no intention of breaking the rules." I honestly meant that. All I wanted to do was go to sleep. It was lame, but true. "I'm tired, Millie. I need to rest."

"Oh, geez." Millie wrinkled her nose, not bothering to hide her disdain. "You are twenty-three years old, girl. It's ten o'clock. You shouldn't be worried about going to bed."

"If you're trying to shame me for following the rules … ."

"Following the rules is an argument for another time," Millie said, cutting me off. "Sometimes rules should be followed and sometimes they should be ignored. I'm not asking you to break the rules, so there's no reason to work yourself up into a snit."

"Oh." I was taken aback. "You're not trying to get me to break the rules?"

"No."

"But you said we were going to a bar."

"How is that breaking the rules?" Millie was full of faux innocence. "Did you sign a morality clause when you came to work for the Legacy Foundation?"

"No," I hedged, looking up and down the hallway.

"Then why can't we go to the bar?"

I didn't have a good answer, so I decided to turn the conversation around on her. "Why should we go to the bar?"

"Because we're in a town the size of a postage stamp," Millie replied without hesitation. "We don't even know who our dead guy is. That seems odd, no matter what that slick tour guide has to say."

Millie's overt distaste bolstered me. "You don't like Zach either?"

"He's smarmy and thinks he's full of charm," Millie replied. "It's my contention that those who really have charm don't need to put so much effort into faking it."

"Good point." To buy myself time, I tapped my chin. "What do you think we'll find at the bar?"

"Gossip."

"What kind of gossip?"

"The kind we're not going to get from a tour guide trying to impress people," Millie answered. "I want to know more about Zach

48

Corrigan. I also want to know more about Dominic Sully and who else might be hanging out at Hooper's Mill. We won't find those answers through official channels."

"You could get that information on your own," I pointed out. "Why do you need me?"

"Because you're fun."

"Why really?"

"Because, as much as I think I'm hitting my prime not everyone believes that," Millie supplied. "I might need someone young and cute to get more information. The way I see it, I have three options. Hannah wouldn't know what to do with her looks if I drew her a diagram. She's completely oblivious."

"Yeah. I hate that about her, too."

Millie snorted. "Laura is too aware of her looks and comes across as bitchy and manipulative."

"So I win by default?" I couldn't help being a little disappointed.

Millie shook her head. "You're the best of both worlds. You don't see your appeal yet, but you're gung-ho to seek out information. You're the perfect sidekick."

She meant it as a compliment – I was sure of that – but I had trouble taking it that way. "Why do I have to be the sidekick? Why can't you be the sidekick?"

"I'm too old to be anyone's sidekick," Millie replied. "Now change your clothes. If you have something that shows off your assets, you should definitely wear that."

"I don't have any assets."

"Oh, geez." Millie pinched the bridge of her nose. "It's going to be a long night. I can already tell. Get dressed. I'm going to need ten drinks to put up with your nonsense."

"Fine. But if we get in trouble I'm totally blaming you."

"I think that's perfectly acceptable."

"THIS IS THE BAR?"

I wrinkled my nose, disappointment rolling over me. I knew it was stereotypical, but I pictured some honky-tonk establishment from a television sitcom, with sawdust on the floor and a mechanical bull in the corner. Instead we got a filthy hole-in-the-wall with a creepy guy standing behind the bar.

"It's got pizzazz," Millie said after looking around for a few moments. "I like it."

"You would."

"Oh, don't bring your bad attitude here," Millie chided. "You'll give yourself bad liquor karma. Nobody needs that."

I had no idea what bad liquor karma was, but it sounded terrible. "Fine. Let's find a place to sit." I pointed myself toward a table in the corner, but instead Millie snagged my elbow and directed me toward the bar.

"We're not going to get information isolating ourselves, missy. We need to talk to the man in charge."

I eyed the bartender, who looked as if he hadn't bathed in the last three weeks. "What do you think he possibly knows?"

"I'm about to find out."

I didn't want to sit alone ... or risk going to the bathroom alone, for that matter ... so I had no choice but to follow Millie to the bar. She seemed to be in her element, the rough and tumble crowd no cause for concern. She hoisted herself onto a stool and patted her hands on the counter as she eyed the drink choices.

"Hello."

The bartender arched an eyebrow as he dried a glass. "You must be the folks in town investigating the murder, huh?"

The question, which seemed to come out of nowhere, made me suspicious. "How do you know that?"

"You're the biggest thing to happen in this town all week," the bartender replied. "We don't get many visitors."

"Yeah, we figured that out when we saw the hotel," I grumbled.

Millie shot me a warning look before pasting a bright smile on her face for the bartender's benefit. "I'm Millie and this is Charlie. What do you recommend?"

The bartender looked amused. "Charlie, huh? You don't look like a Charlie."

"What do I look like?"

"A Heather."

Hmm. I had no idea what to make of that. "I'll have an iced tea."

"No, she won't." Millie shook her head when the man reached for a glass. "She's too high strung for more caffeine. Give her something else ... like a shot of bourbon."

I wrinkled my nose. "I am not having a shot."

"Give her a shot," Millie ordered. "What's your name, by the way? I plan to be here for a few hours and I'll need something to call you."

"Really?" Instead of being annoyed by Millie's bossy attitude, the bartender looked amused. "Call me Lloyd."

"Wasn't that the bartender's name in *The Shining*?" The question was out of my mouth before I thought better of asking it. That's the story of my life, by the way. I have no filter, and it drives people crazy. I can't seem to control the situation, so now I pretend I don't notice.

"I don't believe I've ever seen *The Shining*, but I'll take your word for it," Lloyd said dryly. "As for shots, this one doesn't look as if she can handle a shot. We've got stronger stuff than your standard rotgut here. Maybe she'd be better off with something simple, like a rum and coke."

"That's fine." I was resigned to getting one drink and nursing it for the next few hours. If Millie downed as many drinks as I expected, it was going to be hard enough to get her back to the hotel if I was sober. If I was drunk, we'd both end up lost in the desert.

"No, wait a second." Millie flapped her hand as she surveyed the bar's offerings. "Rum is boring. You guys are close to the border. You must have some good tequila."

"We do," Lloyd confirmed. "You want standard shots?"

"That sounds like a fine idea." Millie beamed. "Don't hold back on the salt and limes."

"I would never." Lloyd grinned as he grabbed a bottle of tequila from the shelf and selected two shot glasses from the rack behind him. He poured the shots, piling a mound of lime wedges on a plate and sliding it between us before putting a salt shaker on the counter. "Bottoms up."

I wasn't much of a drinker. I'd only been out of college a few months and I'd never been fond of the whole party scene. My biggest concern was that I would get drunk, lose control of my magic or let something asinine slip. I followed a firm set of rules when I was in college and now didn't seem the time to stray from them. "I don't know."

"You're drinking," Millie ordered, her tone leaving little room for debate. "Here. Watch me."

I had no choice. I pressed my lips together and worked overtime to keep my eyebrows in place as Millie licked the side of her hand, sprinkled salt on it, licked it again and then slammed back the shot. She then popped a lime wedge in her mouth and sucked on it, a goofy smile on her face.

"Ah," she enthused. "That's some good tequila."

"Thank you." Lloyd was clearly amused as he turned to me. "I think it's your turn."

I was never one to bow to peer pressure, but I couldn't see a graceful way out of this situation, so I capitulated. I mimicked Millie's actions, doing my best not to cough too much when I downed the shot, and by the time I had the lime wedge in my mouth my cheeks were on fire.

"Good girl." Millie patted my back, amused. "Another round, Lloyd."

"Somehow I knew you'd say that." Lloyd set about to pouring, seemingly more at ease now that Millie had shown she was something of a party animal. "I understand you folks went out to Hooper's Mill today. Did you find anything while you were out there?"

"I wasn't part of the group that went," Millie replied. "Charlie was. Did you see anything interesting out there, girl?"

"I don't know," I replied, running my fingers over my hot cheeks. "Is tequila supposed to make my face feel as if it's on fire?"

"Only if it's good," Millie said. "If it's really good, your face should feel numb after the next shot. You clearly have no tolerance. How is that? You were just in college."

"I focused on my studies in college."

"Why? That sounds like no fun at all."

"I had limited funds," I replied honestly. "My parents died when I was eighteen. I had money from them, but it wasn't a windfall or anything. I had to pay for my schooling with the money. I also had to get a part-time job, so I didn't have much time for partying."

"Oh, well, that's a bummer." Millie clearly meant it, because she patted my shoulder while she sympathetically clucked. "That must've been hard."

"Life isn't easy. My mother always told me that. They died in a car accident. It was hard, but ... I wanted to make them proud."

"I'm sure you did." Millie's lips curved into a smile. "Are you ready for that second shot?"

"Okay, but then that's it. I don't think I can handle much more than that."

"Of course that's it." Millie said the words, but the way her eyes lit up caused doubt to roll through my belly.

"I'm serious."

"I know you are, Charlie. I'll take care of you. Don't worry about that. Everything will be okay. Trust me."

Despite my reservations, I did trust Millie. More than everyone else in the group, she opened herself to me right away. I couldn't help but like her.

"I'm going to have a terrible hangover tomorrow, aren't I?"

"Probably." Millie nodded, handing me the shot glass. "You have to bust your cherry eventually, though. This is as good a time as any."

That was an interesting way to put it. "Okay, but if I throw up, I'm blaming you."

"I'm perfectly fine with that."

7

SEVEN

"*I* think I'm having a stroke."

I experimentally pressed my fingers to my cheeks.

"You're not having a stroke," Millie countered. "You're drunk. Enjoy it. Although ... ." She swooped in and stole the shot glass before I could grab it. "I think you should switch to water."

"I'm on it." Lloyd was enjoying himself, as were a few of the locals who sidled closer to the bar.

"I don't need water," I argued. "I'm ready for another shot."

Millie's smile was kind. "Part of me wants to see what will happen if I let you keep going. If anyone needed a night of dancing on a table to shake things up, it's you. I know you, though. You'll insist on going to work tomorrow even if you feel as if your head is going to fall off, which it probably will. You'll thank me in the morning."

Millie shoved the water glass in front of me and downed the shot that I was trying to claim.

"Hey! That's mine. Why can you keep drinking when I can't?"

"Because I'm better at it than you," Millie replied. "Now ... drink your water and shut up."

I wasn't keen on being bossed around, but I didn't feel on top of my game. I sipped my water and watched her work Lloyd for information. It was almost as entertaining as drinking tequila. Almost, but not quite.

"What do you know about Hooper's Mill?" Millie asked before sucking on a lime wedge. "You must have a lot of stories to tell."

"We have a bona fide ghost town twenty minutes away," Lloyd said. "Of course there are stories to tell."

"I heard that kids go there on the weekends and get drunk," I interjected, splaying my fingers in front of my face and staring at them, mesmerized by something I couldn't quite give name to.

"You're drunk, not on acid," Millie snapped. "Don't embarrass me."

"Whatever."

"A lot of the kids hang out there on the weekends, but a lot go to the mall about sixty miles away, too. I guess it depends on the kids."

"I'm guessing the ones who don't like to conform are the ones going to Hooper's Mill," I supplied, resting my chin on my palm. "I would've been all over hanging around at a place like Hooper's Mill when I was a teenager. I wouldn't have cared about the partying as much as the exploring."

"Yes, I'm starting to get a very sad picture of your childhood," Millie tsked. "We'll talk about that later."

"Okay."

Millie made a face I knew I wouldn't remember in ten minutes, let alone in the morning, before turning back to Lloyd. "What do you know about the property development deal?"

"It seems you're up on all the gossip, huh?" Lloyd was amused. "I don't know nearly as much as you'd probably like. That's probably why you're here. All I know is that people in the area were hopeful because they thought it might lead to jobs."

"What will happen to the property now?" I asked, pushing my empty water glass toward Lloyd. "More, please."

"I don't know," Lloyd replied. "I've heard rumors that more than one person was interested in the property. Whether that's true … ." Lloyd shrugged.

"I'd think some people would want to keep Hooper's Mill as it is," I noted, accepting the fresh glass of water. "I mean … it's a historical landmark. Some people don't like the idea of tourists stomping through their backyards."

"I guess that's fair," Lloyd conceded. "The thing is, you need to have a backyard for people to stomp through to care about things like that. The people here don't really have backyards. They're all struggling to make it from day to day. The idea of jobs, of feeding families, is much more important than history."

"I guess."

"I get that," Millie said. "Still, someone cared enough to kill a man. We don't know if it was the developer, but that's everyone's guess. Do you know if he ticked off anyone in town?"

"Not really, but I'm not the center of the gossip mill," Lloyd said. "I was under the impression you were hanging with Zach Corrigan."

"We are," Millie confirmed.

"Not by choice," I added, earning a smirk from Lloyd.

"I'm starting to like you more and more every time you open your mouth, kid," Lloyd teased. "You might try asking Zach. He's up on all the gossip."

"I think he's told us everything he knows," I said. "It's not much, though. He's more interested in picking up women than answering questions."

"Yeah, get used to that," Lloyd said. "That's the way he operates. He romances every woman of a certain age who comes through town. He can't seem to help himself."

"Don't worry about that," Millie said, digging in her purse. "I'll handle our resident Romeo if he gets too fresh."

"No offense, ma'am, but I don't think you're his type," Lloyd offered. "You're definitely mine, though. What if I want to play Romeo?"

"I'm flattered and promise to come back just as soon as I can," Millie said, grabbing my arm. "But now I need to get this one back to her room. She's going to be in a world of hurt tomorrow."

"Yeah, but she's funny," Lloyd said. "Do you need help getting her back?"

"Thanks for the offer but I can manage." Millie took the bulk of my weight on her sturdy frame as she pointed me toward the door. "Walk, drunk."

"I'm not drunk. You're drunk."

"That's the story of my life," Millie muttered. She paused near the door when Lloyd called to get her attention. "Yeah, Romeo?"

Lloyd's smile at the flirty endearment was sloppy. "What I meant to add before you distracted me is that your young friend there is exactly Zach's type. You watch out for that."

Millie stiffened. "Is he a predator?"

"Not like you think, but he has left a string of broken hearts in his wake"

"I'm not worried about that," Millie said. "This one has a knight in shining armor all lined up. He just needs to realize it."

"Okay then."

"Definitely. I'll be around." Millie dragged me through the door. Even though I was little help, she kept up a constant stream of chatter. "Now aren't you glad you went out with me?"

"I don't feel very well," I said, using my free hand to rub my stomach. "My stomach feels a little … um … what's the word I'm looking for?"

"I have no idea, but if you puke on me we're going to have issues," Millie replied. "Keep your eyes up and don't look at the ground. If you vomit in public, you totally ruin my reputation."

"I don't think you care about your reputation," I argued, focusing on putting one foot in front of the other. I'd had four drinks, but I felt as if the world was spinning out of control. "I also don't think you're going to go back and flirt with old Lloyd."

"I might go back and flirt with him. He seemed nice enough. Out of curiosity, though, why do you think I wouldn't go back?"

"Because I think you're dating Bernard."

Millie came to a complete standstill and pinned me with a look. "Who told you that?"

"No one. I figured it out myself."

"And how did you figure it out?"

I shrugged, noncommittal. "I don't know. I've seen the way you two look at each other."

"Yeah, well you need to listen to me." Millie used both hands to prop me up and stared hard into my eyes, waiting a long time until she was satisfied that I was focused. "I'm not saying it's true, because it's not. Theoretically, though, if Myron were to find out I was dating someone in the group he wouldn't be happy. Do you understand?"

I was fairly certain I didn't. "You don't want to get in trouble with Myron?"

"Oh, I couldn't possibly care less about what Myron thinks," Millie scoffed. "But Bernard might care. Myron could fire him. I like Bernard as a friend. He's a good friend." She kept stressing the word "friend" as if it would somehow convince me to change my opinion of her relationship with Bernard. "Do you understand what I'm saying?"

I nodded solemnly. "Mum's the word." I mimed zipping my lips and then almost fell face forward. "Whoops!"

Millie struggled to hold up my weight. "You are a piece of work, girl," she muttered, grunting as she slipped an arm around my waist. "I have no idea why a girl your age is such a bad drinker, but it's something we need to fix."

"Right now?" My mind was muddled. "I don't really feel like going back to the bar."

"No, not right now."

It was a struggle, but Millie managed to get me most of the way back to the hotel without anyone noticing. We were almost to the porch when a familiar voice called out.

"Hey, there." Zach jogged in our direction, his face brightening. "What are you two doing out so late?"

"We were taking a stroll through your lovely town," Millie replied.

"We were getting drunk," I automatically answered, rubbing the back of my hand under my nose and grimacing. "I'm spinning again."

"And I'm going to punch you in the face if you don't stop saying things like that," Millie warned. "We really need to work on your tolerance."

Zach chuckled, amused. "Would you like some help?"

"Absolutely," I said, grimacing as I stubbed my toe on the stair. "Whoops!"

"Ugh. You're going to be a walking bruise tomorrow," Millie complained. "I've got her. We're almost to the stairs."

"I want to help." Zach moved forward and grabbed me around the waist from the other side. "Go ahead and let go. I've got her."

"I don't really think that's necessary," Millie said obstinately, jerking me closer to her side. "I said I've got her."

"You clearly need help." Zach gave me a tug.

"I don't need help," Millie argued, yanking me back the other way.

Thankfully I didn't hear what Zach had to say because my stomach was close to revolting and I jerked away from both of them. "I can walk myself." They were bold words, and they failed me the minute I stepped forward and smacked into a broad chest.

Jack, his dark eyes flashing with fury, caught me before I could go down. "What's going on here?"

"Oh, geez." Millie wrinkled her nose in disgust. "I should've known this would happen. You've got your 'damsel in distress' radar Lo-jacked to her, don't you?"

"I want answers," Jack snapped. "Is she ... drunk?"

"I am." I bobbed my head. "My stomach is upset." Tears leaked out of the corners of my eyes. "It was fun until I had a stroke."

"Okay, well ... ." Jack looked conflicted as he heaved a sigh and slipped his arm around my back. "Hold on. I'll take you upstairs."

"I was about to do that," Zach argued.

"Zach was going to do it, Jack," I offered, smirking. "Zach and Jack. That rhymes."

"Yes, you're a poet and you didn't even know it," Millie intoned, rolling her eyes.

"I want to help," Zach persisted.

Jack silenced him with a look. "I've got it." He grunted as he lifted me off the ground, pinning me with a bossy look that I knew promised retribution in the morning. "We're going to have a talk about this."

"It's not my fault," I argued. "Millie peer pressured me."

"She peer pressured you?"

"What? That's a thing."

Jack slid his eyes to Millie. "Is that true?"

"I haven't decided how I want to answer yet," Millie replied. "I don't want the girl to get in trouble because I genuinely like her, but I'm not keen on you blaming me for this."

"I need an answer," Jack pressed, climbing the steps.

"Fine." Millie rolled her eyes again. "She wanted to go to bed and I made her go with me. Then she wanted iced tea but I made her drink. In my defense, I thought she was being modest when she said she rarely drinks."

"How many drinks did this?" Jack asked, legitimately curious.

"Four," Millie answered.

"A hundred," I interjected. "That's what it feels like anyway."

For the first time since finding us on the street, Jack cracked a smile. "You're going to feel worse in the morning."

"That's what Millie says." I rested my head on his shoulder as he carried me up the stairs. "I guess now I know what I was missing when I didn't drink in college, huh?"

"We'll fix it," Millie offered. "We'll build up your tolerance."

"Or, next time you can just let her have one drink," Jack suggested.

"What's the fun in that?" Millie offered up a half wave before disappearing down the hallway. "I'll see you guys tomorrow. I'd be obliged if you kept this little outing to yourself, Jack."

"No promises, Millie," Jack shot back. He lowered me to my feet and started moving his hands over my butt. It took me a moment to register the presence of his fingers on my posterior, and when I did, I instinctively smacked at him.

"What are you doing?"

"Looking for your key," Jack replied, gesturing toward the door. "I can't open it without a key."

"Oh, well ... ." I dug in my pocket for what felt like forever, finally coming up with the key as I tipped forward. Jack caught me as he collected the key, keeping his arm around me so I didn't list to the side.

"You are going to be so sorry tomorrow," Jack lamented as he ushered me in the room.

I was happy to see the bed and fell face forward on it. I could've passed out right there, but Jack wouldn't allow it.

"Charlie, I need you to roll over."

"I'm not in the mood. I have a headache."

Jack snorted. "I need you to roll over so I can take your shoes off," he said. "I have no idea what you were suggesting – okay, maybe I have a rough idea, but there's no way that's going to happen."

"I know. You think I'm stupid."

"I think you're ... eager to please," Jack corrected. "Roll over."

I did as instructed, groaning when my stomach lurched. "I don't like this."

"Just hold on for a second." Jack unsnapped my sandals and removed them before clapping his hands to get my attention. "Scoot up and put your head on the pillow."

"Ugh. You're so bossy."

"Yeah, yeah." Jack helped me to the top of the bed and then pulled back as I rolled to my side. "I'm going to get you a bottle of water and some aspirin and leave them on your nightstand."

"Okay."

"I'm taking your key because I'm pretty sure you'll pass out while I'm gone."

"Okay."

"I'll leave the key on the nightstand when I leave."

"Hmm."

"Charlie, can you hear me?"

"Shh. It's quiet time. My parents are waiting for me in my dreams."

I didn't miss the sympathetic look on Jack's face before he stood. "I'll be back."

I barely registered his departure. I was so eager to escape in dreams that I could think of nothing else. I was on the verge of unconsciousness when I heard someone futzing with the door handle.

"Just come in, Jack," I muttered.

The rattling continued and was on the verge of driving me insane. "Just come in, Jack. You have the key."

The rattling stopped, allowing me to drift once more. I was out of it when I felt someone pulling the covers over me.

"Did you find the key?"

"I thought you were gone," Jack said. "Why are you still awake? I put aspirin and water on the nightstand. You should be able to find it when you wake with the world's worst hangover tomorrow."

"Thank you."

"What did you say about the key?" Jack asked. "That's right here, too."

"I heard you at the door." I was so far gone I slurred a bit. "You were trying to get in. I reminded you that you had the key."

"Charlie, that wasn't me."

"Sure it was. It couldn't have been anyone else."

"Okay, but ... ." Jack trailed off. "I'll make sure the door is locked. Get some sleep."

"I'm trying. I can't sleep when you're talking."

"Then I'll stop talking."

"Okay. Goodnight."

Jack rested his hand on my forehead, perhaps checking for a temperature, and then moved away from the bed. "Goodnight, Charlie. I'll check on you first thing in the morning."

That was the last thing I heard before I drifted off.

8

EIGHT

*W*hen I woke the next morning I thought there was a very real possibility my head was locked in a vise. My eyes were crusty and my mouth was so dry I figured that maybe I'd been inadvertently dumped in the desert and woken after a week of dehydration.

Dimly, through the murk of my memories, things slowly came together.

Millie.

Zach.

Jack.

Oh, my aching head!

I downed the aspirin Jack left on the nightstand, guzzled a bottle of water and then staggered into the shower. The water temperature was tepid, but it helped clear the cobwebs. By the time I dressed, pulled my wet hair back in a loose bun and slammed the other bottle of water, I felt almost human.

Almost.

Jack was in the hallway when I opened the door. In hindsight, I realized I should have expected him. He was concerned the night before and reluctant to leave me should I drown in my own vomit.

AMANDA M. LEE

The look he gave me now was neither condescending nor haughty. That's the only reason I didn't turn tail and hide.

"I'm sure you want to gloat," I started, rubbing my forehead. "Maybe that can wait until after breakfast."

"I have no intention of gloating." Jack pushed himself away from the wall and stepped closer, his eyes curious as they scanned my face. "You don't look terrible."

"Oh, well, that's what a girl wants to hear first thing in the morning."

"You know what I mean." Jack pressed the back of his hand to my forehead. "You're cool. That's good."

"I don't have the flu."

"I know, but your face was really hot last night, and it had me a little worried," Jack admitted.

"We drank tequila."

"I heard." Jack brightened. "First time, huh?"

The way he said it, the overt glee, caused my cheeks to burn. "With tequila? Yes. If you're wondering if I'm sorry I went, the answer is yes."

"Oh, don't let it get you down," Jack offered. "You'll feel better once you have breakfast in you. And you might be better off wearing sunglasses today. No one will question you if they don't see your eyes."

"What's wrong with my eyes?"

"They're a little bloodshot."

"Oh, well, great," I muttered. "I haven't been falling down drunk since I was a teenager. I guess I smashed my good girl stretch to smithereens last night ... in more ways than one."

"What do you mean?" Jack was confused. "Why would that matter?"

"Oh, well ... ." I trailed off, unsure how to answer.

"Because your parents died and you were instantly an adult from then on," Jack deduced after a moment of contemplation. "I guess that makes sense. I never thought of it from that point of view."

64

THE CHUPACABRA CATASTROPHE

I had no idea why I was embarrassed, but it bothered me. "It doesn't matter."

"It matters to you, so it matters." Jack gestured toward the stairs. "Hannah was on the phone with the medical examiner's office when I came up to collect you. I think she has some information."

"Oh, really?" I was happy to turn my attention to work. "Are we leaving for Hooper's Mill right after breakfast?"

"That all depends on what Hannah has to say."

"Okay, well ... does everyone know Millie took me to the bar last night and I can't hold my liquor?"

"No. I haven't told anyone, and I doubt Millie will. That's not her style."

"But Zach!" I cringed at the memory. "He wanted to take me upstairs."

"I remember." Jack's tone was dark. "Don't worry about him. If he says something, it won't matter. Chris doesn't care as long as you do your job."

"Yeah, except I still feel a little queasy and my head hurts."

"It's a hangover. You'll get over it eventually. The good news is, it won't kill you. If your reflexes are dull, though, the Chupacabra might."

"Ha, ha." I didn't find his attitude funny. "You don't believe in the Chupacabra. You've already owned up to that. What do you think killed him?"

"I don't know, but I hope whatever news Hannah brings will point us in the right direction."

We both hoped for that.

"IT WASN'T DOMINIC Sully," Hannah announced once we were seated, causing everyone to break out talking at once.

"Who was it?" Jack asked.

"Do they know how he died?" Chris queried.

"How did they mess that up so badly?" Bernard asked.

Hannah took the myriad of questions in stride. "The deceased's name is Wendell Morrison," she read from the notepad in front of her. "According to the woman who called, a secretary who seemed agitated to be sharing information, he was putting in a competing bid on Hooper's Mill."

"A competing bid?" Jack leaned forward, intrigued. "No one mentioned a competing bid."

I racked my brain for the conversation at the bar the previous night and something niggled at the back of my brain. I slid a gaze to Millie and found her face drawn as she sat with her hands folded in her lap.

"Actually, I went to the local watering hole last night, and the bartender mentioned that there was a rumor about a competing bid," Millie volunteered, seemingly not caring that she was outing herself. "At the time we were still laboring under the assumption that it was Dominic Sully, so I didn't press the bartender too much."

"You went to the bar without me?" Laura was clearly annoyed. "Why would you do that? I was bored out of my gourd in my room last night. You could've invited me."

"I wouldn't invite you unless I was in the mood for an earworm," Millie shot back.

"So ... what? You went to the bar alone?" Laura narrowed her eyes. "I bet you were cruising for men. That's your regular shtick, isn't it?"

"I believe you have me confused with you," Millie shot back.

"Besides, she wasn't alone," I interjected. "I went with her."

Jack said I didn't have to own up to my actions, but Millie was right. We didn't break the rules, and I saw no reason to lie. Besides, Zach knew. There was every chance he'd slip and tell, so it was better to get it out in the open right away.

"You went to the bar with Charlie?" Laura made an exaggerated face. "You're kidding me."

"I'm not. And she was a very charming wingman." Millie shot me a soft smile. "How are you feeling this morning, dear?"

I shrugged, noncommittal. "I feel ... fine."

"She's got a headache and she's dehydrated," Jack volunteered, shoving a glass of water in front of me. "She'll be fine once she gets some food in her stomach."

"Of course she will." Millie smiled. "She was quite the little helper when I was asking questions, so she's got good karma coming her way."

Jack murdered Millie with a look. "And what kind of karma do you have coming your way?"

"I don't know, but I bet it's drowned in butter and syrup." Millie refused to avert her gaze, instead grinning until Jack was the first to turn away. "Anyway, Lloyd the bartender mentioned that everyone in town wanted Hooper's Mill to be renovated because it would mean more jobs. He couldn't think of anyone who would want to kill Sully over the development."

"I'm not sure why we're focusing on human enemies when we have a potential canine variant out there that is probably to blame," Chris noted.

"I think we should tackle all possibilities," Jack argued.

"I understand that, but … ."

"Ruling in a Chupacabra isn't going to be easy," I supplied. "If you can rule out human culprits that only helps your cause."

Jack shot me a grateful look, which slipped when Zach walked through the doorway. Our tour guide was freshly showered and dressed, and he looked none the worse for wear despite his late night.

"Hello, all." Zach practically sang as he strode toward the table. "It's a fine day for an adventure, isn't it?"

"It certainly is," Chris enthused. "We were just talking over some evidence and making a few decisions. If you haven't had breakfast yet, please join us."

"Yes." Laura's eyes flashed. "Please join us."

"I think I will." Zach was all smiles as he took the open spot next to me and ignored the one on the other side of Laura. "How are you feeling this morning, Ms. Tequila?"

I tugged on my limited patience to keep from exploding and forced a smile. "I'm fine. I apologize if my public drunkenness was too much for you last evening."

Laura, of course, picked up on the tension right away. "What am I missing? Was Zach at the bar, too?" Her expression was accusatory when she turned it on Millie. "Is that why you didn't invite me? You didn't want the competition, did you?"

"Oh, honey, you're no competition for me," Millie drawled. "I didn't invite you because I don't like you. As for the tour guide here, he wasn't at the bar with us. We ran into him on the street on the way back."

"And it was a lovely interlude." Zach grinned at me. "I'm surprised you're on your feet. I thought for sure you'd be down for the count for a few more hours once you had to be carried to your room."

"He carried you to your room?" Laura was practically spitting venom when she glared at me.

"I carried her to her room," Jack corrected.

I expected Laura to relax a bit, but instead she merely turned her hatred to Jack. "I should've seen that coming."

"I guess you should have," Jack agreed. "Millie didn't take into account that Charlie has a very low tolerance for alcohol. She needed help getting to her room. It wasn't a big deal."

"I bet you have a terrible headache this morning," Hannah said sympathetically. "I have some aspirin in my purse if you need some."

"Thank you, but Jack found some for me and left it on my nightstand. I've already taken some."

"Wait a second ... does no one care that I wasn't invited to the bar last night?" Laura challenged.

"Obviously not," Jack answered, pouring me a glass of orange juice from the pitcher at the center of the table. "Drink this. It will make you feel better."

I was happy to have something to do with my hands, so I eagerly obliged.

"I went down to The Watering Hole after I ran into you guys on the street," Zach said. "You were quite the talk of the establishment."

"What is this bar's name so I know to look for it?" Laura asked.

"The Watering Hole," Zach replied, his face blank. "I just told you that."

"Yes, but I thought that was … you know what? Never mind. I'm totally going to that place tonight if anyone's interested." She said the words for Zach's benefit, but he only seemed interested in embarrassing me.

"I thought for sure you were going to pitch forward into the dirt, but luckily Jack was there to catch you," Zach said. "I would've given it a hearty effort if he didn't."

"Yes, my two heroes," I intoned. "Jack and Zach."

"You're a poet and you didn't know it," Millie offered, smirking when my eyes lit up. "I believe you realized that last night, too."

"Let's just nip the rhyming game in the bud, shall we?" Jack urged. "Hannah, I believe you were telling us about Wendell Morrison."

"Wendell?" Zach obviously didn't care that he was interrupting as he leaned forward. "What about Wendell?"

"He's the owner of the body found in Hooper's Mill," Hannah replied. "He was exsanguinated, and I don't know that the sheriff has any information on why he was out there."

"I can't believe it was Wendell." Zach looked lost in thought as he rubbed his chin. "I thought for sure it would be Mr. Sully. Wendell's a local. He's been here for a long time."

"Did you know that he was interested in buying the property?" Jack asked.

Zach nodded, his face drawn. "Wendell has been interested in the property for a long time. I believe he wanted to do the same thing that Mr. Sully wanted to do, only Wendell didn't have deep pockets and had trouble securing financing.

"The last time I heard Wendell had any interest in the property was at least a year ago," he continued. "I thought for sure he gave up the idea when Mr. Sully started talking publicly about his plans."

"Do you think Wendell would've kicked up a fuss if Sully secured the property?" Jack was in full investigator mode.

"I don't think he would've been happy, but Wendell was the type who wanted what was best for the community," Zach replied. "He would've helped however he could if it meant jobs for people. I just can't believe it was Wendell."

"Did you know him well?" Chris asked.

"Well enough, although it's not as if we spent a lot of time together. It's still a shock."

"I'm sure," Jack said, leaning back in his chair. "What else can you tell us about Wendell?"

"He owns a huge ranch about ten minutes outside of town," Zach answered. "He has a few workers out there – and he paid a fair wage. My guess is his daughter Naomi will step up and take over, so it shouldn't be too much of a change."

"What about Dominic Sully, Hannah?" Jack asked. "Has the sheriff mentioned tracking him down yet?"

"Not that he told me, but I didn't specifically ask," Hannah replied. "I can call back."

Jack shook his head. "That won't be necessary. I have plans to touch base with them this afternoon."

"So you're not going to the site with us?" Chris was surprised.

"I might stop in this afternoon, but I have errands to run this morning," Jack replied. "I want to check out Wendell's ranch and talk to the sheriff's boys. I'm sure I will make it to Hooper's Mill after lunch."

"That's not too bad then." Chris was seemingly happy with the answer. "You can take Laura or Bernard with you on your errands if you think they'll be helpful."

"I'll take a pass." Laura feigned sweetness. "I missed out on the haunted town yesterday. I'm not missing it today."

"And if Jack isn't going to be around, I probably should," Bernard supplied. "Someone needs to be able to repair equipment if necessary."

"Oh, well ... ." Chris broke off.

"It's fine," Jack said, flashing a smile. "I don't need Laura or Bernard."

Chris wasn't convinced. "Are you sure?"

Jack nodded. "I'm taking Charlie."

Oh, well, that was nice. Wait a second ... . "Me?" I swiveled quickly. "I want to go to Hooper's Mill."

"I know, but you're still dehydrated, and I think it would be good for you to stay out of the sun for a bit," Jack said. "You can go with me and hydrate through the morning while sitting in an air-conditioned vehicle. I'm sure you'll feel better after lunch."

"Now that right there is a good idea." Chris waved his fork. "It works out well for everyone."

Everyone but me, I internally groused.

"It definitely works out for everyone," Jack agreed, grinning. "I think it's going to be a fine morning."

That made exactly one of us who believed that.

9

NINE

I was still pouting when Jack pulled into the drive-through at a fast-food restaurant one town over. Despite my agitation, I couldn't keep my internal promise to freeze him out.

"What are we doing here?" I asked, peering through the window.

Jack kept his face placid, though I was certain the corners of his lips curved. "I thought a malt would make you feel better."

"A malt?"

"You need the sugar to fight off the hangover, and a malt will help settle your stomach."

"Fought a lot of hangovers, have you?"

Jack nodded without hesitation. "When you spend your life running, that's often what happens."

It was an odd statement, and I filed it away to ponder later. "I don't feel all that bad. You could've let me go to Hooper's Mill with everybody else. I would've survived."

"I have no doubt, but I needed someone with me and my options were limited."

I rubbed my hand over my chin, debating whether that was an insult or simply the truth. "I'm sorry you got stuck with me," I offered after a beat.

"Oh, well, don't turn all martyr on me," Jack instructed. "I'm fine being stuck with you."

"Thanks so much for the compliment."

"You're welcome." Jack pulled up to the microphone and glanced at me. "What's your flavor?"

"Whatever is fine."

Jack narrowed his eyes and ordered a butterscotch malt when the woman asked what he wanted. The choice took me by surprise and I waited until we were free of the microphone to ask the obvious question. "Why did you assume I'd want butterscotch?"

"If you want something else, tell me now."

"That wasn't really an answer to my question."

Jack heaved a sigh, his frustration evident. "Perhaps you strike me as a butterscotch girl. Have you considered that?"

I shrugged, noncommittal. "Butterscotch is my favorite."

"I know. You suck on those hard candies all the time and leave the wrappers around the office so I have to throw them away."

He was stern when he said it, yet I had to purse my lips to keep from laughing. "Sometimes you come off as a mother hen. Has anyone ever told you that?"

"Just you."

"Perhaps I'm the smartest one in the room."

Jack shook his head as he paid for the malt and handed it to me. "I think you're definitely smart, Charlie."

"Really?" I scratched my nose as I studied his serious face. "You don't treat me like I'm smart."

"There's a difference between book smart and street smart," Jack noted. "You're book smart."

"Does that mean you think I'm not street smart?"

"I haven't decided yet."

It was an honest answer, so I decided to let it go and focus on our morning trip. "So we're going to a ranch to ask questions about Wendell Morrison?"

"We are."

"Why?"

"I believe we've been over this." Sometimes I think Jack has infinite patience. This was not one of those times. "I know you want to believe the culprit is paranormal ... or weird ... or rare. More often than not, though, the answer is human when it comes to murder. I'm trying to narrow down our suspects."

"But you're not an investigator," I pointed out. "You're part of the Legacy Foundation. The entire purpose of our group is to discover proof of the paranormal."

"I know. I get that. You probably think I'm an idiot for being part of this group."

"An idiot?" I cocked a dubious eyebrow. I sipped my malt for a moment to collect myself. "I am curious about you, Jack. If you don't care about the cause ... ."

"I didn't say I didn't care about the cause," Jack countered, his temper flaring. "I merely prefer looking for the obvious answers before jumping to the conclusion that we're dealing with something otherworldly. What's wrong with that?"

"Nothing." The edge to his voice made me nervous. "I was just curious."

"I know, and I don't mean to snap at you." Jack adjusted his tone. "I forget you're sensitive."

"I'm not sensitive."

"I didn't mean it as an insult – and cripes, you take everything I say as an insult – but you are sensitive," Jack argued. "You can't help it. You don't know us yet. You're new to the group. You're still feeling your way around. It's to be expected."

That didn't make things sound better. "But?"

"But nothing. I worry you're going to jump in headfirst before thinking things through. You speak before you think. I'm hoping you'll grow out of that."

"You're only four years older than me," I reminded him. "You're not that much older and wiser than me."

"We've lived different lives, Charlie," Jack countered. "I had a wild childhood and then joined the Marines. I learned how to follow rules quickly. You, on the other hand, apparently had a quiet childhood and were thrust into adulthood as soon as your parents died.

"That wasn't fair and it wasn't right that you had to grow up so fast, but you weren't out of control to begin with," he continued. "In some ways I think that was a benefit to you. You never had to hit rock bottom. In other ways, you insulated yourself. You were protected from the hard things that might've roughened your edges."

Whether or not he meant it as an insult, that's how I took it. "You think I was protected from the hard things?" My voice hopped as I fought to control my emotions. Losing control of my tears – or inadvertently my magic – while trapped in a vehicle with Jack would certainly be a bad idea. "I wasn't protected."

Jack slid me a sidelong look. "I wasn't trying to hurt your feelings."

"I don't care." I knew it was unfair to turn on him. He'd been giving and generous with me the past two days. He didn't know what he was talking about, though. Sure, he couldn't fathom how hard it was to grow up with magic and always wonder what I was capable of – including hurting those I loved the most – but I was angered by his ignorance all the same.

"Charlie, whatever I said … ."

"I don't want to talk about it." I sucked hard on my straw. "It doesn't matter. I think I'm just overly sensitive because of my hangover."

Jack didn't look convinced. "If you want to talk … ."

"I don't want to talk," I repeated. "Let's just get these interviews over with. We're talking to Morrison's daughter, right? I think Zach said her name was Naomi. Let's get it done."

"Yeah, let's get it done," Jack echoed, focusing his attention on the traffic.

"I didn't have it easy," I said, my voice low. "I know it probably looks like I did, but I didn't."

"That's not what I meant." Jack matched my tone. "I didn't mean to upset you. That's the last thing I wanted to do."

"It's fine. We're fine."

"Good."

"Great," I agreed, staring out the windshield. "So, what do we know about the daughter?"

NAOMI MORRISON WAS one of those women who was effortlessly beautiful and cool. She wore simple jeans, a set of amazing cowboy boots that set off her shapely legs, and her long blonde hair was pulled back in a stylized ponytail.

It was clear she'd been crying, notification coming from the sheriff's office only an hour before, but she ushered us inside and ordered iced tea before sitting to discuss her father's death.

"We're very sorry for your loss," Jack started, his expression sympathetic. "I know this must be a terrible time for you, but we have a few questions."

"And you're the group investigating Hooper's Mill because everyone thinks a Chupacabra is running around, right?" Naomi's expression was hard to read, but I felt a bit silly asking her about the Chupacabra given her loss.

"That's one of the reasons we're here." Jack chose his words carefully. "Our foundation is often called in on situations like this. It's our job to ascertain the truth, whether it be otherworldly or something more ... human."

"You think my father was murdered," Naomi surmised, leaning back in her chair. The ranch was impressive. It boasted thousands of acres and a house straight out of that old television show *Dallas*. There were cows in the fields when we drove up, and the vaulted ceilings in the foyer were like nothing I'd ever seen. It was a long way from the middle-class suburbs where I grew up, and I felt mildly out of place.

"We can't say that," Jack cautioned. "We merely want to eliminate every possibility we can to narrow our focus."

"To the Chupacabra?"

Jack's shoulders hopped. "If the Chupacabra is guilty, then hopefully we'll be able to ascertain that."

"And yet you're obviously not sure," Naomi mused, thoughtful. She flicked her eyes to me. "You're more open to the possibility of it being the Chupacabra."

I was surprised to be addressed. Naomi had paid very little attention to me since I had entered the house. That was hardly a surprise. She was dealing with the loss of her father. Plus, well, Jack exuded a certain presence. Most people gravitated toward him when it was time to discuss serious issues.

"I guess I am more open to it," I conceded. "It's easier for me to believe a creature killed your father than another human being. That probably makes me naïve." I shot a weighted look in Jack's direction. "Or young and dumb. That's simply how I am."

"Well, I'm with you," Naomi said. "I want to believe an animal did this rather than a human. I'm not sure if that makes it easier, but the notion doesn't turn my stomach quite the way the idea of a man or woman purposely murdering my father does."

"I have a few questions for you on that front," Jack said. "We don't want to take up much of your time. I understand you have other things to focus on."

"If I can help, I want to help."

"Good." Jack leaned back in his chair, stretching his long legs out in front of him. "We've heard that your father was interested in purchasing Hooper's Mill. Is that true?"

"I think he's always been interested in buying Hooper's Mill," Naomi replied. "As far back as I can remember he's been obsessed with that piece of land."

"Why?" I asked. "I mean, it's a cool piece of land, but it doesn't strike me as a solid investment."

"Which is exactly what I told him," Naomi replied. "He wanted the property because his father always took him there to explore when he was a kid. He loved the property ... and he loved his father. He took me there when I was a kid, too, although I wasn't nearly as fond of the property as he was."

Naomi's voice cracked on the last sentence and she swiped at falling tears as she struggled to remain in control. "I'm sorry. I just ... I wish I would've been more interested in Hooper's Mill. If I knew he was going to take off and hang out there, get himself killed, I would've gone with him. Maybe this wouldn't have happened if he wasn't alone."

"That's another question I have." Jack's voice was gentle. "Do you know what he was doing out there?"

"No, but it probably had something to do with Dominic Sully. My father was angry when he found out Dominic had the inside track on the purchase."

"No offense, but this place is huge," I noted. "If your father wanted to buy the land, surely he had the money before Sully started showing interest."

"You would think that, wouldn't you?" Naomi chuckled harshly. "The thing is, the house looks impressive and the land is sprawling. We take in a fair bit of money on the ranch. We also have huge bills that have to be covered.

"My father inherited the ranch. The original parcel was well managed and turned a tidy profit, which allowed my grandfather to build this house," she continued. "My father wouldn't leave things be. He took out a mortgage and bought ranches to the east and west of us."

"And that was a mistake?" Jack prodded.

Naomi shrugged. "I don't know if 'mistake' is the word I'd use. It does add to the value of the ranch in theory. The problem is, we'll be paying off the mortgages for another twenty years."

"So you went from owning property that was free and clear and making a profit to owning more property, potentially bringing in more profit, but you owe on it," Jack mused.

"Exactly, and we can't separate the property now because my father used our ranch as collateral to buy the other ranches." Naomi rubbed the spot between her eyebrows, as if she was warding off a headache. "I don't want to speak ill of my father. It's the last thing I want. But I pointed out to him on multiple occasions that if he hadn't bought the other ranches that he would've had plenty of money to buy Hooper's Mill and do whatever he wanted with it. It was something of a sore spot between us."

"So he wanted the property, but Dominic Sully had better funding," Jack deduced. "Sully was ultimately going to win, and your father didn't like that."

"In a nutshell, yes. My father thought that because he was a local and in good standing with the bank that they'd give him more money. But ever since the loan collapse in 2008, the banks have been stingier in handing out mortgages. That infuriated my father."

"So what was he going to do?" I was intrigued by the story. It sounded like a nighttime soap opera – since the house reminded me of *Dallas* (a show my mother loved) that was to be expected – and I was infatuated with hearing the ins and outs of ranching.

"I have no idea what he had planned," Naomi replied. "I thought he was letting it go because it was rather obvious that Dominic Sully was going to win the bidding war. If he was out at Hooper's Mill, though, that's obviously not the case."

"Had your father and Mr. Sully spent any time together?" Jack asked.

"Are you asking if Dominic Sully had reason to kill my father?"

"I guess I am."

"I don't see how," Naomi replied after a moment of quiet contemplation. "Trust me, I'd like to give you a suspect and sew this up, but I can't come up with a reason why Mr. Sully would want to kill my father. He was going to win the property regardless. There was nothing my father could do. He wasn't a threat."

"What if your father took a gun out there and threatened him?" I asked, shrinking back when Jack murdered me with a look. "What? It's a legitimate question. They have guns on the wall and everything."

Instead of being offended, Naomi mustered a wry smile. "She's not wrong. My father was a gun enthusiast. But I don't believe any of his weapons are missing, and the sheriff didn't mention finding a gun with him."

"I don't believe a weapon was found in the general vicinity," Jack said. "Is there any way to know for certain if one of your father's weapons is missing?"

"I can have one of the ranch hands run inventory," Naomi said. "I don't really care to do it myself. I've got other things to deal with."

"Of course." Jack slid a quick glance to me. It was clear we were being dismissed. "I'm sorry for your loss, Ms. Morrison."

"Thank you." Naomi extended her hand. "Please keep me informed if you hear anything."

"Absolutely." Jack nodded. "I don't suppose we can talk to a few of your ranch hands before leaving? We're just trying to pin down a timeline for the evening in question."

Naomi shrugged, her mind already elsewhere. "I don't see why not. You can show yourselves out. The barn where most of the workers are this time of day is to the east. It will be easier to drive there."

"Thank you so much for your time."

10

TEN

"**W**hat do you think?"

I waited until we were in the rental and heading toward the large barn we saw during our trip to the main house to ask the question.

"I'm not sure what to think," Jack replied. "It seems to me that there might've been a little more anger and hostility between Sully and Morrison than Naomi wants to admit."

"She's going through a tough time. Her father died, and she's feeling guilty for not supporting his dreams."

"I think she was pretty matter of fact," Jack countered. "It sounds to me like her father wanted to be a big fish in a little pond, but he created his own barriers to doing that."

"That doesn't change how Naomi feels," I pointed out. "Her father might've made mistakes, did things she didn't agree with, but she still loved him. She can't stop herself from feeling guilty about the things they fought over – especially recently – because she'll always wonder if that's the last thing he thought about before … well, before it happened."

Jack didn't immediately respond. In fact, he was silent for so long I had no choice but to look in his direction. His eyes snagged with mine when I finally risked a glance.

"Is that what happened to you?" he asked after a beat.

I swallowed hard, frustrated. I shouldn't have said that. It exposed me in a way I wasn't comfortable with. "Why would you ask that?"

"That's not an answer."

"I ... don't know what you're talking about." I averted my gaze and stared at the approaching barn. "What do you hope to get from the workers?"

"I just want a feel for Morrison," Jack answered, pulling into a parking spot in front of the structure. "I don't expect this to take long."

"Shouldn't the sheriff be handling this part?" I turned to face him as I unfastened my seatbelt. "I mean ... I'm not trying to tell you what to do."

"Sure you are."

I ignored his tone. "It's just ... I don't get it. I would assume the sheriff is asking the same questions you are. I know you told Naomi you were asking questions because it makes it easier to eliminate certain things, but I think you're actually interested in solving this case."

"I am interested in solving this case."

"As long as the Chupacabra didn't do it, right?"

Jack pursed his lips. "I know this is difficult for you to understand – especially given what I do for a living – but I prefer having documentable proof," he explained. "As for the Chupacabra, even if I was predisposed to believe in the supernatural I wouldn't believe in the Chupacabra. It's just too ridiculous for me to wrap my head around."

"Scientists are discovering new species all the time," I argued. "They even found a species of fish a few years ago that they thought was long extinct. It could happen."

"They've found more than one species of fish that they thought was extinct," Jack countered. "I think you're probably talking about the Coelacanth."

I was dumbfounded. "Excuse me?"

"What? Don't look at me that way." Jack's cheeks turned pink as he pocketed the keys and opened the door. "I watch a lot of nature documentaries. Sue me. The giant squid was thought to be extinct at one time, too. It's still alive and kicking ... er, waving its multiple arms around."

"I'll alert Peter Benchley," I drawled.

"I'm sure he already knows."

Jack met me at the front of the vehicle, taking me by surprise when he grabbed my arm before I could turn toward the pathway that led to the barn.

"What?" Part of me expected Jack to let loose on a diatribe so I was surprised when his voice turned soft.

"Whatever you said to your parents before their accident, I guarantee it didn't matter," Jack said. "If you're carrying that around ... don't. It's clear that they loved you and you loved them. Feeling guilty about something you can't change is only going to give you a complex."

His words shook me. "I don't ... I ... what?" I was flustered.

Jack merely shook his head. "You'll end up giving me an ulcer before this is all said and done."

"I hope not."

"That makes two of us."

Jack was all business when he strode inside the barn, making quick introductions before focusing on a ranch manager brushing a big horse. His name was David Stevens. He was a big, burly guy with bright green eyes and he seemed amused by my reaction to the horse.

"Naomi said it was okay if we asked a few questions," Jack said.

"I have no problem with that." Stevens looked me up and down curiously. "I want to help as much as I can. Wendell was a good guy – and a good boss – and I want to know who did this to him."

"I promise it won't take too long."

"No problem." Stevens shifted so he was facing me. "Do you want to pet him? I can tell by the look on your face you've never been this close to one before."

"That's not exactly true," I replied, sheepish. "I've seen horses before ... in parades and stuff. I've just never really been close to one."

"This is Clyde. His girlfriend is over there. Her name is Bonnie." Stevens grinned as I tentatively raised my hand to the horse's snout. "It's okay. He's gentle."

I looked over my shoulder toward Jack, worried he would think I was being unprofessional. But he offered me a nod of encouragement. He looked amused at my wonder.

I pressed my hand to the horse's forehead and grinned. "He's so big."

"Don't take it to a pornographic place, Charlie," Jack warned, shaking his head as he turned his full attention to Stevens. "You said that you wanted to know *who* did this. You didn't say you were interested in knowing *what* did this. Can I take that to mean that you don't believe all the Chupacabra stories flying around?"

"Well, that's an interesting question." Stevens rubbed his chin as he shifted from one foot to the other. "I happen to believe in the Chupacabra."

"You do?" I flicked my eyes to him, surprised. "Have you seen it?"

"I have. I saw it out in the desert one night. I was out with some friends – you know, drinking and stuff – and I saw one clear as day. It stood on a slight incline, its spine raised like a cat about to strike its prey. I thought for sure we were dead men, but it stared at us for a few minutes and then disappeared into the night."

"I don't suppose you ever thought the liquor might've contributed to that sighting some, huh?" Jack asked.

"I wasn't all that drunk," Stevens replied. "It doesn't really matter anyway. I do believe in the Chupacabra, but I don't believe the Chupacabra killed Wendell."

"You don't?" I was so enamored with Clyde I didn't bother to glance in Stevens' direction. "Why not?"

"Because Wendell had a particular personality defect that caused him to fight with humans more than animals," Stevens explained. "He was a good boss and he paid well. He was also a righteous pain in the ass when he wanted to be. He sometimes made me want to punch him in the testicles."

I raised my eyebrows and flicked a glance to Jack. "Wow."

Jack ignored my exclamation. "You think he ticked off the wrong person."

"That was his way," Stevens confirmed.

"Do you have any idea who he might've ticked off enough to want to kill him?"

"That list is long and sundry," Stevens replied. "He's been fighting with some land developers who want to lease some of the property for wind turbines. He's also been fighting with Dominic Sully about Hooper's Mill."

"Naomi made it sound as if he'd given up on Hooper's Mill," I said, rubbing my cheek against the horse's flank. "She said he wasn't happy about it but knew he didn't have the funds to compete with Sully."

"Yeah? I'm pretty sure that's what Wendell wanted Naomi to believe." Stevens was blasé. "He wasn't giving up. He was trying to work with the county to secure a grant. He thought that might give him the edge on the property – you know, if the county could have a say in the development – but I have no idea how far he got on that plan."

"The county, huh?" Jack scratched the back of his neck, something I noticed he did when he was deep in thought, and he stared at his feet. "Do you think Dominic Sully was worried enough about Wendell to kill him?"

"I can't answer that for you. I've never met Sully. And, as much as I loved him, Wendell was a real piece of work when he wanted to be. I don't know what happened at Hooper's Mill. I have trouble believing the Chupacabra swooped in at the exact right moment and ended a potential property feud."

Jack nodded in agreement. "Yeah. I have trouble believing that, too."

"Not me," I offered, rubbing my nose against the horse's snout. I was pretty sure I was in love. "I think the Chupacabra did it. Why else would his body be exsanguinated?"

Jack's expression was grim as I flicked my eyes to him for an answer. "That's exactly what I plan to find out."

I LET JACK TAKE THE lead when we got to the clerk's office, mostly because I had no idea what he was looking for. The woman behind the desk seemed eager to help, her smile flirty and friendly when Jack walked up to the window.

"I need some information on Hooper's Mill," Jack explained, mustering a flirty smile of his own as he read the woman's nameplate. "Alanna is a beautiful name. Has anyone ever told you that?"

"You're the first." Alanna's voice was breathy. "Are you new in town? Did you just move here?"

"Actually I'm only visiting." Jack adopted a rueful smile. "I'm regretting that a little bit right now."

"You and me both, honey," Alanna lamented. "I'll see what information I can find. I'm assuming you want everything."

"You assume right."

I barely bit back a groan at the ridiculous exchange and crossed my arms over my chest so I could look stern when Jack shifted in my direction. "You're shameless."

Jack's lips quirked. "I have no idea what you're talking about."

"You know exactly what I'm talking about. You're playing with that poor girl's emotions."

"That girl is only here until she meets a husband," Jack corrected. "I'm guessing she flirts with everyone. She'll be over me within five minutes of us leaving."

He sounded awfully sure of himself. "How do you know she's here to meet a husband?"

"I can read women. She's got 'I want to snag a man' face."

"That's a little condescending."

"Don't worry." Jack patted my head as if I was a stray dog and he was trying to comfort me. "You don't have that face. If you do, you manage to hide it pretty well because I've only seen it once or twice."

I was insulted ... and horrified ... and insulted. "I do not have 'I want to snag a man' face," I hissed, frustrated beyond belief. "Not ever. That is condescending. How would you like it if I told you that you had 'I want to snag a woman' face?"

Jack's expression was bland. "Most men always want to snag a woman … at least for one night."

"That's rude!"

Jack snorted. "You're so easy." He flicked my ear. "Are you this keyed up because your hangover is making you touchy or are you always like this?"

"Whatever." I turned my face from him. "I'm done talking to you."

"Best news I've had all day," Jack teased, poking his finger into my side. "Tell me what I did to earn this fate. I might want to do it again."

I had a sharp retort on the tip of my tongue, but the second Jack touched me I lost my train of thought, because my mind was invaded by a series of flashes. It wasn't the first time my psychic senses took over at an inopportune time, but this one was different.

Usually I see images from the past, things that have happened, and it's my job to make sense of them. This time I was certain I was seeing something from the future.

I saw several things at once. Putting them in order, understanding what I was seeing, would prove difficult.

Charlie!

Jack screamed in my head, the night sky filling with lightning. Thunder echoed between my ears as the rain pounded down. We were in Hooper's Mill, Jack in the middle of the street and me watching from inside a building, although I couldn't tell which one. Jack looked panicked.

I opened my mouth to answer him, but the cry died on my lips as a dark figure moved in at my left. Jack was looking for me, but someone else had already found me. I couldn't see a face – or put a name to the presence – but I knew I was in real trouble.

Charlie!

"Hey." Jack snapped his fingers in front of my face, drawing me back to the here and now. "Where did you just go?"

I swallowed hard, searching for an answer that would placate him. "I ...."

"Here's your information," Alanna announced, appearing at the window.

Jack kept his eyes on me for a beat before swiveling. His smile was back in place, although it was obviously fake. He paid for the documents, thanked Alanna profusely, and then gripped my arm tightly as he led me out of the building. He didn't as much as glance back to gauge Alanna's disappointed reaction at his hasty retreat.

"What was that?" Jack asked as soon as we were outside. "What just happened?"

"What do you mean?" I needed to come up with a story he'd buy, but all I could do was rub my hands over my cheeks as I tried to anchor myself in reality. "Nothing happened. I was standing right next to you."

"You went somewhere," Jack prodded.

"I didn't leave."

"You know what I mean!" Jack's temper was on full display. "Your head went somewhere. I could see it on your face. You kind of went ... slack. That's the only word I can think to describe it. Your eyes glazed over and you froze."

"I didn't." I felt bad for lying to him. He looked so concerned, as if he wanted to pick me up and carry me to the nearest hospital. I couldn't tell him the truth. It wasn't that I never told anyone the truth. Okay, it wasn't *only* that. It was also the fact that he didn't believe in the supernatural. He worked for a paranormal investigative group and he didn't believe in the paranormal. He most certainly wouldn't believe this.

It was altogether ridiculous. The entire thing. I had magical abilities – something the Legacy Foundation would love to know about – and I was hiding in their midst. Jack didn't believe at all, and he was head of security.

The group seriously needed to rethink its hiring practices.

"Charlie, if something is going on ... ." Jack trailed off, uncertain.

"I didn't mean to frighten you." I found my voice and held firm. "I kind of have a headache and zoned out. It's not a big deal."

Jack clearly wasn't convinced, but he didn't push the issue too far, instead resting his palm on my forehead. "You're not hot."

"Thanks so much for that."

Jack chuckled, easing the pall that had settled over us. "I didn't mean that. I keep forgetting you don't often have hangovers so you don't know how to deal with them."

At least he believed me. That was something. "Maybe we should stop at a pharmacy so I can buy more aspirin."

"That sounds like a good idea." Jack perked up. "Then we'll get some lunch, go over the documents Alanna got for us, and go from there."

"Sure." I forced a smile. "You know you probably broke that poor girl's heart the way you ran out without flirting a bit more. She's going to be self-conscious, perhaps wonder if it's because her hair was so big."

Jack snorted, genuinely amused. "You're funny when you want to be."

"Thanks. I'm here all week."

"Let's get some food into you," Jack said. "Hopefully that will help you shake off the dregs of that hangover. Remind me to smack Millie upside the head next time she tries to get you drunk."

"You'll have to beat me to it."

Unfortunately for Jack, he couldn't understand that the hangover was the least of my worries. No, I'd apparently seen the future ... and in it I was in grave danger.

That couldn't be good, right?

11

ELEVEN

"*W*here have you been all my life, handsome?"

The waitress at the restaurant Jack picked for lunch had a smile so wide I thought she could swallow every burrito in the place in one attempt. She barely paid me any attention as she positioned herself next to Jack, her low-cut flower top allowing a nice view of her rather ample goods as she bent over.

"I guess I've been hanging around in the wrong places," Jack answered smoothly. "It's good to know I've found my way into the light."

I was dumbfounded by his flirting. I wouldn't have guessed it was possible to make a grown woman melt into a big pile of goo in the middle of a restaurant with only a smile, but somehow he managed it.

"Good answer," the waitress said. "I'm Mercedes, by the way. I'll be your server ... and hopefully more." She offered an exaggerated wink that made my stomach twist. "What can I get you?"

"I'll have a wet burrito with all the fixings," Jack replied. "Charlie, what do you want?"

I was simply impressed he remembered I was at the table. The way Mercedes was hawking her wares there was a very real chance he'd be blinded and forget all about me. "I'll have the mini-burrito dinner," I replied. "That's not too spicy, right?" Even though I didn't want to admit it, my stomach remained a bit iffy.

"No, that's gringo food," Mercedes said, her smile slipping. "Your friend can handle the spicy stuff, I'm sure." Mercedes collected our menus before promising to return promptly with our drinks. "Don't miss me too much while I'm gone, sugar. I swear I'll be back before you get too lonely."

"I'm not sure that's possible, but I'll do my best." Jack kept his smile in place until she turned on her heel. Then he was all business. "Let's see what documents Alanna got us, shall we?"

I accepted the sheets of paper he slid in my direction, never moving my eyes from his handsome face.

"What?" Jack asked after a beat, shifting uncomfortably on the booth seat. "I haven't eaten yet, so I know I don't have food on my face."

"What is it with you and women?" I probably should've thought better about asking the question – or at least phrased it differently – but my mouth often seems to have a mind of its own and that mind is regularly belligerent, cocky and rude.

"Do you want to be more specific?"

"Sure. Women take one look at you and throw themselves at your feet. Why is that?"

"I think it's the hair," Jack said dryly, sipping from his glass of water.

"I think it's something else – and it's weird."

"It's weird?" Jack cocked an eyebrow, amused. "How is it weird?"

"Well, for starters, you're not a very charming guy. I know from firsthand experience."

"Ah, well, if you say it then it must be so," Jack drawled.

"It's not meant as an insult," I argued. "You're simply … withdrawn."

"I'm not withdrawn," Jack countered. "There are times in life I like quiet. You're never quiet. That's why we butt heads."

"I'm quiet."

"When?"

"I … was quiet when we interviewed Naomi. I was quiet when we interviewed David Stevens."

"You weren't quiet when we interviewed either of them," Jack countered. "Although, I will say you were almost quiet when we interviewed Stevens. Of course, that was only because you were considering running away with the horse."

"Ha. That shows what you know. As beautiful as I found Clyde, I'd never run off with him. I can barely take care of myself. A horse is far too much work."

Jack snickered. "I think you do a fairly decent job of taking care of yourself. But you're not quiet."

The insult was mixed with a compliment, so I wasn't sure how to react. "You're kind of a pain in the ass. You know that, right?"

Mercedes just happened to pick that moment to return with our iced teas, and the look she graced Jack with was nothing short of smoldering. "Honey, if he's a pain then set me up for one of them sadomasochistic relationships," she said. "Bring on the pain."

The statement set my teeth on edge, but I opted not to respond. Even Jack looked a little uncomfortable with the woman's enthusiastic reaction.

"Um … thank you for the drinks, Mercedes."

"Don't mention it, honey." She patted Jack's shoulder, smiling as she gripped the muscles there before turning her attention to a nearby table when a patron called for her attention. "I'll be back to check on you guys."

"Thanks." Jack rubbed his cheek as Mercedes added a little swing to her step – most likely for his benefit – as she crossed the room. "Maybe you're right about flirting with people."

"You should give it some thought," I agreed, turning my attention to the documents. "So what are we looking for here?"

"It's the history of Hooper's Mill, but from a government standpoint, not a historical one." Jack was eager to have something to focus on besides Mercedes' overt interest. "I have no idea what we're looking for, but occasionally you can pick up interesting tidbits from these things."

"I found one." I raised my hand.

"You found one already?" Jack's expression reflected doubt. "You've barely looked at the sheets I handed you."

"That doesn't mean I haven't found something." It was hard to hold back my ego given how annoying I found it to watch women fall all over themselves to get Jack's attention, but I managed it – barely. "I've definitely found something."

"And what would that be?"

I turned the sheet of paper in my hand so Jack could see it and touched the bottom. "This says that Hooper's Mill was started by three people. Richard Hooper, Michael Forest and Donald Morrison. I'll bet that if we do a search on Donald Morrison we find he's the great-great-great grandfather of Wendell Morrison, or at least some shirttail relation."

Jack's eyebrows flew up his forehead as he snagged the document. "Crap! You did find something."

"And you doubted me," I tsked, shaking my head.

"I didn't doubt you," Jack clarified. "I simply ... huh. So, you have three men who founded a silver rush town. Why'd they name it after only one of them?"

I hated to admit it, but that was a good question. "I don't know. You'd think there'd be a fight to call it something like Hoopison Forest or something, right?"

Jack snorted. "Your mind is always working, isn't it?"

"I think that's what happens when you try to figure out a potential murder."

"And I don't think that most people have a mind quite as quick as yours," Jack countered.

I stilled, surprised. "I think that's the nicest thing you've ever said to me, Jack."

Jack lifted his eyes until they linked with mine. "I've said nice things to you before. The problem is you don't listen. Heck, sometimes I say nice things and you assume they're insults."

"Name one time I've done that," I challenged.

"Okay, two weeks ago I said your knowledge of computer equip-

93

ment and how things worked was impressive," Jack started. "You said I added 'for a woman' at the end when I didn't. You then spent the next five hours adding 'for a woman' to everything I said until I wanted to snap your head off your shoulders."

That was quite the visual. "But you said 'for a woman.'"

"No, that's what you heard," Jack argued. "That's your biggest problem. You only hear what you want to hear."

"I'm pretty sure that's a big, fat lie."

"And I'm pretty sure it's not. I didn't say it. I would never say that. I was raised by a mother who would smack me around for saying anything like that. Just because you heard it doesn't mean I said it."

Hmm. Could that be true? "But … ."

"No." Jack wagged a finger to silence me. "I didn't say it. You heard it because it was what you expected to hear. If you plan to continue in this job – and I think you should, because you'll be good at it – you need to learn to open your ears and shut your mouth."

Huh. He had a point. Darn it! "That doesn't change the fact that you're a flirting fool with strangers and mean to those you know."

"I've never been mean to you."

"I'm sure you have."

"I haven't."

"You have."

"Just … keep reading the documents." Jack made a face as he returned his attention to the sheet I handed over moments before. He muttered something under his breath, something that almost sounded like "I know you're going to make my head explode one day" before he cracked his knuckles and fell silent.

I turned my attention to the next document in my stack and quickly found myself engrossed in it. "I found something else."

The look on Jack's face when I glanced up was nothing short of murderous.

"What?"

"How can you have found two big things in less than sixty seconds?"

"That sounds like the premise for some very intriguing erotica," I replied dryly.

Jack took a moment to consider what I said and then barked out a laugh. "You're definitely quick on your feet. What have you got?"

"Well, it seems that three individuals were involved in purchasing the property but less than a year later it was transferred to one person. That's what it says here, right?" I held up the document for Jack's perusal. "I don't deal with county land deeds all that often, so I'm not one- hundred percent sure."

Jack narrowed his eyes as he read the line in question. "That's exactly what it says. Hooper took over the property a year later. It doesn't look like it mentions a sale, does it?"

I shrugged. "I don't think so. If he didn't buy it, how did he get it?"

"No idea," Jack replied. "You have to keep in mind that it was a long time ago. Things might've been run differently back then. Or, perhaps the other two recognized it would be a boom-and-bust town and wanted out."

"If our dead Morrison is related to the Morrison in these documents – which we should be able to find out with a computer search, right? – that might explain why he was so hot-to-trot to get his hands on the property," I supplied. "Maybe he thought of it as a birthright or something."

"That's possible. And a good explanation," Jack said. "We can run the family tree easily enough. We could call and ask Naomi."

"Yeah, I would rather not bother her if it's not necessary."

"I can conduct some research tonight," Jack said. "I'm not sure how the sordid purchase history of the town will come into play."

"It might if we knew how Hooper lost the property," I pointed out, scanning the document. "It says here that property rights shifted to an Adelaide Hooper in 1920 and then completely lapsed ten years after. The state has owned the property ever since – except that two years ago it reverted to the county. I'm not sure if that means the county bought it or simply absorbed it."

"It's probably a mixture of both," Jack said. "Whoever owns the deed is responsible for liability and keeping it up. The county probably didn't buy it. If I had to guess, the state probably signed it over as long as the county agreed to take over maintenance and upkeep."

"I don't think there's a lot of upkeep going on there."

"No, but if the county could sell it – especially to a guy who wants to bring jobs to the area – that would be a boon."

"Why wouldn't the state sell it?"

"I don't know." Jack's expression was thoughtful. "Maybe Mercedes knows." He sat back, his smile in place, and focused his attention on Mercedes as she delivered our meals. "I will just bet you're up on all the area history, aren't you, Mercedes?"

Mercedes brightened at the obvious flattery. "I know a lot about a great number of things. I can prove that to you whenever you're up for it."

Jack's smile didn't slip, but I sensed the unease rolling off him.

"That's a tempting offer, but I need to focus on work first," Jack said. "What can you tell me about Hooper's Mill?"

"Oh, are you the folks searching for the Chupacabra up there?" Mercedes brightened. "I heard we had a group of people searching for that fiend. It's about time."

Even though Mercedes' interest in Jack rubbed me the wrong way – and not because I'm jealous or anything, because that would be ridiculous – I couldn't help being intrigued. "Are there a lot of stories about the Chupacabra?"

Mercedes appeared annoyed by the question, probably because it came from me, but she answered all the same. "This area is thick with Chupacabra stories. It's like the county mascot."

"That's ... fun."

"My daddy saw the beast when I was nothing but a kid, and he told the story for years even though people laughed at him," Mercedes volunteered. "He was out hunting one day and he swore he felt something watching him. He knew it wasn't a man by the way the hairs on the back of his neck stood up.

"He told the story much better, mind you, but it always took him a whole hour to get through it," she continued. "Anyway, he decided to head back to his truck, but he heard something in the bushes behind him. Every time he turned, there was nothing there. Now, my daddy was a brave one, but he said that he was filled with such fear that he couldn't bring himself to look in the bushes, so he hurried on up and almost ran to the truck.

"He swore he could almost feel something breathing down his neck when he finally got there. He refused to turn around and look over his shoulder because he thought it might end up with him dead at the end of some teeth," she said. "He opened the door, hopped in, and the second he closed the door something hit it really hard – so hard that it shook the whole truck."

"Did he see it?" Jack asked, cutting into his burrito. "Did he see what it was?"

"He did see it." Mercedes was solemn as she nodded. "He looked down and saw red eyes staring back at him and a tail that was straight off an alligator."

That didn't sound right. "I've never heard of the Chupacabra having an alligator tail," I argued.

"Have you ever seen the Chupacabra?" Mercedes challenged, her eyes flashing.

"Well … no."

"Then you can't comment on it, can you?"

Jack shot me an amused look as he dumped a small bowl of salsa over his burrito. He seemed as eager to hear the rest of the story as he did to eat. "What happened after that?"

"What do you mean?" Mercedes' face was blank. "He high-tailed it out of there."

"Did he ever go back?" I asked. "I mean – once he calmed down – didn't he want to go back and get a photo of it?"

"Honey, when you escape the Devil you don't go back a second time so you can shake his hand." Mercedes was dismissive. "Everyone knows that beast is running around these parts. It doesn't just hang around Hooper's Mill."

"Have other people seen it at Hooper's Mill?" Jack probed.

Mercedes nodded. "That's where it seems to spend most of its time. It sets out for other places when it's got a mind to. There's nothing stopping that beast when it decides to attack."

"Yes, well ... thank you." Jack flicked his eyes to me. "I guess that should be our next stop, huh? We need to check up on the others."

Finally, something I wanted to do.

12

TWELVE

"I think we should spend the night."

Jack was lost in thought for the duration of the ride to Hooper's Mill. I tried to follow his example – mostly because he thought I was a chatty beast – but it didn't work out well. Ten minutes into the ride I felt the need to make my opinion known.

"Spend the night where?" Jack asked absently.

"At Disney World. Where do you think? Hooper's Mill."

"Absolutely not." Jack was firm. "That's a terrible idea."

"Why?"

"Because we have no idea what's out there."

"That's why we should stay the night," I argued. "The Chupacabra is more likely to visit if we're there after dark."

"And how do you figure that?"

"Because … it makes sense."

"To you."

"To anyone with a brain," I fired back. "It's probably nocturnal. That means it only comes out at night, so that will make it easier for us to see it."

"I know what nocturnal means," Jack said dryly. "I'm mildly curious why you think the Chupacabra is nocturnal."

"Because people have seen it only at night."

"Mercedes said her father saw it during the day, that he at least started out there when it was daylight, and some of the other stories we've heard happened during the day, too."

"Yes, but Mercedes' father also said it had an alligator tail, which is ridiculous."

"Yes, of all the conversations we've had about the Chupacabra, the alligator tail is the ridiculous part."

I cast him a sidelong look. "Nobody needs the sarcasm."

"If we didn't have sarcasm we would have absolutely nothing to talk about," Jack muttered, tilting his head to the side as the road turned to gravel. "It's pretty open out here," he noted after a beat. "If the Chupacabra does live in these parts, where do you think it burrows when it sleeps?"

"You're assuming it sleeps," I pointed out. "How do you know it sleeps?"

"Everything sleeps."

"Sharks don't."

"Are you saying the Chupacabra is a land shark?"

"No, I'm saying … you know what? I'm done talking about this. I'll just bring up my suggestion to spend the night to Chris. He'll be more open to it."

"You go right ahead. I'm head of security. When it comes to the safety of the group, I overrule him."

I swiveled to face him full on. "Is that true?"

"It is," Jack confirmed, folding his arms across his chest. "Myron is the true head of the Legacy Foundation. He generally steps back and allows Chris to make all the decisions. However, Chris is his nephew and he would never forgive himself if something happened to him. That's why he put me in charge of security. My orders stand when we're talking about the safety of this group."

Huh. You learn something new every day. "I'm glad to know Myron cares about Chris. The day I met him all he seemed to care about were my boobs."

Jack shot me an interested look. "Did he say something to you?"

"Not exactly. He was more a lecherous gazer than verbal sexual harasser."

"You're not the first person I've heard that from," Jack noted. "I don't think it's acceptable. I'll have a talk with him."

"You'll have a talk with him?" I was doubly surprised. "How can you do that? Isn't he your boss?"

"Kind of."

That was an evasive answer. "Kind of?"

"Don't worry about how my contract is arranged," Jack ordered. "It's under control. If he makes you feel uncomfortable, I'll talk to him."

I considered the offer for a moment and then shook my head. "Don't do that."

"Why?"

"Because I haven't seen him since that first day and I don't want to be considered the problem employee," I answered honestly. "It's not as if I have to put up with constant sexual harassment or anything. He just ... stared, which I don't get, because I'm not exactly well-endowed."

"No, but you're young and pretty," Jack said. "You've got that hipster thing going for you that a lot of people find attractive." The way he said it left no room for doubt whether he did. That was a definite no. "You shouldn't have to put up with a bunch of crap simply because you're young and this is your first real job."

"I know we had this argument yesterday, but I'm only four years younger than you," I reminded him. "You might think you've lived more than me, but ... ."

"Not more," Jack clarified. "Differently. I've lived differently than you. I didn't mean to upset you when I said that yesterday. You've been through more than most people should have to go through at your age."

He had no idea. If he knew about the magic, about the flash I had a few hours ago, he would probably blow a gasket ... and then proceed to call the men in white coats and have me locked up. He wasn't a believer. I had to keep reminding myself of that.

"I get the feeling that you think I talk down to you," he continued. "It's not on purpose. I have to keep this group safe. You're part of the group. I take my job seriously."

I'd never really considered things from his point of view, and the plaintive way he spoke made me realize I was doing him a disservice. That hardly seemed fair, especially given the fact that he'd come to my rescue a few times – mostly when I did something stupid and needed to cover my tracks.

"I'm sorry."

"What?"

"I'm sorry," I repeated. "I'm not being very nice to you. Sometimes my heart gets ahead of my mind and I act before I think."

"That seems to happen fairly often."

He wasn't wrong. "I still think staying out here is the smart way to go."

"No, you think staying out here sounds like an adventure," Jack corrected. "I get it. I'm not ruling it out, Charlie. But we have procedures to follow. That means we need to set up cameras and watch the area before we put ourselves at risk. There's a reason we follow rules. You might not understand them, but you do have to follow them."

"I get it." I did. "When I wear you down and you allow an overnight stay, you'll include me in the group, won't you?"

Jack rubbed his forehead as he made a hissing sound. "You are … something else."

"Thank you."

"It wasn't a compliment."

"It was in my head."

"Just … be quiet for the rest of the trip. Can you do that?"

It would be tough, but I was gung-ho to try. "Sure."

"Great."

"Um … Jack?"

"Oh, who did I tick off in the universe to deserve you?" Jack lamented.

"I'll start in twenty seconds," I promised. "I just have one more question."

"I've been rendered temporarily deaf. I won't be able to answer."

"Let's just see if that's true."

JACK SEEMED ONLY TOO happy to dump me on Millie when we landed in Hooper's Mill. He grabbed my shoulders and shoved me in her direction as she sat under an eave by the saloon, drinking a bottle of water.

"Watch this," he barked before stomping down the street in search of Chris.

Millie, her eyes lit with amusement as she used the back of her hand to wipe her brow, chuckled as she turned her full attention to me. "What did you do to him?"

"I didn't do anything to him." I sat next to Millie and grabbed a bottle of water from the cooler to her right. "I think he's naturally sensitive or something."

"He's the mellowest person I know," Millie countered. "You're the only one who seems to get to him."

"I guess that must be my little gift."

"I guess so," Millie agreed, leaning back so she could stretch out her legs. "What did you guys do today?"

I related our morning, including the information we found on the documents from the clerk's office. When I was done, Millie was nowhere near as excited as I felt.

"That sounds like a boring day."

"Did you miss the part where I got to pet a horse?"

Millie snorted. "I keep forgetting you lived in the city ... and that city was in the Midwest. There probably weren't a lot of horses running around where you were, huh?"

"Only at parades and carnivals."

"That's kind of a bummer. When we get back to the office and have a break I'll take you to the big house and we can go riding."

The offer caught me off guard. "What big house?"

"The Biggs house," Millie explained. "It's where I used to live when

Myron and I were married. I still come and go as I please. It was part of our divorce decree."

"So ... you still go to the house you used to live in?" That was flabbergasting. "Myron doesn't care?"

"Myron likes to whine about everything, but I don't care to listen," Millie replied. "It's fine. He won't put up a stink, and there are plenty of horses there for you to ride. It will be fun."

It sounded fun – and a bit daunting. "Okay."

"Sounds good." Millie licked her lips as she shifted her eyes to Chris. He was animated as he walked out of what used to be a hotel of some sort. Jack tailed behind, the duo in deep conversation. "What do you think that's about?"

"Probably me. I suggested we spend the night here and Jack acted like I wanted to spend the night in shark-infested waters with a pork chop tied around my neck. He's such a mother sometimes."

"He's not a mother," Millie corrected. "He's good at his job. We're his responsibility and he's very serious about shouldering his responsibilities the right way."

"You sound just like him."

"And you sound a bit petulant," Millie fired back. "Have you ever considered that Jack spent years of his life overseas risking his own life to save others and losing quite a few of them in the process?"

Millie's tone caused me to shrink back. "I didn't mean to ... ."

"What?" Millie quirked an eyebrow.

"I wasn't talking bad about him," I started. "I just ... he's bossy."

"Oh, Charlie, so are you," Millie said. "Kid, I know you don't mean to sound like a spoiled brat. That's honestly not your intent. Your age makes it impossible for you to sound any other way sometimes.

"Jack is good at what he does," she continued. "You might not like how protective he is, but there are times the man has the weight of the world on those broad shoulders. If something were to happen to you – to any of us, really – he'd carry that the rest of his life.

"Now, I know that you've seen death because of your parents, but you're young and the young often think of themselves as immortal," she said. "You're not immortal, and while your death would be a tragedy for all of us, Jack would never recover."

"We're honestly not that close," I argued.

"Not because of that." Millie made a face. "Because he's in charge. It's easy for you to sacrifice yourself, because you wouldn't be around to take the blame. Jack constantly lives with the knowledge that he's the be all and end all when it comes to security."

"I ... um ... huh." I pressed my lips together as I absorbed Millie's words. "I never thought of that."

"That's another thing that comes with age." Millie's expression softened. "I like you, Charlie. You make me laugh. I like your enthusiasm ... and how you're kind of a prude ... and how you're always ready for an adventure. You simply need to remember that not everything is about you."

"I know that."

"Good." Millie scratched at the back of her neck as she stood and stretched. "We've almost finished the camera grid. Hannah and Laura are around the back of the saloon making casts of some prints we saw. Chris was excited by them, but they looked like coyote tracks to me. I don't think it will be long before we call it an afternoon."

"So ... we definitely won't get to stay here tonight?" I couldn't help being disappointed.

"Definitely not," Millie agreed. "We'll set up the cameras and check the feeds. If we see something, we'll come up with a plan. If we don't, we'll come up with a different plan. That's how we operate."

"Okay, well ... ." Since Millie was angry with me – or at least that's how it felt – I decided to give her some space. "I'm going to look around the saloon again before we go. There's more light today."

"Don't wander too far." Millie smiled. "If Jack has to go looking for you, he won't be a happy man when he finds you."

"Yeah, I think I figured that out myself."

I left Millie to do ... whatever it was she was doing and shuffled across the rotting wood that made up the front porch. The fact that the wood remained intact at all was something of a mystery to me, and I dropped to my knees to run my hands over it.

The wood was weathered but nowhere near to the point of the saloon floor. I crawled through the open doorway, staring hard at the spot where they intersected. Someone had built new porch walkways. That much was clear. How old they were was anyone's guess, but there was no way the outdoor porches were original.

I continued crawling until I hit the bar area, peering around the corner to see if the wood matched the internal or external look of Hooper's Mill. The spot behind the bar was clearly original, but the hallway looked newer and stronger.

I crawled in that direction, doing my best to ignore the bug carcasses scattered about. I was almost to the junction when an image invaded my mind and caused me to rear back on my haunches. It was me. I saw me. I saw myself exactly as I was, crouched on the floor in the murky darkness. Only ... I didn't see myself from my vantage point. I saw myself from the end of the hallway, as if something crouched in the darkness waiting for me, something I couldn't see but somehow felt.

My heart skipped a beat and I let loose a gasp as my mind brushed against something. I had no idea what, thanks to the murky gloom. I screamed at myself to get away, to scramble back, but as before, I was frozen in place. I couldn't make myself move. Thankfully, nothing else seemed to be moving in the darkness, at least there was no sound to signify movement. Whatever was down there remained unmoving ... and watchful.

"What are you doing?" Jack's agitation was evident when he stepped through the doorway.

"I ... ."

"Are you hurt?" Jack strode to my side, grabbing me under the armpits and hauling me to my feet. "Did you fall?"

I swallowed hard. "No. I was looking at the floor."

"Why?"

"I ... the outdoor wood is newer than the indoor wood."

"Okay." Jack brushed off the knees of my jeans and looked me over before meeting my gaze. "Why are you so white? You look like a ghost."

"I thought I heard something." That was a safe answer, right? I couldn't tell him I hopped into someone – or something – else's head and looked at myself. He'd think I was crazy.

"Where?" Jack was instantly alert.

I hated the way my finger shook as I pointed toward the hallway. Jack pulled a flashlight from his belt and flicked it on, pointing it in that direction. The hallway, of course, was empty.

"What do you think you heard?" Jack asked.

"I don't know. Shuffling, I guess."

"Well, there's nothing down there now." Jack put his hand to the small of my back and directed me toward the door. "You're okay."

His words were gentle, and I felt a bit like an idiot when I realized how I probably looked in his eyes. "I know. I just freaked out a second. I thought the Chupacabra might be down there."

"I thought it only came out at night," Jack teased.

"It's dark enough that it might've been fooled into thinking it's night. Plus, well, it does need a den. Maybe the saloon is its den."

"That's exactly where I would make my den if I was the Chupacabra," Jack said. "Come on. Chris wants to show everyone the grid and test the cameras. Then we're heading back to town for dinner."

"Okay." I was thankful to walk into the bright and airy outdoors, shaking off the last strains of dread as the sun hit my face. "I still think we should spend the night here."

"Why doesn't that surprise me?"

"Because you're a smart guy."

"I am, and you're not spending the night here, so let it go."

"Okay, I'll let it go for tonight, but I'm going to start bugging you first thing tomorrow morning."

"I can't wait."

13

THIRTEEN

"*E*verything outside is gridded."

Chris was rarely boastful, but that's how he acted when Jack and I joined him in front of what used to be the hotel.

"Are you sure you got every angle?" Jack asked.

Chris nodded. "Absolutely."

"Do you care if I walk the perimeter to check?" Jack didn't sound like a man trying to protect his fellow co-worker's feelings. He didn't sound like a guy worried about what the boss's nephew would say. He was very matter of fact.

"I think that's probably a good idea," Chris replied. "You have good ideas and you might see something I missed."

"Okay." Jack smiled. "I'll walk through once on my own and drop flags where I think cameras are necessary. Then we'll take your camera locations and compare them to mine and make some adjustments."

Chris beamed, not bothered in the least. He was all about the science, after all. That's all he cared about. "That sounds like a plan."

Jack flicked his eyes to me, uncertain. "If you want to come with us …."

"I'm fine." I shot him a pointed look. I didn't want Chris to think I was some sort of panicky weakling. "I want to check out the hotel. I haven't been inside yet."

Jack shot me a sidelong look. "Maybe … ." He didn't finish what he set out to say. I had an idea what it was – some variation of me not being alone – but he kept it to himself. "Be careful."

He didn't let his gaze linger, instead clapping Chris on the back to prod him into motion. "Let's take a look at the cameras. It shouldn't take us more than an hour to get them exactly right. Then we can head back to town and get dinner."

"I've been thinking," Chris hedged.

"That's always a dangerous proposition," Jack drawled.

Chris plowed forward, ignoring the teasing. "I think we should spend the night and monitor the cameras ourselves."

I was in the middle of sneaking away to the hotel when I swiveled and landed on the other side of Chris. Now we were getting somewhere. "I agree with Chris," I volunteered immediately.

Jack scowled, annoyance evident. "We've talked about this, Chris." The security guru's tone was calm but I could see the fire kindling in his eyes. "We need to follow procedure."

"But this is different," Chris protested, sounding a bit like a whiny child trying to get his way. "This town is abandoned. If several of us stay here together … ."

Jack cut off Chris with a firm headshake. "Absolutely not."

"But there's no danger." Chris wasn't ready to give up. "The town is completely abandoned. We haven't seen a single soul. There's nothing to worry about."

My mind drifted to the presence I felt in the saloon. They might not have seen anyone – souls notwithstanding – but something was here. I was certain of that. Whether man, beast or something else entirely, I had no doubt there was something here.

Jack didn't share my sense of distress, but he refused to waver. "We're not staying here tonight. We're setting up the cameras. That's procedure. You can watch the footage live all you want. Tomorrow, I'll go through the footage with you. We'll make our next decision after that."

"But ... ."

"No. It's not going to happen, Chris."

It was fascinating to watch the man I thought of as the boss crumble as Jack put his foot down. Chris heaved a sigh and shrugged. "Fine. You're always such a stickler for the rules."

"That's why you're still alive." Jack smirked as he pointed toward the edge of town. "Let's start over there."

"Sure." Chris hurried down the steps, Jack following.

Jack stopped long enough to give me a considering look. "Do not wander off ... and if you hear something again, call out to me. I'll come running. I promise."

Charlie!

My mind flashed to the vision I had of Jack looking for me. "I know. I'll be fine. I freaked myself out in the saloon. I won't let it happen again."

"I don't care about that." Jack lowered his voice. "Just be careful."

I watched him go, a combination of feelings I couldn't quite put a name to flitting through my stomach, and then I turned my full attention to the hotel. It looked stronger than the other buildings, more protected from the elements for some reason. I was eager to see inside.

The feeling lasted exactly thirty seconds until I strode into what used to be the lobby and found Laura and Zach looking around. It was obvious they were flirting – Laura's expression suggested they might even be considering getting filthy – but they both looked in my direction. Zach smiled, the expression coy and lazy. Laura glowered. I had no doubt we would never be friends.

"I just want to see the hotel," I offered lamely. "It looks kind of cool from the outside."

"It's definitely cool," Zach agreed, his lips curving into what I'm sure he considered a sexy smile. "And how was your day, Miss Charlie? I hope you're over that pesky hangover. You were absolutely delightful last night when I ran into you on the street."

I stared at him for a long beat. "I'm sorry if my drunkenness caused you extra work."

"I like my work." Zach offered up a saucy wink, causing me to roll my eyes.

"Is there a reason you constantly wink?" I challenged. "I mean … do you have something in your eye? Do you wear contacts? Do you have an aversion to the sun and your eyes tear when it's too bright?"

Zach balked. "No. I … ."

Laura snorted, catching me off guard. "The winking is a little much, Zach," she agreed. "You look like you have a nervous tic or something. You should probably stop doing that. It makes people uncomfortable."

Zach made a face before moving toward the door. "Yes, well, I think I'll check on the rest of your group. The light won't last long. We need to be out of here within the hour."

"You do that," Laura said dryly, her expression unreadable as she watched him go. She waited until she was sure he was out of earshot before speaking again. "You don't like him."

It was a statement, not a question, and I had no idea how to respond. "No. He's fine. Um … I think he's swell."

"Swell, huh?" Laura didn't bother to hide her amusement. "I really want to dislike you, but then you say things like that and I can't help but think you're funny."

"You want to dislike me? Why?"

"Because you're competition." Laura's answer was simple, and she didn't seem bothered to admit it. "The second I saw you walk through the door I knew you were going to be trouble."

"Because I'm competition? Exactly who am I competing with you over?"

"It's not like that." Laura was matter of fact as she smoothed her auburn hair. I had no idea how she could look so put together in this heat. "You're looking at it the wrong way."

"How should I look at it?"

"We're not competing for people, but status," Laura explained. "Before you came I was the young one everyone wanted to take under his or her wing."

I had serious doubts about that. "Isn't Hannah younger than you?" She certainly looked it.

"Hannah doesn't count because she's in her own little world," Laura replied. "She can't compete because she simply doesn't believe in competition."

"And you think I do?"

"I think you're competing whether you know it or not. The thing is ... you like the work. I guess that's to be expected because of your age. You're enthusiastic because you're just starting out. You need to take it down a notch or two."

"And what about you?" I challenged. "Have you ever considered that making things a competition isn't healthy?"

"No." Laura was blasé. "Without competition I'd be bored."

"Well, I think that says a little something about you."

"It might, but I'm fine with that." Laura flicked her eyes to the door over my shoulder at the sound of footsteps, forcing me to swivel quickly.

I wasn't expecting the Chupacabra to appear in the doorway, but dread filled me all the same. It disappeared when I found Millie standing there, her gaze speculative.

"What's going on here?" Millie asked.

"Nothing." Laura adopted an air of innocence. "We were simply chatting. You know ... getting a feel for one another."

"Oh, joy." Millie rolled her eyes until they landed on me. "I saw you talking with Jack and Chris. What was that about?"

I saw no reason to lie. "Chris wants to spend the night and Jack thinks it's a bad idea."

"Well, I happen to agree with Jack for a change," Laura said. "There's no way I'm spending the night in this dusty rat hole."

"What if Zach decides to spend the night?" I challenged. "Something tells me you might change your mind then."

"Zach isn't stupid enough to spend the night here," Laura replied. "Speaking of that, you might want to look elsewhere if you're hoping for a little thrill while we're here. I've decided that Zach is going to be my thrill, and I'm not keen on sharing."

"You're more than welcome to him."

"Because you don't like him," Laura mused. "I can see it on your face when you're around him. Why is that?"

"He just ... irritates me." I could hardly tell her that he made me feel uncomfortable. Laura was the type to use that to her advantage.

"Plus, you're interested in Jack," Laura added, tapping her bottom lip. "Be careful with that. He's never going to give you what you want."

My irritation bubbled as she moved toward the door. "I am not interested in Jack!"

Laura let loose a derisive snort. "Yeah, you keep telling yourself that. By the way, if you're heading upstairs, use the front staircase. The back one's so rickety it looks like it's going to fall any day. I would hate for you to take a tumble and die." She disappeared through the doorway before I could think of something nasty to say.

When I risked a glance at Millie I found her smiling. "What?"

"Nothing." Millie made a clucking sound with her tongue. "You do bring a lot of drama to the group. I like it. What are you doing here?"

I shrugged as I worked to rein in my temper. I liked Millie. She wasn't the irritating one. I had to keep reminding myself of that so I didn't take out my frustrations on her. "It's a cool building. I thought I'd look around while they're finishing the camera grid."

"I haven't been in here yet either," Millie said. "Let's see what this place has to offer."

"I bet it won't be much."

"It's still worth a look. Normally I don't listen to Laura, but I don't want to die, so we'll avoid that back staircase."

It didn't take long to search the main floor. The ravages of time and weather had turned the furniture into dust-covered lumps, and there was very little of interest. The second floor was something else entirely.

After a nerve-wracking climb up a set of narrow stairs that I was certain was about to give way – seriously, if the second staircase was worse I didn't want to see it – we stopped at the head of the hallway so I could drop to my knees and study the floor.

"This is newer, too," I said after a beat.

"Newer than what?"

"Some of the floors look to be original and are giving way," I answered. "The porch on the front of the saloon and these stairs look newer, though. I wonder why that is."

"Maybe someone thought about restoring Hooper's Mill at another time that was more recent," Millie suggested. "As much as I don't like the town – and I don't, because it feels as if someone is watching me – I can see why a developer might try to save the place. It has a certain amount of ... charm."

Her words caught me off guard. "You feel as if someone has been watching you?"

"What? Oh." Millie shrugged, noncommittal. "It's just a feeling. I can't explain it."

I knew that feeling well. "Let's look around the rooms. By the time we're done I'm sure Chris and Jack will be ready to go."

"There aren't many rooms, eh?" Millie wrinkled her nose as she walked with me. "Only six. I wonder if that was standard for the time."

"I have no idea, but I guess that most of the people who came to a town like this camped close to wherever they were working. Hooper's Mill was probably a place to stock up on supplies and blow off steam."

"Oh. You mean that this was probably a brothel masquerading as a hotel."

That's not what I meant, but now that she said the words it made sense. "Probably," I conceded, flicking on my flashlight as I turned into the first room. It faced the street and a decent amount of sunlight poured through the intact window, so I lowered my flashlight. The bed in the middle of the room was long gone, but pieces of the frame remained. "Do you think they just up and decided to walk out one day?"

"What do you mean?" Millie asked, running her fingers over the aged metal.

"Why leave the furniture?" I challenged. "They must've had some sort of hint that the town was fading. Why wouldn't they pack up the furniture when they left?"

"Maybe there was no one left by then to pack the furniture."

"Because the Chupacabra ate them?"

Millie snickered. "I think it's far more likely that the town dwindled – and quickly – to the point where only one or two people were left when they decided to abandon ship."

"I guess that makes sense." I rolled my neck as I stepped to the window, frowning as the view of the street overlapped with the flash I had of Jack.

Charlie!

This was where I stood in the vision. I was sure of it. I looked down, saw the spot where Jack would scream my name, and glanced to my left. In the vision, someone approached from that direction. For now, it was empty ... except for a small something that gleamed on the floor.

I knelt, holding up my flashlight so I could see better. When I was sure the item was something other than critter eyes, I reached down and wrapped my fingers around a discarded earring.

"What is that?" Millie asked, drifting closer.

"I'm not sure." I flipped the earring over and rested it in the palm of my hand. It looked old, and expensive. It certainly didn't appear to be costume jewelry. "Do you think this belonged to one of the ladies of the house?"

Millie shrugged. "I don't know. It's interesting, though. Bring it with us. We might be able to learn more about it."

"Good idea." I pocketed the earring as I stood, shifting my eyes to the open doorway at the sound of footsteps. Jack appeared two seconds later.

"I was looking for you two." Jack ran a hand through his straggly hair. He looked tired. "The camera grid is good to go and Zach is on us to get out of here before it gets dark. Are you ready?"

I nodded without hesitation. "If we're not staying the night, I see no reason to stay longer than necessary."

"Don't push me on that," Jack warned. "If you're not careful I'll ban you from staying if I ultimately allow an overnight visit. You won't like it if that happens."

He wasn't wrong. "My lips are sealed."

Jack cocked a dubious eyebrow. "That would be a neat feat since I've yet to see that happen."

"I guess you'll have to wait and see, huh?"

"I guess so." Jack ushered me through the door and met Millie's steady gaze. "What?"

"I didn't say anything." Millie's lips curved. "You guys are like a snarky sitcom. I think it's funny."

"You can be quiet for the ride back to town, too," Jack ordered. "I want a little peace and quiet."

"Sir, yes, sir." Millie snickered as she mock saluted.

"You two have been spending way too much time together," Jack complained.

"Should we march, sir?" I asked, grinning.

"Just move." Jack pushed me toward the stairs. "I'm officially going to need a drink with dinner if this keeps up."

"Me, too," Millie enthused.

"Not me." I shook my head. "I think I'm going to become a teetotaler."

"If you do we can never be friends." Millie was solemn. "You simply need to build up your tolerance. Trust me."

On that particular front, I wasn't sure that was true.

14
FOURTEEN

*M*illie and Bernard rode with us back to town, opting to sit in the backseat and whisper to one another. I watched them a bit, my earlier suspicion that they were in a secret relationship only solidifying when I saw the way she smiled at him. After a few minutes, I realized Jack was watching me and I ceased spying.

"What?" I asked, uncomfortable.

"You know what." Jack kept his voice low. "Mind your own business."

The look on his face intrigued me. He clearly suspected the same thing I did. In fact, he might actually know something. I would have to feel him out about that later. For now, I changed the subject. "How was the grid?"

"Fairly decent. We added two cameras. I think we have the entire town covered – at least for the most part."

"That's good, right?"

Jack shrugged. "It is for Chris. I think he's going to be watching the monitors tonight rather than television in his room."

"Why is that bad?"

"It's not. It's just … labor intensive. I'd let the cameras record all night and then speed them up in the morning, but that's just me. Chris is more dedicated on that front."

"Chris is definitely dedicated," I agreed. "He wants to spend the night at Hooper's Mill. Are you going to let him?"

"I haven't decided yet."

"I could stay with him," I offered. "We could eat dinner and turn around and go back. That way he wouldn't be alone."

"No offense, Charlie, but you're not exactly a good chaperone. You can't even keep Millie out of trouble."

"I resent that," Millie said, turning her full attention to the front of the vehicle. "I was her chaperone."

"That's even more frightening," Jack said. "If that's how you see it, you definitely fell down on the job last night."

"How was I supposed to know she was a lightweight?" Millie protested. "She just got out of college. I assumed she could hold her own."

"I didn't drink all that much in college," I admitted. "In fact, I think I drank three times the whole four years."

"Why?" Bernard looked pained. "The best thing about college is the drinking."

"Word." Millie solemnly nodded and bumped fists with Bernard, causing him to grin.

"I didn't go to college to drink," I said. "I had limited funds. I worked thirty hours a week and held down a full class schedule. I had to graduate in four years."

"Why?" Millie asked. "If I were you, I would've dragged it out to five years."

"I didn't have the money for that."

"Oh, well ... I didn't think about that." Millie had the grace to look abashed. "You mentioned it before, but I kind of forgot ... or maybe I thought you were exaggerating a bit."

"Not everyone has a fat divorce settlement to live on, Millie," Jack reminded her. "Some people actually need their salaries to survive."

"I said I was sorry." Millie turned petulant. "I forget sometimes that I have it easy in a lot of respects. I didn't mean anything by it."

"And that's why I'm not angry," Jack said. "Hannah, Charlie and I all live on our earnings. I believe Bernard does, too."

"Mostly," Bernard agreed, turning to stare out the window. "Do they pay you well enough to have your own place, Charlie?"

"I have a small apartment. One bedroom." It wasn't terrible. It was nothing like the house I lived in as a kid – and had to sell or face financial ruin – but I didn't own much and the apartment served my needs because we were always traveling. "It's fine."

Jack slid me a sidelong look. "Do you need more money?"

The question jolted me. "I'm not accepting money from you."

"That's not what I asked. If you're not being paid enough, I'll talk to Chris."

"I'm paid fine." It was true. "I didn't expect to make buckets of money coming out of the gate. I have more than enough to pay my rent and put some away each month."

"Okay." Jack dropped it. "Did you guys see anything while you were at Hooper's Mill today?"

"Nothing of interest," Bernard replied. "The town is sort of desolate and depressing."

"You said you felt as if someone was watching you, Millie," I reminded her. "Do you think it was a person?"

"As opposed to the Chupacabra?" Millie grinned, legitimately amused. "I don't know if it was a man or monster. I'm not even sure it was real. It was just a feeling."

"Maybe it was a ghost," Bernard suggested. "I'm guessing that place is thick with them."

"Not that I've seen," I murmured, my mind flashing back to the vision of Jack screaming my name.

"Do you see many ghosts?" Jack asked.

I realized what I said too late to take it back. "No. I wish I did, though."

Jack's eyes were lasers as they locked with mine. "You wish you could see ghosts?"

He was making me nervous. "Doesn't everyone?"

"Not last time I checked." Jack focused on the road. "Charlie thought she heard something in the saloon, but when I flicked on the flashlight there was nothing. Were you inside the saloon, Millie?"

"Of course. It's a saloon. I've always wanted to hang out in a vintage saloon. Of course, to be fair, that saloon is a little more vintage than I'd like."

"Word." I bobbed my head, thinking I was merely fitting in with the group. When Jack, Bernard and Millie burst out laughing I realized that probably wasn't the case. "You guys suck."

Jack chuckled, the sound light and easy. "You'll learn to love us."

One look at his strong profile told me that was potentially true ... and worrisome. "I'm hungry," I volunteered, shifting the conversation again. "I assume we're having barbecue again tonight."

"That seems to be the only thing the one diner in town offers," Millie said. "You guys were out of town today. Please tell me you got something different."

"Mexican," I said. "It was good. The waitress hit on Jack."

Millie seemed happy to turn the conversation toward the taciturn security chief. "Oh, I bet that's the story of his life. What do you think, Jack? Is she your type?"

"No." Jack answered without hesitation.

"What exactly is your type?" Bernard asked.

"Inquiring minds want to know," I teased.

Jack heaved a sigh. "I'm kind of wishing we'd made a rule about being quiet for the ride."

"Too late."

"I'll remember for next time."

AFTER DROPPING BY MY ROOM to wash up and run a brush through my hair, ultimately giving up and returning it to a loose bun because it looked gross thanks to the nonstop sweat, I headed down the street. We all agreed to meet at the diner. I wasn't surprised no one waited for me. I was the last to arrive, and the only open spot was between Zach and Jack.

I took my seat, flashing a friendly smile at Hannah across the table, and grabbed a menu as I tried to ignore my growling stomach.

"You smell divine," Zach offered, leaning in to sniff me.

I shifted away from him and almost ended up in Jack's lap. "Um ... okay."

"Don't do that," Jack ordered, glaring at our erstwhile guide. "That's invasive."

"I was just sniffing her," Zach argued. "She smells like coconuts."

"It's body spray," I said. "I used it to mask the fact that I smell like a stinky armpit underneath thanks to all the sweating I did today."

Zach made a face. "Well, that sort of ruins the illusion."

"I think it adds to her mystique." Jack's lips quirked as I shifted away from him. "Try not to sniff her, okay? She clearly doesn't like it."

"Yes, sir." Zach's response was sarcastic, and I didn't miss the way the muscle in Jack's jaw tightened.

"It's cuter when I do it, huh?" I whispered, trying to ease the tension. It apparently worked because Jack's expression softened.

"Infinitely."

"So, what's the plan with the cameras?" Laura asked, clearly growing bored with the sideshow at our end of the table. "Are we going to watch the footage in the morning and make a new plan?"

"In theory, yes," Chris replied, sipping his water. "I'm hoping we'll see something definitive. If we don't, we'll still return to Hooper's Mill in the morning."

"What if we do see something?" I asked. "Does that mean we'll spend the night tomorrow and try to get photographs – like up-close-and-personal style?"

"You need to let that go," Jack warned.

I ignored him. "It's just ... we might see something that the cameras miss."

"I happen to agree with you, but it's up to Jack," Chris said. "I'm in charge of everything but security. Jack has to give his okay for something like an overnighter."

"That sounds like a bummer because Jack is such a dull dude," Zach said.

Laura chortled as I scorched him with a hot glare.

"Jack has a job to do," I barked. "He's responsible for us. I'm sure you have no idea what that means, because you're barely responsible for yourself. So you might want to shut your hole instead of attacking him."

I had no idea I could be so vehement in my response until the words were already out of my mouth, and when I shifted I found Millie watching me with delight. Jack, however, seemed dumbfounded.

"Well, thank you for that," Jack said after a beat. "Does that mean you'll stop bothering me about spending the night in Hooper's Mill?"

"No."

"I didn't think so." Jack rolled his neck and smiled at the diner owner, Donna, as she approached the table. "Your food is delicious. We're looking forward to another wonderful meal."

And the charm was back and on full display. I had no idea how he did it.

"You don't need to blow smoke up my behind," Donna said dryly. "The barbecue is good, but it's hardly going to win awards. That's why I'm out here. I'm doing ribs tonight. They'll take another twenty minutes. They're one of my best dishes, so I suggest waiting for them."

"Sounds good to me," Jack said.

"Me, too." Chris was enthusiastic as he closed his menu. "While you're out here, I was wondering if you might have some insight into the history of Hooper's Mill. We pulled some documents from the county clerk's office but we have more questions than answers."

"I don't know how much help I can be, but I'll certainly give it a try," Donna said. "Lay it on me."

"Well, for starters, why is some of the wood older?" Jack asked the first question before Chris had a chance. "Charlie noticed that the front porches are newer and less likely to fall apart. The stairs in the hotel are the same. Also, there looked to be some sort of weird construction that happened at some point on the second floor – a room that is no longer a room maybe – but it was hard to ascertain with the limited light."

Hmm. I noticed the odd floor patterns, but I hadn't paid any attention to the corner Jack mentioned. I would have to look closer when we returned.

"I can't be certain, but I seem to remember a story about a developer coming in, oh, it must have been in the late nineties, and he did some work at Hooper's Mill while the paperwork was still winding its way through the state. Ultimately his mortgage didn't go through and he couldn't take it over, so all the work he did was for nothing."

"That seems a shame," I said. "Most of the buildings look like they're one good storm away from falling down."

"I think that's why Dominic Sully wants to get in there as soon as possible," Donna said. "He's been making noises that he wants clearance – and soon – because he's certain the buildings won't last much longer. He wants to fortify them."

"Does he plan on keeping the original work?" Jack asked.

"I think he plans to keep the original feel," Donna clarified, tucking a strand of her dirty blonde hair behind her ear. She looked sweaty and tired, but seemed eager to answer questions rather than return to kitchen duty. "That wood is so old it can't be saved."

"Do you go out there often?" I asked.

"I've been out there a few times over the years. I'd be more willing to visit if it wasn't so creepy. Plus, well, with everyone saying they've seen strange beasties out there I don't have much interest in hanging out."

"So you've never seen the Chupacabra?" Chris was disappointed.

"I didn't say that." Donna smiled. "I said that I don't want to see strange beasties. The Chupacabra isn't strange. It's misunderstood."

Jack exchanged an amused look with me. "How so?"

"Well, for starters, it's half dog and half lizard. You would be confused if you were like that, too." Donna's face lit up as she warmed to her subject. "I saw it one day out behind the shed. It was just hanging out, panting like a dog. Seemed okay to me."

"Panting like a dog?" Chris' expression was hard to read, but I got the feeling that Donna's story didn't sit well with him. "I've never heard of a Chupacabra panting like a dog."

"Then you haven't been talking to the right people." Donna clapped Chris' shoulder, amused. "I have a boatload of stories for you if you're interested."

"I'm definitely interested." Chris was nothing if not a gentleman.

"Well, I'll get your ribs and then come back and join you," Donna said. "Give me twenty minutes. I'll have a waitress come and take your drink orders."

"That sounds like a plan." Chris was practically giddy when he turned back to us. "Isn't this great?"

"Yes, I can't wait to hear about the panting lizard," Jack said dryly. "I actually have something I want to talk to Donna about when she gets back, though. I want to see if I can arrange a meeting with Dominic Sully, although I have no idea if he's been found since his disappearance or if he's even open to talking with me."

"Why do you want to talk to him?" Chris asked.

"Because he's going to buy the town and he and Wendell Morrison were competing to own it," Jack replied. "If we're trying to rule out human suspects, we should start with Sully. He seems to have the most motive for wanting Morrison gone."

"Yes, but Morrison was exsanguinated," Chris pointed out. "Humans don't usually do that."

"Vampires do," I offered. "Maybe we're not looking for the Chupacabra at all. Maybe we're looking for a vampire."

"Do you think that's helping?" Jack asked, his eyebrows migrating up his forehead.

I shrugged. "I didn't know I was supposed to be helping. I'll do better next time."

"That would be great," Jack gritted out. "As for Sully, I'm guessing I'm going to have to go through layers of corporate B.S. to speak with him."

"If you think it's necessary," Chris said. "I believe we're clearly dealing with something else, though."

"You pursue your suspect and I'll handle mine." Jack grabbed a breadstick from the basket at the center of the table. "I'll start making calls in the morning."

"You don't have to do that," Millie said, taking everyone by surprise. "If you want to talk to Sully, I'll arrange it for you. There won't be any hoops to jump through."

Jack licked his lips, his mind clearly busy. "You'll arrange it for me?"

"That's what I said, isn't it?"

"But ... how?"

"I know people who know people," Millie replied. "I can arrange it. I'll make a call in the morning and get you a time."

Jack didn't look convinced, but he capitulated all the same. "Okay, well, thanks."

"You're welcome." Millie smiled. "Now, let's talk about the panting lizard. I think that would be a great name for a porn star."

The table erupted in laughter, giving me a chance to watch Millie with fresh eyes. She was full of surprises. I risked a glance at Jack and found him doing the same.

"What do you think?" I kept my voice low.

"I have no idea what to think. I guess we'll simply have to see how things work out."

I wasn't keen on the idea, but we were at a crossroads. "Thanks for not sniffing me, by the way." I was trying to lighten the mood and I knew it worked when Jack cracked a grin.

"You do smell fabulous," he teased. "I especially love the hint of armpit you exude. It's ... delightful."

"That's what I was going for."

15

FIFTEEN

*M*y dreams were muddled.

Millie did her best to get me to go out to the bar with her again, but my head – and liver – politely declined. I was more than happy to roll into bed and slide into slumber. Unfortunately, what followed wasn't exactly restful.

I found myself wandering through a dreamscape. I was in Hooper's Mill – I recognized it – but it didn't resemble the ramshackle place I'd visited in the present. No, this was something from the past. Whether it was my mind filling in the gaps or how the town really looked, I couldn't be certain.

The sun was high in the sky, although there was something of a mist hanging about. The streets were empty. The town looked like it should be bustling with activity, but it was as if the residents suddenly disappeared for no apparent reason, which made it all the eerier.

"What are you doing here?"

Jack's voice jolted me, and I swiveled quickly, widening my eyes when I found him sitting in front of a small building, his feet propped on a split-rail fence and a cigar in his hand.

"What are you doing here?" I challenged, stepping closer. He wore a tin badge on his chest. It was faded, and he looked to have an antique gun in a holster on his hip. "You look like an extra from a western."

"You don't look like you belong here," Jack challenged. "Why aren't you in costume?"

I smiled at his outrage. "I guess my imagination is running away from me ... again. You look nice in the outfit. The hat looks adorable with your hair."

Jack made a face. "Whatever." He puffed on the cigar, wrinkling his nose as he coughed. "Why am I smoking this? I don't smoke."

"I don't know. I guess I associate movie sheriffs with cigars. I can't explain it."

"I think that says a little something about you," Jack muttered, shaking his head. "Why am I here, Charlie?" The question was so plaintive I could do nothing but shrug.

"I don't know. I don't know why I'm here."

"I think you do," Jack countered, getting to his feet. "You're here because you think there's a mystery to solve. You like solving mysteries."

"You barely know me. How could you possibly know that?"

"Because I know you better than you think. It might be argued that you don't know yourself very well so you can't see it, but it's true."

"Is that because I'm young and dumb?" My voice, tinged with bitter resentment, wasn't pretty.

"I didn't say you were dumb. I said you were young. That's not an insult."

"It feels like an insult."

"Which is only something you believe when you're young." Jack's eyes lit with mirth as he tipped back his hat and flicked the cigar to the ground. "What do you think you're going to find here?"

I shrugged. "I don't even know what I'm looking for ... and you shouldn't litter. Pick that up."

"This isn't real, so I'm not littering."

He had a point. "It's still gross."

"Whatever." Jack rolled his neck. "I know what you're doing here. You're looking for answers, but I haven't figured out the question you want answered yet. Are you looking for the Chupacabra or something else?"

That was a very good question. "Chris is convinced that the Chupacabra killed Wendell Morrison. He won't even consider anything else. You're convinced it's a human and won't budge from that. What if the answer is somewhere in the middle?"

Jack furrowed his brow. "What? Like Dominic Sully took his pet Chupacabra to Hooper's Mill and killed Wendell Morrison because the guy was moving in on his business venture?"

Well, when he said it like that. "Just because Morrison was probably killed by a human doesn't mean the Chupacabra isn't hanging around Hooper's Mill."

"Fair point. But I still don't believe the Chupacabra is real."

"I know." I tilted my head back and stared at the sun. "This isn't real. It should hurt to stare at the sun like this. That's how I know this isn't real."

"I'm going to play devil's advocate here. Just because you know it's a dream, that doesn't mean it's not real."

"Oh, apparently I've turned you into a weird philosopher spouting messages that surely must come from fortune cookies in my subconscious."

"Maybe that's who I am in real life."

"Doubtful." I pressed my eyes shut and clasped my hands. "Something bad is going to happen, Jack. I feel it."

"Have faith. It might not be as bad as you think."

As if on cue, I heard it again, a loud rumble of thunder even though it was a sunny day. Then the screaming started.

"Charlie!"

I wrenched open my eyes, but the Jack who stood next to me only moments before was gone. I was alone again, in my hotel bed, with nothing but his bellow on the imaginary wind in my head.

"Something bad is going to happen," I repeated. "I don't think I can run from it this time."

. . .

I WAS DRAGGING WHEN I woke the next morning, the dream weighing me down. Everyone was already at the breakfast table in the hotel restaurant when I made my way to the main floor and took the seat between Zach and Jack. I barely registered that it was the same configuration from the night before when Jack pushed a glass of orange juice in front of me.

"You didn't go out with Millie again last night, did you?" Jack scorched Millie with an accusing look.

"Hey, Bucko," Millie fired back. "I was good, and went to bed early last night."

"So did I," I offered. "I didn't go out."

"Then why do you look like roadkill on a barbecue spit?"

That was a lovely visual. "Thanks so much for that compliment," I muttered, annoyed.

"Sorry." Jack held up his hands in a placating manner. "You look as rough this morning as you did yesterday. I thought you'd get some sleep."

"I had weird dreams." I rubbed my cheek as I grabbed a doughnut from the plate at the center of the table. "Have you guys already ordered?"

"We were waiting for you." Jack's expression was contemplative. "Did you have nightmares?"

"I don't think 'nightmares' is the correct word," I replied. "They were weird dreams, interactive or something. I don't know how to explain it."

"Well … ." Jack took me by surprise when he pressed the back of his hand to my forehead. "You don't feel warm. Are you certain you're not sick?"

"I'm not sick, Mom." I rolled my eyes. "I'll be fine once I get some fuel into me."

Jack didn't look convinced. "Then eat two breakfasts, because you look like something the Chupacabra dragged in."

"You've got a weird thing for checking people's temperatures, don't you?" I challenged. "I think you missed your calling. You should've been a nurse."

"I'm going to be the guy who locks you in your hotel room all day if you're not careful."

Millie snorted. "You two are a trip. Leave her alone, Jack. She's still waking up."

"You shouldn't really talk to women that way," Zach chided. "They don't like being told they're ugly."

"Ain't that the truth," Laura muttered.

"You're not ugly, Charlie." Zach gripped my hand tightly and stared with a look I'm sure he thought was soulful into my eyes. "You're a beautiful woman."

"I think I changed my mind about being sick," I said.

"Knock that off." Jack slapped Zach's hand away. "You're bugging her."

"I think you're both bugging her," Millie suggested. "Let the girl eat her breakfast in peace."

I was grateful for the assistance, but I felt Millie's probing gaze, so I avoided eye contact. "Was there any action on the camera last night?"

"Not that we've seen so far, but there are a few shadows that bear further examination. And we haven't checked the night-vision equipment yet," Chris supplied. "I know you want to go back to Hooper's Mill, Charlie, but before that happens I was hoping you and Millie could go to the zoo. There's an expert there we want to look at the footprint casts we took."

"Sure." I wasn't especially bothered about being sent out of town. In fact, it sounded like a pleasant afternoon. "We can get lunch wherever the zoo is, Millie. It will be a nice to have a little variety."

"Just no barbecue." Millie rubbed her stomach. "I had heartburn hotter than a Chupacabra's tongue on a skillet last night. I don't want to go through that again. In fact, we need to stop at a pharmacy so I can get some antacid."

"No problem."

"What about you, Jack?" Chris asked. "Have you heard from Dominic Sully yet?"

"I don't expect to hear from him. Millie said she was handling it." Jack's opinion on putting Millie in charge of tracking down Dominic

Sully was obvious when he crossed his arms over his chest and kicked back in his chair.

The look Millie shot him was pure haughtiness. "And I handled it, Mr. Attitude."

"Really?" Jack cocked a dubious eyebrow. "How?"

Millie gestured toward the door. "That's him right now."

I followed Jack's disbelieving gaze and focused on the man striding into the room. He looked to be in his early fifties, strong and well built. The suit he wore looked to cost more than the entire hotel. I recognized him from the photos we saw during the flight to Texas.

"Are you the members of the Legacy Foundation?" Sully asked.

"We are," Chris confirmed, hopping to his feet and extending a hand. "You're Dominic Sully, right?"

"I am." Sully offered a curt nod. "My mother called and insisted I was needed here ... so here I am." Sully didn't look thrilled with the turn of events. "Which one of you is Jack?"

Jack tentatively raised his hand as he snagged Millie's gaze. "How did you manage this?"

"I happen to be on a charity board with his mother," Millie replied dryly. "I didn't realize it until after we'd already ascertained the body in Hooper's Mill didn't belong to this guy." She jerked her thumb in Sully's direction for emphasis. "I called in a favor last night. It wasn't easy, but I'm nothing if not determined ... er, or annoying, if that's the word you prefer."

Despite his rather obvious agitation, Sully barked out a laugh. "You are exactly how my mother described you."

"I'm not sure if I should take that as a compliment, but have a seat anyway." Millie pointed to the chair on her left. "We're ordering breakfast."

"I don't believe I want to eat anything this place has to serve." Sully's lip curved. "Couldn't you have picked a nicer hotel?"

"Not in close proximity to Hooper's Mill," Jack replied, recovering from his earlier shock. "Mr. Sully, do you understand why we're here?"

"If I'm to believe my mother, it's because you're looking for the

Chupacabra," Sully replied. "I'm hoping she was merely morning drinking when she let that little tidbit slip."

"No, we're definitely looking for the Chupacabra." Chris' face was serious. "Do you know why you were initially thought to be the victim?"

"Because I took a three-day respite and apparently that was cause to call out the National Guard," Sully replied.

"Respite?" I was curious. "What does that mean? Is that code for rehab or something?"

"Charlie." Chris shot me a warning look, but Jack merely shook his head and chuckled.

"That's code for a spa," Sully corrected. "I was getting some Botox."

He didn't seem embarrassed, so I saw no reason to press him on the issue. "Oh, fun."

"So, when you returned from your respite you realized that a lot had happened," Jack noted. "Are you surprised that Wendell Morrison is dead?"

"Not in the least," Sully replied, not missing a beat. "The man had the personality of a rabid possum. He was a complete and total pain in the – pardon my French, ma'am – ass."

It took me a moment to realize I was the "ma'am" in question. "Do I look old enough to be a ma'am?" I turned to Jack for confirmation, but he merely held up his hand to silence me.

"I understand you had some issues with Morrison," Jack pressed. "Has the sheriff questioned you in regard to his death?"

"Yes."

"And?"

"And my alibi is airtight and they've moved on to other suspects," Sully replied, his temper flashing. "I didn't come here to be insulted."

"I'm not trying to insult you," Jack said. "We're struggling for answers."

"I thought the Chupacabra did it," Sully deadpanned. "I'm seriously hoping that becomes the official cause of death. That will only increase visitor traffic when I finally open the town to tourists."

"And that's still your plan?" I asked.

Sully nodded. "I've had my eye on that parcel for years. Morrison's death – however tragic – doesn't change that. Why should it?"

"I don't really care about that portion of it," Jack replied. "I care about finding out exactly who killed Morrison. It's a priority for us. The only thing we have to go on is the fact that Morrison wanted Hooper's Mill because he was determined to maintain the integrity of the town."

Sully let loose with a laugh so ragged and raucous it almost knocked me out of my chair. "Is that why you think Morrison wanted the property?"

Jack blinked several times in rapid succession. "Why else would he want it?"

"Oh, I don't know," Sully drawled. "Perhaps it has something to do with the legend."

Legend? Now we were getting somewhere. "There's a legend? Is it about the Chupacabra?"

"Shh." Jack squeezed the back of my neck to quiet me. It didn't hurt, but I found it annoying. "We're not from around these parts. We need more information on the legend."

"I don't know how it will help you, but it's not exactly a secret," Sully said. "For more than a century people have been buzzing about the former owners of the town and how they sold their interests for some silver."

"That would explain how they lost ownership of the town," I mused.

"Shh," Jack hissed. "I will gag you if it becomes necessary."

He looked serious, so I shut my mouth.

"The town had one owner after the first couple of years. The town went belly up because the silver rush was fast and furious," Sully explained. "It was over quickly. There was a rumor that the owner had his own stash of silver, and he packed it up in the middle of the night and abandoned Hooper's Mill, stealing away like a ghost. They say he had so much silver he had to leave some behind because he couldn't carry it all."

"And rendering it a ghost town within twenty-four hours," Jack said. "That explains why all the furniture was left behind. Do you believe the legend?"

"No," Sully waved the question away with his hand. "I'm not interested in the silver. I'm interested in an entertainment venue. I do believe Morrison thought the legend was true."

"Why?"

"Because I found him nosing around the property numerous times. He was keeping track of his progress on a map," Sully replied. "I don't own the property yet – although it's only a matter of time – so I couldn't bar him. He knew it was coming, though, which probably explains why he was there after dark."

"Did anyone else believe the legend?" Jack asked. "Could other people have been spending time at Hooper's Mill looking for the silver?"

"I guess it's a possibility, but I don't see the point of it," Sully replied. "Even if there is silver, I doubt it's enough to make anyone rich. Plus, that place has been party central on the weekends for teenagers for years. If there was anything hidden out there I think they would've found it long ago."

"Morrison obviously believed it was out there," I pressed. "Maybe he was right."

"And even though the silver isn't enough for you to care about, that doesn't mean that the poorer people of this area feel the same way," Jack added. "The legendary silver could be a motive."

"If the killer is human," Chris argued. "We don't yet know who or what killed Wendell Morrison."

"We don't," Jack agreed, maintaining his calm. "This is a good lead. It could explain a few things."

Chris wasn't happy with the observation. "Or it could be the Chupacabra."

"I didn't say otherwise." Jack kept his voice flat, but irritation practically rolled off him in waves. "We need to investigate more."

Chris' eyes were flat. "We definitely do."

16

SIXTEEN

*J*ack met Millie and me outside, keys in hand. I was certain he was about to invite himself along for the ride. I was torn on the issue – he was smart and always asked the right questions when it came to an investigation – but ultimately I wanted a break from him and his overbearing attitude.

"You're coming with us?" I did my best to cover my disappointment, but it wasn't a stellar effort.

Jack stared at me for a beat. "Maybe. How would you feel about that?"

"Like you're suddenly asking questions a television therapist would," I muttered.

Jack's lips curved as he shook his head. "You need to develop a poker face, Charlie. Other people might not take the fact that you don't want them tagging along so well."

"That's not the issue," I lied.

"Whatever." Jack shook his head. "The zoo is about an hour away. I programmed the directions into the GPS."

I blinked slowly, absorbing the news. I didn't know whether to be happy he wasn't coming or annoyed that he thought I couldn't find my way. "So ... you're not coming?"

"I have other things to check on, including Sully's supposed alibi. I also want to do some research on that silver legend. I'm suspicious that we haven't heard mention of it until now."

"Oh, well … ." I held out my hand to take the keys. "I guess I'm the captain for a change. That's exciting."

Jack pressed his lips together and moved the keys toward my hand, veering at the last second and handing them to Millie. "You're not the captain."

"Oh, come on," I complained. "I want to be the captain."

"You can be the co-pilot," Jack countered. "Think of yourself as Spock … or Chewbacca."

"Ugh. You're a geek. I didn't see that coming."

Jack's eyes went dark. "I'm fine with being a geek."

"I didn't say there was anything wrong with it," I argued. "I'm a geek, too. I like it."

"You're … something," Jack muttered, making a tsking sound with his tongue before focusing on Millie. "The footprint casts are in the hatchback area. You're looking for Desmond Sharper. He's a zoologist who has agreed to look at the casts to see if he can identify what made them. He's expecting you. Just tell the woman at the ticket window why you're there and she'll call him to collect you."

"No problem." Millie's reaction was flat. She clearly didn't care either way about our excursion. "I'll have my phone if you want to check in."

Jack tilted his head to the side, confused. "Why would I want to check in?"

Millie slid me a sidelong look, amused. "I thought you might want to make sure Charlie wasn't finding trouble at the zoo. You know, climbing into the lion habitat or swimming with the otters."

Well, that was insulting. "I wouldn't do that," I argued. "I might hang out with a kangaroo or something, but that's only after I finished my work for the day." I offered up a smirk to let them both know I wouldn't forget this slight.

"I like you more and more each day," Millie cackled. "You have an absolutely fabulous personality."

"I think the idea of you two wandering off on your own adventure is going to give me an ulcer," Jack said. "I don't have options, though. Chris needs Hannah and Bernard at Hooper's Mill, and I don't think we'd ever see Charlie again if we sent her off with Laura."

"Because she thinks we're in competition?" I asked, fixing my hair in the window reflection.

"Did she say that to you?" Jack's tone was sharp.

"She said it yesterday. She said we were in competition and then proceeded to essentially call me an idiot. Oh, she also warned me away from Zach, even though I'd rather bathe in piranha-infested waters than touch him."

"Just ... steer clear of Laura and I'll have a talk with her," Jack said, pointing me toward the passenger side of the vehicle. "Now ... get going. I expect you two will have lunch over there so you can have something other than sandwiches or barbecue – and that's fine – but take pity on me and get back here in plenty of time for dinner. I don't want to have to come looking for you."

"I think we can manage a trip to the zoo," I argued.

"I hope you're right." Jack took me by surprise when he rested his hands on my shoulders and stared into my eyes. For a second I thought he was going to kiss me goodbye – which was ridiculous because he thought of me as the younger sister he never wanted. "Do what Millie says. She's in charge. Try to think before you speak. And, for the love of all that's holy, don't wander off and get lost."

Oh, well, geez. That was pretty far from romance. "I've got it under control."

"No, I've got it under control," Millie corrected. "Don't worry about us, Jack. Everything will be fine."

"See, I have trouble believing that, but I have no choice but to let you go." Jack took a step back. "If you run into trouble, call me."

"We won't run into trouble," Millie said. "We're going to the zoo and having lunch. What could possibly go wrong?"

"I THINK WE'RE LOST."

137

I held back as long as I could before expressing my obvious frustration. We were lost in a catacomb in the center of the wolf display, and I was fairly certain the zoo workers would have to send a search party to find us.

"We're not lost," Millie argued. "There's no need to panic."

"I'm not panicking."

"You're kind of a dramatic soul. I don't think you can help yourself. It's fine. Trust me."

We found the zoo and even lucked out on a parking spot. Once we told the woman at the ticket booth who we were she waved us back and told us to follow the signs to the wolf exhibit. Once there, we were to go through the employee door carved into the habitat wall and walk until we found the end of the hallway. Unfortunately, the hallway had five or six branches. It was also dark, chilly and kind of dank.

"I'm not that dramatic," I argued, keeping my stride short so I wouldn't accidentally trip and smack my face into one of the fake cave walls. "What do you think this material is?" I ran my hand over the cool wall.

"What are you, a builder now?" Millie asked. "It's some sort of brick masonry or something. It's meant to look like a cave. This is all manmade. You're not really in a cave."

"I figured that out myself."

"Then why are you walking as if you expect a hand to rise from the earth and drag you to hell?"

"I'm not." I squared my shoulders and increased my pace. "You're kind of mean when you want to be."

"Yes, well, I'm looking forward to margaritas at lunch," Millie replied. "I expect you to serve as the navigator on our way back, by the way."

"I don't think Jack will like that."

"What Jack doesn't know won't hurt him," Millie shot back, causing me to smile. "Ah, well, here we go."

The hallway opened into a large room resembling a veterinarian's office, which made sense because we were meeting a zoologist. The laboratory centered the room and was surrounded by modified cages. The animals in the displays burrowed down in their dens when they were tired of running around outside, and the cages were located at the back in case someone needed to approach the animals. It was a convenient set-up.

"Are you Desmond Sharper?" Millie asked the man staring through a microscope at the center table.

He lifted his eyes and smiled as he ran a hand through his gray hair. "I am. You must be Millie and Charlie. I've been expecting you."

"I'm sure you have." Millie hefted the footprint cast onto the table and then took a better look around the room. "This is kind of neat. The animals come to you on some levels."

"There's a false wall behind each den," Sharper explained. "The animals are completely closed off most of the time, but we just had a cleaning crew come through and I've yet to raise the walls. We only lower them when we need to run tests. It gives the animals the illusion of privacy."

"And who doesn't love the illusion of privacy?" Millie drawled, amused. "Still, it's kind of neat down here."

"Plus it's cool," I added. "I imagine Texas gets pretty hot, so it's nice that you can escape down here."

"It's fairly comfortable," Sharper agreed, removing a pair of latex gloves and getting to his feet. "So what do we have here?"

"We've been investigating the death out at Hooper's Mill," Millie explained. "We found these tracks. There's some ... unexplained ... aspects to Wendell Morrison's death, and we're trying to find answers."

"I see." Sharper was all business as he shifted toward the casting. "Where did you find these in proximity to the body?"

"Oh, ... it was a good hundred yards away," Millie replied. "My understanding is that the body was found in the middle of the street. The prints were found on the other side of the buildings. I wasn't there when they were cast, so I'm not one-hundred percent sure."

"We've heard rumblings about Hooper's Mill for years," Sharper supplied, tilting the cast so he could see it better under the light. "I've been fascinated with the history of the place ever since I moved here from Austin twenty years ago."

"Do you mean the Chupacabra rumors?" I asked.

"I've heard those rumors." Sharper's lips quirked. "You believe in the Chupacabra?"

I shrugged, noncommittal. "I don't know. I believe there are things that can't be explained."

"That's a good answer." Sharper moved to a drawer and pulled out a metal contraption I couldn't identify before returning to the print.

"What's that?" I asked.

"It measures the size of the print," Sharper replied.

"Do you know what it is?"

"Give him a few minutes," Millie chided, shaking her head. "It's nice and cool down here, comfortable. We're in no hurry."

"I thought you wanted margaritas with lunch," I challenged.

"The margaritas aren't going anywhere."

"If you're looking for good margaritas I can point you toward the perfect place when we're done," Sharper offered. "It doesn't open for another hour."

"That sounds good." Millie sat in a chair and watched Sharper work. "You said you've heard stories about Hooper's Mill. Have you ever heard one about hidden silver?"

"I have," Sharper confirmed, squinting at the casting. "That was one of the first ones I heard. The Chupacabra story followed not long after. I always thought they were tied together."

"In what way?" I asked, my eyes widening when a huge wolf wandered in from the outside and settled in his climate-controlled cage. "Wow! He's awesome."

"That's Lobo." Sharper smiled at my enthusiasm. "He's a handsome boy. He was raised in captivity, so he's not afraid of humans. He's more dog than wolf."

One look at the animal's wild eyes made me think otherwise. Still, it wasn't my place to argue. Sharper was helping us and seemed eager to chat, so I figured it was smart to take advantage of that. "What did you hear about the silver?"

"Just that the former owner had so much of it that he couldn't carry it all when he left," Sharper replied, furrowing his brow as he all but pressed his nose against the cast. "Most people think he hid it in the buildings – like in the walls or floors – and planned to come back for it. The story I heard was that Richard Hooper died before he could return.

"I've always been a history buff, so I did a search on him," he continued. "He lived until the 1940s, but I believe he transferred ownership of Hooper's Mill to a sister during the 1920s, and then moved to Arizona. He didn't die before he could return – in fact he lived to be quite old, especially for back then – so it doesn't make sense to me that he would leave a huge pile of silver behind for no apparent reason."

"Do you think a lot of people have been out there searching for it?" I asked.

"I think a lot of people I know have been out there looking for it," Sharper replied. "It's a regular Saturday outing for some. People are determined there's silver out there, and they believe they'll be the one to stumble upon it.

"It's the age-old wish," he said. "People want to get something for nothing. It's human nature to dream. It's human nature to build up stories until they take on a life of their own. I think that's happened with the silver … and, quite frankly, with the Chupacabra."

What he said made sense, but I wasn't quite ready to let it go. "You said before that you think the silver and Chupacabra stories go together. Why is that?"

"Because I think one was manufactured due to the other," Sharper replied, his somber eyes landing on me. "Think about it. The silver stories have been around for a long time. Everyone wants to search the area. What's the best way to cut down on the searches?"

I shrugged. "I don't know."

"I do." Millie's eyes lit. "You think someone started the Chupacabra story to scare people off. If people think there's a beast out there they're less likely to search for the silver."

"Exactly." Sharper nodded. "I think the two stories are linked."

"But what about Wendell Morrison?" I challenged. "Something killed him out there. He was exsanguinated."

"You don't know that was a Chupacabra," Sharper pointed out. "That could've been a human trying to take the legend to the next level. Everyone knows Dominic Sully is going to buy the land. When that happens, he'll probably cut off access to the property while he renovates. People think they're running out of time to find the silver."

"And you figure someone was willing to kill a man to buy more time to search for the silver?"

"I think the area surrounding Hooper's Mill is extremely poor, and that amount of money could change someone's life," Sharper replied. "I think the Chupacabra makes a handy … well … scapegoat-sucker."

"Ha, ha. Good one." Millie grinned. "You know, I hate to say it because Chris won't like it, but this theory makes a lot of sense. It's far more likely someone killed Morrison and made it look like the Chupacabra did it than it is to believe the Chupacabra is really running around an old silver town."

I wasn't ready to give up the dream. "But what about the prints?"

"These prints?" Sharper gestured toward the cast. "These belong to a coyote."

"But look at the odd spacing on the right one there," I protested.

"I have," Sharper said. "That's what took me so long. This animal broke its foot at some point and it never healed correctly. That's why it looks off."

I couldn't help being disappointed. "Are you sure?"

"Yes." Sharper shot me a sympathetic look as he chuckled. "I'm sorry. I know you were hoping for a different answer."

"We were hoping for the truth," Millie countered, getting to her feet. "You gave us the truth. We're grateful for it."

"It was my pleasure." Sharper was quiet for a moment as he watched me pack the print cast. He spoke again before we could leave the laboratory. "Be careful, ladies. If I am right, that means someone

THE CHUPACABRA CATASTROPHE

isn't going to be happy about you guys running around Hooper's Mill. You could be stepping on a murderer's toes, so ... watch your backs."

"We always do." Millie offered a half-hearted smile. "So, you were going to tell me where to get some good margaritas."

"Right. Let me draw you a map."

17

SEVENTEEN

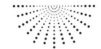

*D*esmond's restaurant served great Mexican food according to the locals and some of the largest margaritas I'd ever seen. I was perfectly happy letting Millie sip her pear margarita while sticking to iced tea as we waited for our food.

"Are you disappointed the print isn't from a Chupacabra?" Millie played with her straw wrapper as she searched my face.

"I guess." I wasn't sure how to answer. "I'm not sure I ever believed it was a Chupacabra print. I'm not sure what I believe about this one, truth be told."

"In other words, you think there's too much evidence pointing toward a human culprit," Millie mused. "That makes sense."

"I didn't say that," I cautioned. "It's just … it's too convenient."

"Meaning?"

"Meaning that Wendell Morrison reportedly wanted the property and he knew he was running out of time because Dominic Sully was going to get it. When you combine that with the fact that a bunch of people believe there's a hidden fortune on the land … well … it seems like a really convenient time for the Chupacabra to attack."

"It does," Millie agreed. "It seems like a great time for people to become interested in the Chupacabra again, doesn't it? Gives the property a little mystique before Sully starts his renovations."

"Do you think he did it?"

Millie held her hands palms up. "I have no idea. Jack will check his alibi today and I'm sure we'll know more this afternoon. Sully doesn't strike me as the type to get his hands dirty, so if he did it he most likely paid someone to do it."

"You're friends with his mother," I pointed out. "Do you believe she raised a murderer?"

"We're not exactly friends," Millie hedged. "Friends is a relative term. We're members on a couple of those snooty boards I was forced to participate in when married to Myron. That doesn't make us friends. I would say we're acquaintances. I called in a few favors to get her to reach out to her son. She wasn't happy about it, but she did it to make sure I stayed off her back … and out of the other women's ears."

That was an interesting way to phrase it. "What kind of favors?"

"Never you mind." Millie wagged her finger. "You're turning into a regular busybody. You remind me of … me."

"Uh-huh." I wasn't convinced, but I let it go. "Hopefully Jack will come up with some good stuff on the silver legend, too. I think he said he was going to research Sully and the legend all morning."

"Jack is good at what he does. He'll be fine."

"I didn't say he wasn't good at his job."

"And yet you almost panicked when you thought he was going with us this morning," Millie noted. "Why is that?"

Uh-oh. She was trying to pin me down. I recognized the move from when my mother was still alive and she figured out I liked a boy. Once that happened, she stalked, harped, hounded and badgered until I owned up to the crush. The realization caused a pang in my chest. "I have no idea what you're talking about," I lied.

"You know. You just don't want to talk about it." Millie regarded me. "You like him, don't you?"

I thought I was prepared for the question. It was only a matter of time before someone asked it, of course. I'd seen the curious looks. I knew Laura believed it. Still, I was caught off guard by Millie's bluntness. "He's very good at his job. He's a decent co-worker. Of course I like him for those reasons."

"Oh, that was cute." Millie grinned. "You like him more than that," she prodded. "In fact, I think you have a crush on him."

I was absolutely mortified. "I don't get crushes."

"Everyone gets crushes. I have one on Sean Connery. There's nothing to be embarrassed about."

"Who is Sean Connery?"

Millie narrowed her eyes to dangerous slits. "Are you messing with me? Are you doing that thing younger women do regarding older stars when they pretend not to know them to make someone feel old?"

I thought about dragging it out longer, but her reaction made me believe that would be a poor idea. "I know who he is."

"You'd better."

"He's the guy from *Highlander*. I know because I like those movies. There's something about a dude with a sword."

Millie made an exaggerated face. "*Highlander*? He's James Bond, honey."

"No, Daniel Craig is James Bond."

"There's more than one."

"Why?"

"Ugh. I can't even look at you right now." Millie shook her head. "What were we talking about again?"

"Your crush on an old dude," I replied without hesitation.

"No, we were talking about Jack," Millie corrected. "I've seen the way you look at him."

"As if I want to find a baseball bat and hit him over the head?"

"Sometimes," Millie conceded. "He drives you crazy. There's no doubt about that. You do the same to him."

"So why would you possibly think I have a crush on him?"

"Because you two have chemistry." Millie sipped her margarita and smirked as I shifted on my booth seat. "Oh, you've already figured that out yourself. I wasn't sure on that one. You seem to block things out you don't want to deal with."

"And what kinds of things would those be?"

"Your feelings for Jack," Millie answered. "Your feelings of inadequacy."

"I'm not inadequate."

"You're not," Millie agreed. "You're smart and funny. You have a charming sense of humor and your dramatic flair is delightful. But in your mind, you feel inadequate because you were the last to join the team. That's perfectly natural, by the way, and you'll get over it."

"Since when did you turn into a therapist?"

"You make jokes about therapists a lot," Millie noted. "That tells me it might be a good idea for you to see one. But you don't need a therapist to tell you that your feelings for Jack are perfectly okay."

She was starting to agitate me. "I don't have feelings for Jack. That's ridiculous."

Millie took another sip of her margarita and waited for me to fill in the silence.

"I don't," I snapped, making a face. "I mean ... I have feelings about him being in charge and bossing me around. I have feelings when he talks down to me as if I'm a child. I have feelings when he tells me I talk too much and to be quiet. Those are the only feelings I have for Jack."

Millie chuckled, legitimately amused. "You keep telling yourself that."

"I will ... because it's the truth."

"Honey, it's so far from the truth that you can't even see truth on a map right now," Millie argued. "It's fine. You're not ready to admit it."

"There's nothing to admit."

"There's a lot to admit, but it's not important now," Millie said. "It's good you're taking your time. Jack isn't ready to admit it either. That boy has been on a dry spell since the day I met him. It will be nice to see him relax when he finally ... ." Millie made an odd movement but I recognized it for what it was. She was simulating a sexual act.

"Stop that," I hissed, leaning forward. "You're going to draw attention to yourself."

"You act as if I should care about that," Millie drawled. "I don't. I don't give a moldy crap what other people think about me. That's how I choose to live my life."

"It must be nice."

"It is. It's freeing. That's how I got freed from my marriage to Myron."

I stilled. "What do you mean?"

"I mean that I thought I wanted one life, so I went for it," Millie replied. "I married Myron – and I did love him for a time – but ultimately that wasn't the life I really wanted, because I couldn't be myself. Myron wanted to be something he wasn't and I didn't. That's how we ended up here."

"What did you want to be?"

"The kooky woman in the corner." Millie grinned at my furrowed brow. "You're young, Charlie. I know you're sick of hearing that, but it's true. Soon you'll realize that being what everyone else wants you to be is exhausting. It's much better to be what you are."

"I don't pretend to be something I'm not." Even as I said the words I thought about my abilities. I hid those from everyone. There was a reason for that, of course, but I couldn't be the person I was born to be, because that would instill fear and suspicion in people. I didn't want that.

"I don't think you're pretending to be someone you're not," Millie said after a thoughtful beat. "I do think you're hiding something. I don't know what – I've given it a lot of thought and come up empty – but you're hiding something."

Her intense gaze made me feel uncomfortable. "I'm not."

"It's okay if you are." Millie lowered her voice. "You don't have to share your secrets with the world. You don't have to be uncomfortable being yourself either. I think you're pretty great."

"Except I talk too much and don't think before I speak," I muttered.

"Is that what Jack said?"

I nodded.

"Ignore him. Those are my favorite two things about you. I think they're Jack's favorite two things, too, although he's not ready to admit it."

"And I think you're seeing things that aren't there."

Millie wasn't about to be dissuaded. "I guess we'll have to see, won't we?"

I ASKED MILLIE IF we could make a stop before heading back, and she was more than happy to oblige. She limited herself to one massive margarita during lunch, and seemed in a good mood, only mildly tipsy. She was flummoxed when I pulled into a jewelry store parking lot.

"Are you going to buy Jack a promise ring?"

I ran my tongue over my teeth as I tugged on my limited patience. "No. I thought I'd see what they had to say about this." I pulled the earring I found the previous day from my pocket. "I thought maybe they could tell us when it was made."

"Oh. I forgot all about that." Millie was suddenly intrigued. "Good idea. You're getting good at this investigative stuff. Jack would be proud."

"Don't make me hurt you," I warned. "Just because you're older and I'm supposed to treat you with respect doesn't mean I won't kick you when you deserve it."

Millie snorted. "Honey, I could take you with a margarita in one hand and a burrito in the other. We both know it. Age is a state of mind."

Sadly, she was probably right. She was made of stern stuff, and I'd never been in a physical fight with another woman. "Just … stop with the Jack stuff. It's not true and makes me feel icky."

"That's because you know it's true but you don't want to admit it," Millie countered. "Still, if you don't want me to mention it, I won't."

"Thank you."

"For three days."

"What? That's absurd."

"I'm giving you a three-day moratorium. Then I'm going to start mentioning it again."

"You are un-freaking-believable."

"That's what my business cards say."

Millie didn't bother hiding her smug smile as she followed me into the jewelry store. The woman behind the counter – her nametag read "Sue" – offered us a bright smile.

"Welcome. Is there something specific you're looking for?"

"Yes." Millie grinned like an idiot. "Where are your watches?"

"The case at the far end."

"Great. While I'm looking at those, Charlie has something she'd like to ask you about."

Millie left me and drifted toward the watch case. "Do you take credit cards, by the way?"

Sue nodded. "Of course." She turned her bright eyes to me. "And what questions do you have?"

"I found this earring, and I was wondering if you could tell me a little about it." I drew out the item in question and held it up for Sue's perusal. "It looks old to me, but I'm not an expert."

Sue took the earring and flicked on a counter lamp so she could study it closer. "It looks like a nice piece. Where did you find it?"

"Out at Hooper's Mill." I saw no reason to lie. It wasn't as if I stole the earring.

"Really?" Sue was intrigued. "Well, it's certainly authentic. These are real diamonds and pearls. Do you think someone dropped it?"

"We're there in conjunction with the investigation into Wendell Morrison's death," Millie volunteered. "She found it in one of the old hotel rooms. We're a little curious how it ended up where it did."

"Could it be from the original time period when the town was booming?" I asked.

"This is certainly a beautiful piece – and it looks to be original – but that would be original from the 1920s," Sue explained. "It doesn't date as far back as Hooper's Mill."

"Oh." I couldn't help being a little disappointed. "So it's newer but hardly new."

"Correct." Sue chewed her lip as she pulled out a loupe and closed one eye to focus on the gemstones. "The diamonds are not only real, but high quality. The earring itself is probably worth a couple thousand dollars. It would be worth more if the backing was original, but it's still a good find. Do you want to sell it?"

The question took me by surprise. "It's not mine. I found it."

"Yes, but I doubt anyone is going back to Hooper's Mill to look for it," Sue noted. "What is that saying … finder's keepers? I think you found it, so it's yours."

"I agree," Millie said. "But don't sell it. At least not yet."

I had no intention of selling it, mostly because the thought unsettled me. I felt as if I were dealing in stolen goods or something, which was ridiculous, but I was something of a goody-goody when it came to issues like this. I needed to buy time so I could think.

"You said the backing isn't original," I prodded. "What does that mean?"

"Do you see the metal here?" Sue pointed at the gleaming back of the earring. "That's much newer."

"How much newer?"

"I would say within the last two years or so, because it's in really good shape," Sue replied. "It's not uncommon to rehabilitate older pieces like this. People have been doing it for years. I like it because it maintains the integrity of the older pieces, but makes it so they're less likely to fall apart."

"Hmm." I rubbed the back of my neck as I lobbed a gaze toward Millie, who was watching me with a thoughtful expression. "If the earring was updated within the last few years, that means the person wearing it was there within that timeframe."

"And from where you found it, I'm going to guess it was more recent than that," Millie said. "It wasn't even dirty when you discovered it."

"That's how I found it," I said. "That room was dark, and it glinted in the sunlight."

"What are you thinking?" Millie asked. "Do you think Wendell Morrison somehow dropped it?"

"I'm sure it's not his style, but that doesn't mean someone he knew didn't drop it."

"Like his daughter?"

I thought back to Naomi Morrison and shook my head. "This doesn't seem like her style either. She wasn't wearing jewelry. But she might know who it belongs to."

"Oh, good, another trip. Do you think Jack would approve of us handling this leg of the investigation?"

That was an interesting question. I had another one. "Do you care?"

"Not in the least," Millie replied. "But before we go, I want to buy a watch."

"Why do you need a watch?"

"It's for you."

I balked. "I don't need a watch. In fact … you don't have to buy something for me."

"I want to, and you do need a watch," Millie argued. "Look at the rest of the group. Everyone wears a watch. They're important."

"But … ."

"No." Millie shook her head. "It's obvious you've been on your own for a long time and you're used to doing for yourself. This is a gift. You're going to take it and suck it up."

I was both mortified and touched. "I don't know what to say."

"Start with 'thank you.'"

That seemed simple enough. "Thank you."

"Good." Millie's smile was benevolent. "I want you to remember this moment when I start bugging you about Jack again. I've earned some good will here."

Yup. I should've seen that coming. It was too late now, though. "I'll try to remember."

"That would be great. Wrap her up, Sue. We've got a grieving daughter to question, and I wouldn't mind finding some ice cream on our way out of town."

Well, at least not all her ideas were bad.

18
EIGHTEEN

*N*aomi's ranch was quiet as we drove along the driveway, somber, almost as if the house and land were mourning Wendell Morrison's death. I was nervous when I knocked on the door. The man who answered seemed surprised to see us. He cocked an eyebrow, almost as if he suspected us of being Texas' version of solicitors.

"May I help you?"

"Hi." I shifted from one foot to the other and did my best to appear professional. "My name is Charlie Rhodes. I was here the other day and interviewed Naomi. I'm with the Legacy Foundation. Um ... I was hoping to talk to her again."

"Ms. Morrison is indisposed."

"Does that mean she's crying or drinking?" Millie asked. "I don't care if she's doing either – or both, for that matter – but we really only have a quick question, and it might help with the investigation into her father's death."

The man was quiet for a long moment, the only movement his blinking eyes.

"I swear we won't take long," I added. "It's simply a question she might know the answer to. Um … we don't want to bother her. We know she's dealing with a lot."

"She is." The man nodded gravely. "I will discuss this with her and return shortly." Instead of ushering us inside he closed the doors in our faces, leaving us alone on the front porch.

"So … do you think he wants us to wait?" I asked, confused.

"I think so," Millie confirmed. "He's not very friendly, is he?"

"He's probably just serious about protecting his boss. She is going through a hard time. I mean … think about it. Say your father died in the middle of a ghost town and all his blood was drained and you had no idea if it was the work of man or beast. How would you feel about that?"

"Like *Ripley's Believe it or Not* would be getting a call and I would be getting some money."

I slid Millie a sidelong look, dubious. "Do you really believe that?"

Millie huffed out a sigh. "No. I get it. She's in mourning. In her position, I'm not sure which outcome would be more welcome."

"She seems pretty matter of fact about her father and the way he interacted with her, but … well … he's still her father."

"You're essentially saying she loved him even though he was a douche nozzle."

I blinked back my surprise at the term. "I'm pretty sure I would never use those words."

Millie snorted. "I think it's funny that you have no filter and say whatever comes to your head, but you're offended by the term 'douche nozzle.'"

"I didn't say I was offended."

"You didn't have to say it. Your face said it for you."

I heaved a sigh and blew my bangs away from my forehead. "There are times you make me want to take a nap."

"I have that effect on everyone. You'll learn to live with it."

The door opened a second time, the man returning to his previous spot. He looked resigned rather than happy. "Ms. Morrison will see you in the parlor."

"Thank you so much."

The butler – whether he was really a butler or an assistant, I didn't know, but he looked like a butler to me – ushered us into the same room Jack and I visited previously. He didn't offer refreshments or snacks, which I had to figure was by design, and left us to wait for Naomi.

"I'm starting to get the feeling that he really doesn't like us," Millie said once he left.

"Yeah. That's pretty obvious. I wish he would chill. It's not as if we're going to steal the silver or anything."

"He's paid to be uptight," Millie noted. "He's good at his job."

"He certainly is."

We sat for about three minutes before Naomi walked into the room. She was dressed in simple yoga pants and a T-shirt, her hair swept back in a ponytail. She wore no makeup and her eyes were red-rimmed. She was clearly struggling through her day-to-day responsibilities.

"You're back." Naomi spoke it as fact rather than recrimination or excitement. Her affect was flat and she looked largely disinterested in our visit.

"I am, and I'm sorry." I rubbed my hands over my knees as my nerves returned. "I don't want to take up a lot of your time – I know you're really going through it right now – but I do have a few questions."

"You know I'm really going through it right now?" Naomi's response was dull. "I see. Did you lose your father to the Chupacabra?"

"No, but I lost both my parents in an accident when I was eighteen and was left completely on my own from that day forward."

Naomi relaxed a bit. "I'm sorry. That was an awful thing to say. I don't know why I said it. I'm simply exhausted. That's no excuse for taking my grief out on you."

I waved off her apology. "It's fine. I know you're dealing with a lot. We really don't want to take up much of your time."

"Fair enough. Why are you here?"

"We heard about the silver legend," Millie replied, getting straight to the point. "A lot of people in town say that your father was obsessed with buying Hooper's Mill because he believed the legend and wanted the silver."

If the statement upset Naomi, she didn't show it. "My father believed the legend, but that's not why he wanted Hooper's Mill."

"He believed the legend? Did he tell you that?"

Naomi nodded. "I was raised on the legend. He kept calling it my birthright, but I learned pretty quickly when I got older that not everyone believed the same story."

"He thought it was your birthright because his ancestor was one of the original founders of the town, right?" I asked.

Naomi's eyes widened. "I'm impressed. How did you know that?"

"We pulled the land deeds for the town. There was a Morrison listed," I replied. "It wasn't hard to put the pieces together. Apparently Donald Morrison sold his share of the town to Richard Hooper a few years after, right?"

"It was more like a year later, if I'm remembering it right," Naomi corrected. "I'm familiar with that story, too. My father is convinced that Richard Hooper scammed his great-great-however many greats it is-grandfather. He's been obsessed with righting that wrong ever since."

"Scammed how?" Millie asked. "I thought the original Morrison sold the property."

"He did." Naomi rubbed her cheek, weariness evident. I felt bad for bothering her, but it was necessary. "I've spent a lot of time researching this. To be fair, I believed my father's stories when I was younger. I thought that we were somehow swindled and was righteously ticked off on behalf of our entire family.

"Then, when I was about fourteen, I went to this event at the library," she continued. "It was all about the history of Hooper's Mill. I'd always been interested because of the things my father said – and he took me there from time to time when I was a kid – so I went to this talk to learn more.

"Imagine my surprise when the historian started talking about a bunch of things that I didn't know about," she said. "I thought he had to be making it up. I asked my father about it, and he said that there were all kinds of lies being bandied about regarding Hooper's Mill. That only frustrated me more, of course.

"I decided to do some research. I was going to write that historian an angry letter when I was done, because I thought that would somehow show him – I was naïve at that age – but I actually uncovered a lot of things that made me realize my father was the one spinning tall tales," she said. "I don't think he meant to. I think he honestly convinced himself they were true. You couldn't talk to him about Hooper's Mill. He was absolutely crazy when it came to talk of that place."

"Do you believe the stories about the silver?" I asked. "A lot of people we've talked to say the legend is true and that Richard Hooper died not long after leaving town and couldn't return to reclaim the silver. I did a little research, though, and found that's not true. I have trouble believing that he would purposely leave a small fortune in silver behind."

"And I'm right there with you," Naomi said. "I do think there's still room for debate, but if there was silver there – and I'm not ruling out the possibility – I think it was a much smaller quantity than what's been reported. And it was probably discovered and removed from the property a very long time ago.

"The thing is, the areas surrounding Hooper's Mill are poor, so even the thought of five stray hunks of silver sitting around is enough to entice people to head out there and take a look," she continued. "When you're struggling to put food on the table, you're more willing to believe wild stories."

"I can see that." I dug in my pocket and retrieved the earring. "The other thing I wanted to ask is if you recognize this."

Naomi accepted the earring, her eyebrows coming together as she stared. "Am I supposed to recognize this?"

"No, but it's a distinctive piece. I found it in the hotel yesterday," I explained. "At first I thought it had been there since the town was abandoned. It's an antique, after all. But we took it to a jeweler, and she said the setting is antique but not old enough to date back to the days when Hooper's Mill was in operation."

"I still don't understand why it's important," Naomi said.

"The backing on it is new and refurbished," I supplied. "She thinks it was done within the last year or two. It was out in the open when I found it, no dust or anything. I think that means it was discarded or lost recently."

"I guess." Naomi dropped the earring in my hand. "Teenagers are running around Hooper's Mill all the time."

"They are, but this isn't something a teenager would wear," I pointed out. "It looks like an heirloom of some type. I'm sure if we take it to the right people, a historian maybe, we might be able to drill down and figure out the family it came from."

"Hmm." Naomi didn't look convinced. "Perhaps it was someone looking for the silver."

"Could be. The jeweler said the earring was valuable, so if you have money for an earring like this why are you rooting around in the dark for silver that probably isn't there?"

"I ... um ... don't know how to answer that," Naomi replied after a beat.

"I was just hoping maybe you'd recognize the earring," I admitted. "I thought maybe your father had a friend or someone he hung around with. If he took her to the town and she was wearing this earring ...."

"Ah." Realization dawned on Naomi's face. "I see what you're saying. Unfortunately, I don't recognize the earring. I don't know what to tell you."

"It was a shot in the dark. Thank you for your time."

"Don't mention it."

MILLIE AND I DECIDED TO surprise our co-workers and picked up sundaes from the nearby ice cream shop before returning to the hotel. The shop was just around the corner, so the ice cream wasn't overly melted when we delivered it.

Chris, Hannah and Bernard were thankful. Laura and Zach weren't in the lobby, so Millie and I ate their sundaes (after already eating sundaes of our own at the shop). Jack merely smiled when I delivered his.

"Vanilla ice cream with butterscotch sauce," he mused. "How did you know this was my favorite?"

I was caught off guard by the question … and the hint of amusement in his eyes. He looked sweaty and tired, grime edging his forehead and cheeks. He immediately dug into the ice cream with gusto.

"I don't know," I hedged. "You got me a butterscotch malt yesterday."

"I did. How was your day today?"

I shrugged. "The zoologist was a bust. He says the print belongs to a coyote that once broke a foot that healed poorly."

"Did you expect a different outcome?" Jack's gaze was probing.

"I don't know. I guess not. The setup at the zoo was really cool. They had a laboratory in the middle of the habitat, and I got to see a huge wolf named Lobo. He was really beautiful."

Jack smiled. "You like animals, don't you?"

"Yes. I want to make a pet out of the Chupacabra and walk him on a leash," I said dryly.

"Not that." Jack shook his head as he spooned more ice cream into his mouth. "You liked the horse. You're gaga over the wolf. You like animals. I like animals, too."

"I wanted to stop and see Clyde while we were at the ranch today, but Millie thought it was a waste of time." I was a little wistful, so I barely registered the shift in Jack's stance. "Now I wish I had put my foot down and forced her to let me see him."

"You went back to the ranch?" Jack's tone was decidedly chilly. So was his gaze when I risked a glance in his direction.

"Oh, well … ."

"Don't even think about running," Jack warned, as if reading my expression when I swiveled toward Millie. "Talk."

"Ugh. I have such a big mouth," I complained.

"I've been telling you that for days. Talk."

159

"Fine." I related our trip to the jeweler and the ranch, bracing myself for an explosion when I finished. Instead of yelling, Jack looked intrigued.

"So Naomi said her father was a bit delusional." Jack scraped his spoon against the bottom of the sundae container, digging for the last bit of butterscotch. "I'm starting to think that Wendell Morrison was unbalanced and that might have played a part in his demise."

"Naomi is interesting," I said after a beat. I kept expecting a meltdown, but Jack seemed content to let my detective work slide. "She's obviously very sad about her father's death, but she knows that he was a bit of a kook. I feel bad for her."

"I do, too. You made a smart move this afternoon," Jack noted. "I wouldn't have thought to show her the earring, but it adds credence to the idea that someone else has been hanging around Hooper's Mill – and it's not the sort of someone who is poor and looking to scrape out a few pieces of silver."

"Naomi didn't recognize it."

"No, but it was still a good idea."

"We have no way to track the owner," I reminded him. "We also have no way of knowing if the earring was there for five days or five months. I mean … we could take it to someone who knows antiques, a historian or something, but that's probably a longshot."

"You said that it wasn't dirty and was out in the open," Jack pointed out. "That indicates that it wasn't there very long. If people are visiting the town every week and searching … someone would've snagged that earring and tried to sell it, even if they thought it was worth only a few dollars."

"It's worth more than that."

"Which means someone would've taken it if they saw it," Jack said. "That means it wasn't there very long."

"We don't know that this earring has anything to do with Morrison's death, though."

"We don't, but the earring solidifies my belief that a human is responsible here and not an animal."

"Chris won't like that."

"Chris is more convinced than ever that it's the Chupacabra. He won't listen to my arguments. He's too far gone."

"What do you mean?"

"You'll find out at dinner. Chris has new video footage and he's absolutely determined he's got proof of the Chupacabra."

"Sounds exciting."

"You're only saying that because you haven't seen the footage yet."

"It still sounds exciting."

"Let's see if you feel the same way after you've watched the footage."

NINETEEN

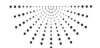

J headed to my room to wash my face and chill in private for thirty minutes or so – I wasn't used to so much "together" time with people and was still coming to terms with the group dynamics. I pulled up short when I entered the room.

It was cool, the air conditioning unit in the window working over-time, but something felt … off. I furrowed my brow as I glanced around, instinctively leaving the door open. The room wasn't big enough for someone to hide. I could see inside the tiny bathroom, including inside the grim shower. It was empty. There was no closet, only a rack in the corner, and there was no way anyone could fit under the bed.

Despite that, I felt as if I wasn't alone.

"What are you doing?" Jack appeared in the doorway behind me, his gaze curious.

I jolted at his sudden appearance, unsure how to respond. "Oh, well … um … I was going to wash my face and lay down for twenty minutes."

"Are you sick?" Jack instantly went into mother hen mode and pressed his hand to my forehead.

"You keep doing that and it bugs me," I groused, pushing his hand away. "I'm not sick."

"Well, excuse me for looking out for you," he shot back. "If you're not sick, why are you standing here with the door open?"

I wanted to be angry – he was a pain in the butt, after all – but I remained unsettled from my initial reaction to walking into the room. I couldn't quite shake my discomfort. "I don't want to tell you because you'll think I'm being crazy."

Jack's expression softened. "I won't think you're crazy."

"Really?" I had my doubts. "What if I told you I thought a ghost was in my room?"

"I'd tell you to be careful when changing your clothes in case it's a perverted ghost."

He answered a little too quickly for my taste. "What if I told you I felt as if someone had been inside this room while I was gone?"

Jack's eyes narrowed. "Why do you say that?"

"I don't know." That was the truth. "It's just a feeling. I ... ."

Jack opened his mouth to say something, seemingly changing his mind mid-thought and offering a reassuring smile. "I won't laugh at you. I won't think you're crazy. Tell me why you think someone was in here."

"I don't know."

Jack remained calm. "Has anything been moved?"

I scanned the room and shook my head. "I don't think ... ." I broke off and moved toward the duffel bag at the end of the bed. "I think someone went through this."

"Why do you say that?" Jack's tone wasn't accusatory. It wasn't exactly sympathetic either.

"This wasn't on top." I pointed at the raggedy T-shirt on the top of the pile. "It was at the bottom. I know, because I saw it there when I was deciding which shirt to wear today."

"Okay." Jack didn't act as if he doubted me. Instead, he grabbed the bag and upended it on the bed. "Look through here and tell me if anything is missing."

"I don't have anything of value."

"Look anyway." Jack watched as I sorted through the clothes, pressing his lips together when I grabbed a handful of bras and panties and shoved them to the side. My cheeks burned, but I refused to acknowledge the clothing. "Do you have any jewelry? Even if it's not valuable, that might not stop someone from stealing it."

"I don't have any jewelry. Er, well, that's not entirely true. I have my mother's engagement ring and a few necklaces from her, but they're in a safety deposit box. I don't leave them out because we travel so much."

"That's probably wise." Jack bit his bottom lip as he glanced around the room. "It could've been the maid. She's obviously been in here. Maybe she went through your things."

That was a possibility ... yet it didn't feel right. The energy I felt upon entering the room was much more sinister. A thief wouldn't leave that sort of vibe behind. "Jack ... ."

"Don't panic." It was almost as if Jack read my mind when he rested his hand on my shoulder and squeezed. "If someone was in here, they're gone now. You said yourself that you don't have anything to steal."

"That doesn't mean it's not creepy."

"No, definitely not," Jack agreed. He gave my shoulder another squeeze before moving to the door and hunkering down to study the lock. His expression was hard to read, but I didn't see joy there ... or relief. In fact, he looked annoyed. "This lock would be easy to bypass. All you need is a credit card."

I shifted from one foot to the other, uncomfortable. "Do you think someone was in here?"

"I think you believe it, and that's all that matters to me," Jack replied. "You should be able to feel safe in your own hotel room. I'll talk to the owner about switching out the lock."

"Thank you."

"Don't mention it." Jack moved toward the hallway and then stilled. "You're okay. My room is right across the way. No one will come in here while you're sleeping. I won't allow it."

He was so full of himself, so puffed out and determined, I couldn't help but smile. "Thank you."

"Do what you need to do. I'll be downstairs with the owner. If I have to change that lock myself, I'll do it before you go to bed."

"I'm probably just being an idiot." I ran a hand through my hair, my fingers snagging. "The heat is making me act crazy."

"I don't believe that, and I don't think you do either," Jack argued. "I'll take care of it."

"You're going above and beyond."

"I'm head of security. This falls exactly on my shoulders."

"Well … thank you anyway."

"It will be fixed. Trust me."

TRUE TO HIS WORD, Jack had a maintenance man at my door in twenty minutes. I never got the rest I wanted, but the relief I felt watching the man switch out my lock was profound. There was also an amusement factor, because Jack oversaw the entire endeavor, arms crossed over his chest, and he didn't wander away until he'd double-checked the lock himself, testing it three times before allowing the maintenance man to leave.

"Better?"

I nodded, grateful. "Thank you."

"Don't thank me, Charlie. This is part of my job. It's important you feel safe."

"Well, I definitely do now."

"Good. It's time to head over to the diner. Chris has already left. He's dying to show you guys the footage he found from last night."

I locked the door and pocketed my new key before following Jack down the hallway. Even though the hotel cooling system wasn't great, it felt as if an oven blast smacked into my face when we hit the street.

"I'm not used to this heat." I rubbed my forearm over my forehead. "I like it in the low eighties. That's my happy place."

"You and me both." Jack pressed his hand to the small of my back as he directed me to the side so I wouldn't collide with a few of the locals walking down the sidewalk in the opposite direction. I was already hot, but the feel of his hand on me seemed to ratchet up the temperature. "Chris will be looking for people to agree with him when he shows his footage."

The change in conversation threw me for a loop. "Excuse me?"

"Chris is looking for people to agree with him," Jack replied. "He's angry I don't see what he sees in the footage."

"And what does he see?"

"Well ... ." Jack broke off. "I want you to look at it yourself. I don't want to force you to see what I want you to see."

"Fair enough." Jack was a pragmatic sort. Whatever Chris saw was enough to alarm Jack. He might not agree with our leader, but he was worried enough to try to get me on his side. "Is it an animal? What? You can at least tell me that."

"I want you to see the footage for yourself," Jack pressed. "Chris is extremely excited. You tend to land on the excitable side of things, too."

"What about the others? What do they see?"

"Bernard sides with me. Hannah sides with Chris."

"That seems normal. What about Laura and Zach?"

"Laura and Zach are a little too worried about Laura and Zach right now," Jack supplied. "They're much more interested in flirting with one another than casting a vote in the great Chupacabra debate."

I snickered, genuinely amused. "So Chris thinks he has footage of the Chupacabra?" That was definitely an exciting prospect. "You disagree."

"It's not that I disagree. It's that ... well ... I don't see what he sees. Or, rather, I don't come to the same conclusion about what's on the footage."

"Oh, I'm practically salivating."

"That's because you're getting barbecue again tonight," Jack teased. "We're all practically salivating."

My smile slipped. "Yeah, I love barbecue as much as the next person, but I'd kill for a nice stir-fry right now ... or pasta. Oh! Olive Garden sounds divine."

Jack snickered as we crossed to the diner. "I hate to say it, but

Olive Garden does sound divine. Some nice seafood alfredo with breadsticks. Yum."

"That's my favorite, too."

"I'll eat just about anything from Olive Garden, but that's definitely my favorite. Unfortunately for us, for the time being, we're stuck with barbecue." Jack held open the door, and before I could duck inside he lowered his voice and held my attention before I could find our group. "Please keep an open mind when you watch the footage. Don't say the first thing that comes to you. Just ... think about it first."

"I promise." He was so earnest I felt the need to return the emotion in kind. "Everything will be okay."

"HOLY CRAP! The Chupacabra is real and we have actual footage!" I jumped to my feet and clapped my hands ten minutes later, almost knocking Chris' laptop over in my zest.

Jack slapped his hand to his forehead. "I told you not to say the first thing that came to your mind."

"I didn't. I said the second. The first was, 'Holy moly, we're going to be on the news.'" I flashed Jack the prettiest smile in my repertoire. "This is exciting, Jack." I grabbed his hand and gave it a good shake. "Why aren't you excited?"

"Because this is unbelievable idiocy," Jack shot back. "There's a slight glow on one camera's footage."

"And a shadow that is very obviously an animal with it," I replied. I looked at the footage Chris caught. I looked hard. I knew Jack was being pragmatic when he tried to reel us in. I also knew that I saw something that couldn't be ... well, normal ... when I looked at the footage. There was definitely something out there. "It's the Chupacabra, Jack."

"I need a drink," Jack muttered, shaking his head.

Millie moved up beside me so she could look, allowing Chris to show her the footage three times before she spoke. "That could be fireflies."

"Thank you!" Jack threw up his hands. "Finally a voice of reason."

"I said it could be fireflies," Millie cautioned. "It could be something else."

"You don't mean ... ." Jack looked distraught. "I expected you to be one of the rational ones."

"That is so not something I want on my business cards," Millie drawled. "It's not about being rational, Jack. There's something there. I don't know what it is, but there is definitely something there."

"None of us knows what it is," Jack barked.

"Which is why we have to investigate." Millie adopted a pragmatic tone, as if she was talking to an overwrought child and reasoning was imperative. "You're not a natural believer, Jack. I'm not either. But I can't say that I don't see anything in this footage. That wouldn't be the truth."

"So what do you suggest?" Jack's frustration oozed so hard it was enough to cast a pall over the room. "What do you think we should do about the possible glowing eyes in the abandoned town? Should we get some humane traps and see if we can catch it?"

"That's certainly something we can consider down the road," Chris replied. "I don't think that's a prudent move now."

"Really? And what do you think a prudent move would be?" Jack was at the end of his rope, and it just so happened to be a rope I thought he might be considering using to hang Chris.

"We have to stay in Hooper's Mill tonight so we can be on hand to catch the action," I answered, hoping to take the onus off Chris. "It's the only answer."

Jack extended a warning finger. "We've talked about this."

"We have," Chris confirmed. "We need to talk about it again. We have evidence here that suggests we need to take the next step."

"What evidence?" I thought there was a very real chance Jack was about to lose his world-class cool, his cheeks red as he sputtered. "We have what may be Chupacabra eyes or what may be fireflies."

"You're a poet and you didn't even know it," I commented.

"Don't go there again," Jack hissed, his eyes flashing. "I can take only so much."

"It's not about what you can take, Jack." Chris drew the security chief's eyes back to him. "We're supposed to investigate unexplained phenomena. I understand you have a job to do. I do, too. My job requires that I camp out at Hooper's Mill tonight. If you have a problem with that … ."

"I have a huge problem with that!" Jack exploded.

"Then take it up with Uncle Myron," Chris suggested. "I've already talked to him. He agrees with me and has given his permission to go overrule you on this one. That's what I'm doing."

Jack, eyes wild, turned to Millie. "You can exert control over Myron. Call him. Force him to change his mind."

Millie looked caught. "I can't do that, Jack. You know I respect you – no, I really do – but Chris has a right to see this through. If he wants to go to Hooper's Mill and watch the town for himself, I don't see how you can stop him.

"It's important to him," she continued. "It's important to this group. I think this one has to be Chris' decision."

"I just want to … ." Jack mimed strangling an invisible figure. I had no idea if he was picturing Chris, Millie or me, but it was clear he wasn't happy.

"I'm taking volunteers for the overnighter." Chris raised his voice. "Who wants to be part of this?"

"I'm definitely in," Zach enthused.

Laura shot him a coy look. "I'm in, too."

"Me!" I shot my hand into the air. "Please, please, please!"

Chris smiled at my enthusiasm. "You're in, Charlie. I don't think I could do it without you." He glanced around the table, everyone else remaining silent. "We'll have our phones and be in constant contact. This will be good. You'll see."

"I can't wait." I clapped my hands. "I'm even excited for the barbecue tonight. This is … totally amazing!"

I risked a look at Jack and found him glowering.

"It'll be okay." I patted his knee, a jolt of hurt going through me when he jerked away. "Jack … ."

"Don't talk to me," Jack barked. "I've had my fill of you for one day."

The words were painful – as was the overt distaste on his face – but I didn't back down. "I'm sorry."

"You're not," Jack shot back. "But you will be if something happens, won't you?"

"I …."

"Shut your mouth," Jack ordered, his face flushed with anger. "For once, just shut your freaking mouth."

Even though I was understandably offended, I did as he asked. He felt betrayed. I couldn't take it back or make him feel better. I could only do what he asked – so I did.

2 0

TWENTY

I was excited to the point of giddiness when we loaded the vehicle for our overnighter at Hooper's Mill. Jack refused to talk to me, which was a small tear in the heart department, but I figured I could eventually get him to ease up. After a night left to his own devices, a lot of brooding and pouting on the menu, I figured he'd get over it.

I realized I was wrong when Jack appeared in the parking lot and threw another bag into the vehicle's rear.

"What are you doing?"

Jack's eyes, like dark lasers full of disgust, locked with mine. "I'm still head of security."

"You're going with us?"

"No, you're coming with me. Now … get in the backseat and fasten your seatbelt."

His tone was unbelievably chilly. "Jack … ."

"Get in the truck, Charlie."

The edge to his voice left no room for debate, so I did as instructed.

The ride to Hooper's Mill was uncomfortable. Jack took the wheel, and Chris settled in the passenger seat. That left Zach, Laura and me to wedge ourselves in the back. Zach seemed happy with the configuration and purposely selected the middle spot as he split time smiling at both of us. By the third time his hand "accidentally" brushed my thigh I was ready to explode.

"Do you mind not touching me?" The question was out of my mouth before I thought better about uttering it. "Can you please keep your hands to yourself?"

Zach wasn't insulted. "Oh, you know you like it." He winked as Laura shot me a challenging look.

"Keep your hands to yourself," Jack hissed.

"What if I don't want him to keep his hands to himself?" Laura challenged. She was clearly spoiling for a fight – with Jack, at least – and her voice was laced with disdain.

"I don't care if he touches you," Jack shot back. "You can do what you want."

"So you only care about Charlie, huh?" Laura's expression was hard to discern, but I was certain there was a mixture of several emotions there ... and one of them was hurt. That was weird.

"I didn't say that." Jack adjusted his tone. "She clearly doesn't want to be touched, and I'm not going to sit back and watch her be sexually harassed."

"I'm hardly sexually harassing her," Zach countered.

"Keep it that way." Jack was firm. "Once we get to Hooper's Mill, we need to set up a base camp. No one – and I mean absolutely no one – is allowed to wander off on his or her own. Do you understand?"

"That's a good idea." Chris was focused on the night vision equipment in his hands, so he didn't notice the dark look Jack lobbed Zach in the mirror.

"I don't think you have to worry about me wandering around alone," Laura said. "I plan to wander around with Zach."

"Oh, you're so cute." Zach beamed at her, making my stomach twist.

"I was talking to Charlie," Jack said. "No wandering around alone, Charlie."

I was fairly certain I should've been offended at being singled out. "I know. I'm not stupid."

Jack muttered something under his breath, something that sounded suspiciously like, "You're a freaking idiot," but otherwise remained silent. Chatter ceased for the remainder of the ride, and by the time we hit Hooper's Mill the sun was close to setting.

"Which building should we set up shop in?" Chris asked Jack. Now that he'd gotten his way he was more than willing to be deferential on the small things.

"We're not sleeping inside of a building," Jack replied. "That's not wise or safe. We can build a fire off to the side of the saloon over there. Everyone has sleeping bags and it's warm enough to sleep under the stars."

Laura was the first to balk. "Why can't we sleep inside? It seems weird to sleep outside with all the bugs when we don't have to."

Jack shot her a withering look. "There will be more bugs and scavengers inside the buildings than outside. They'll avoid us outside."

Laura didn't look convinced. "Is he lying to me?" She turned to Zach for an answer.

"He's actually right." Zach beamed at Jack, as if those three little words would be enough to eradicate the rampant dislike continually growing between the two men. "We'll be better outdoors."

"If you say so." Laura was blasé. "I'll grab the sleeping bags."

"I'll grab the cooler," I offered.

Jack shook his head, refusing to meet my eyes. "Leave the cooler in the back. That will attract scavengers. We'll grab water out as we need it. Make sure no garbage is left behind."

"I won't." I wanted to say more to him, apologize for taking Chris' side even though I wasn't exactly sorry for doing it. Jack's mood had me feeling guilty, and it wasn't a feeling I liked. "Jack … ."

"Gather some wood for a fire," Jack ordered, cutting me off. "There's some stacked along the side of the hotel. Grab it quickly, because I don't want you wandering over there by yourself once the sun sets. Get a lot because it's going to be a long night."

I didn't want to let it go, but he seemed adamant about getting camp set up before doing anything else. "Okay."

Jack turned his full attention to the darkening street. "Chris, check the camera and give me that night vision camera and scope. We're setting both of those up at the campsite perimeter."

Chris looked disappointed. "I thought I'd take a look around with the scope and see if I can find anything of interest."

Jack forced a smile that was more annoyed than amused. "Not until camp is set up ... and then not alone."

"But ... ."

"No."

"Come on, Chris," Laura said, appearing at his elbow. "If you help us set up camp for Captain Bad Attitude, we'll go with you to look around." She gestured toward Zach. "I think we'll all want a break from the gloomy wonder here."

Chris beamed. "Sounds like a good idea."

IT TOOK AN HOUR TO set up the camp and get the fire going. Chris was eager to take off, so Jack ultimately relented as long as Zach and Laura went with him. It was so dark by the time they wandered away that it took only about thirty seconds for them to disappear into the murk.

That left Jack and me by the fire, which was cozy and yet unbelievably uncomfortable at the same time. I wanted to go with Chris and check the equipment, but that would've left Jack alone. It wasn't that I was worried about his safety as much as I knew that would mean Jack would follow us wherever we moved around the town. I decided to take one for the team and stay with him so everybody's fun wasn't ruined.

Unfortunately for me, the silence was oppressive, but I was determined not to be the one to break it. I hadn't done anything wrong. Not really. Sure, I felt guilty and didn't enjoy the way he pouted, but I was not going to break the silence. I was going to force him to do it. I would make him apologize.

My resolve lasted exactly two minutes.

"How cold do you think it will get?"

Jack slid me a sidelong look. "I don't know. Probably not too cold. You'll be fine in your sleeping bag."

"I'm not worried I'm going to freeze to death or anything. I was just asking."

"You were uncomfortable with the silence because you want me to pat you on the head and say 'all is well,'" Jack countered. "There's a difference."

I scowled. "I don't want you to pat me on the head."

"No?" Jack arched an eyebrow. "You could've fooled me." He dug into the bag at his side and returned with a flask, causing me to widen my eyes.

"What is that?"

"Whiskey."

"You're drinking when you're supposed to be running security?" I wasn't exactly scandalized, but I'd never seen him carry a flask. The fact that I drove him to drink increased my guilt. It also made me feel a bit puffed out, which was probably the opposite of what he wanted.

"I'm having some whiskey because I'm annoyed with all of you and I need something to focus on." Jack made a face as he took a swig and swallowed. "Want some?" He tilted the flask in my direction.

"Probably not. Thank you."

Jack's eyes were so dark they almost looked demonic thanks to the flickering fire. "You should have a shot and relax. I'm not telling you to get drunk. I'm telling you to relax. You're too keyed up."

"I'm excited."

"I've noticed."

For lack of anything better to do, I accepted the flask and took a swallow. "Ugh." I managed to down the acrid liquid without choking. "That tastes like gasoline or something."

Jack snickered as he reclaimed the flask and tucked it into his bag. "You really haven't done much drinking, have you?"

"It was never important to me."

"It should never be important to you. I always thought of it as a rite of passage, though. Some of my best stories start with, 'I was drunk with my Marine buddies.' It's not that I'm proud of it. It simply is what it is."

"I've never been one for losing control." I arranged my backpack so I could lean against it and stare at the sky. "I simply didn't have time for drunken nights out when I was in college. I needed to pass my classes on the first go-around, and I worked when I wasn't studying. That didn't leave time for much else."

"I'm sorry."

"Why are you sorry?"

"Because you had to grow up much faster than most people, but you still get treated like a kid."

Jack's response caught me off guard. "I'm the new kid on the block," I clarified. "I think that's probably normal."

"Yes, but you get bossed around by everyone. That probably doesn't seem fair to you."

"I learned long ago that life isn't fair." I scratched my anxious fingers against the front of my jeans. "You don't have to feel guilty. You've been nothing but nice to me - even when you're furious and yelling."

"It doesn't seem that way sometimes." Jack grabbed my hand and stopped the scratching. "Did something bite you?"

I shook my head, lifting my eyes to his. I couldn't tell what he was thinking, but there seemed to be a soupçon of ten different emotions flitting across his face. "I'm antsy."

"I think that should be listed as one of your special skills on your résumé," Jack said. "It will be fine. Even if the Chupacabra is really out here, he won't kill you. I promise."

"What if he kills you first and you can't protect me?"

"Then my ghost will avenge my death and you'll still be fine."

"I see you've got this all figured out."

"I do indeed."

He still had his fingers wrapped around my hand. I couldn't decide if he knew it or not, but I didn't move to pull away. I liked his proximity and the way his face looked in the firelight. It was a terrible idea, but Millie's words kept echoing in the back of my brain. Maybe I really was attracted to him. If so, I should like this. Did I like this? I had no idea. My heart was pounding too hard for debate.

"It's a nice night at least." Jack turned his eyes to the sky and released my fingers. His demeanor was often hard to read, but he seemed relaxed. "I guess things could be worse. Imagine if it was storming when we decided to hunt down the Chupacabra."

I exhaled heavily as my heart rate returned to normal and I shifted to get more comfortable. The fact that I was disappointed that Jack released my hand – a move that was friendly rather than romantic from the start – made me feel like an idiot. I tried to hide my internal strife as I followed his gaze. "Yeah. It's nice."

"Sadly, I think we're going to spend the entire night watching Chris run around with his equipment, while Laura and Zach try to feel each other up behind the buildings."

"I doubt they'll stop at feeling each other up."

"True."

Something occurred to me and now seemed the best time to bring it up. "Did you and Laura date?"

"Excuse me?" Jack's eyebrows flew up his forehead.

"Did you and Laura date?" I repeated.

Jack made a tsking sound with his tongue as he shook his head. "You just say whatever comes to your mind, don't you?"

"Usually."

Jack smirked. "I keep telling myself that's because you're young, but I honestly don't know if it's true. I think you're just one of those people who will always be effortlessly blunt."

"Is there anything wrong with that?"

"No."

"You haven't answered the question."

"What was the question?"

I let loose a long sigh as Jack smirked.

"Ah, I remember now," Jack said. "You want to know if I ever dated Laura. Before I answer that question, can I ask why you want to know?"

177

"She's said a few things to me that seem odd," I replied. "She also looks at you in a very specific way when she thinks no one is looking."

"And what way is that?"

"As if she's starving and you're the only thing on the menu."

"You have a way with words." Jack shrugged his shoulders. "For the record, I have not dated Laura."

I was secretly relieved, although admitting it – even to myself – was difficult. Would it have changed anything if he'd said yes? Probably not. That didn't stop me from internally crowing all the same. "I wonder why she acts the way she does if you've never been involved."

"Probably because there was an incident about a year ago where she tried to entice me to get involved that ended with her being mortified," Jack said.

"Really?" I was intrigued. "Do tell."

"Since when are you such a gossip?"

"I don't drink. Gossip sustains me."

Jack snorted, his earlier anger seemingly forgotten. "I'm not going to get into the nitty-gritty, but suffice it to say she got drunk at the company Christmas party and made a move in the laboratory."

"Wow!" This was even better than I'd hoped. "What did you do? Wait, let me guess. You crushed her heart in a vise and she's been mooning after you ever since."

"Good grief." Jack flicked me between the eyebrows. "You have a mind that's better suited for writing soap operas. You know that, right?"

I shrugged. "I can't help it. Laura is nasty."

"And she's decided to focus on you because you're the newest member of the team," Jack surmised. "She thinks you're an easy mark. She hasn't spent enough time with you to know that's the exact opposite of the truth."

"Just tell me … did she cry when you turned her down?"

Jack's chuckle was warm and throaty. "No, she got angry and threatened that if I told anyone she would make me pay."

"Were you worried she'd make good on the threat? Her father is one of the company bigwigs, after all."

"I don't let bullies worry me," Jack replied. "It's not my way."

"No, I guess not." I pursed my lips. "I need you to tell me every-thing that happened from the beginning to the end. Also, if you want to reenact it – do voices and stuff – I'm all for it."

"I'm not doing that. It would take forever."

I settled back against my pack, truly comfortable for the first time in a long while. "We have all night."

"No."

"I'll have another drink of whiskey if you do. That should be enough to knock me out so you can have quiet before bed."

Jack tilted his head to the side, considering. "Fine. I'll tell the story, but I'm not reenacting it."

"Fair enough. Now … what was she wearing?"

"How should I know? It was a year ago. I can't remember that."

"You're a terrible storyteller."

"Yeah, I'm going to need another shot."

TWENTY-ONE

"They've been gone a long time."

An hour later and Jack and I were still talking. We'd finished half his flask. I wasn't drunk as much as warm and comfortable. He related a few of his "drunk" stories from his military days, making me roar with laughter because he was a much better story-teller than I ever gave him credit for, and I lost track of time. Then I realized we'd been alone for a long time.

"They have been gone a long time," Jack agreed, grabbing a flash-light. "I guess we should look around."

"We can always look for the Chupacabra while we're doing it," I suggested. "That way it wouldn't be a completely wasted effort when we find them sitting in a corner staring at fireflies."

"Good idea." Jack stood, dusting off the seat of his jeans before extending a hand to help me to my feet. He met my gaze in the fire-light and I thought for a moment he would kiss me. It was one of those fleeting ideas – one I'd had at least three times now – that caused my heart to seize. The moment was thick with tension and unexpressed chemistry, and I realized that I wanted him to kiss me. Then he ruined the moment. "Stay close to me and don't wander off. If you get lost, I'll have you sent back to the hotel."

I sighed. "I have no intention of wandering off."

"Because you're worried about your safety and want to do the smart thing?"

That was an interesting question. "Because I don't want to get bitten by the Chupacabra and have to go through rabies shots. I hear they hurt."

"Yeah. That's what I thought." Jack made a disgusted sound in the back of his throat as he surveyed the town. "Where do you want to start?"

"Let's check the saloon."

Jack furrowed his brow. "We're camped in front of the saloon. We would've seen them if they went in there."

"Yes, but we're looking for the Chupacabra, too," I reminded him. "If I were the Chupacabra – surely a cagey and smart animal – I'd hide in the nearest building to avoid detection."

"Uh-huh. And how did the Chupacabra get into the saloon without us noticing?"

"I'm sure there are holes in the walls, maybe even hidden corridors."

"Good point." Jack handed me a flashlight before gesturing toward the saloon. "Let's do it."

"Great." I couldn't help being excited. "Do you really think we'll see the Chupacabra?"

"Not even a little."

"You have no sense of adventure, Jack."

"I'm in the middle of a supposed ghost town with you looking for a mythical creature that's apparently part dog and part lizard. What's more adventurous than that?"

He had a point.

Hooper's Mill was eerily silent as we made our way to the saloon. I'd been comfortable when we sat next to the fire and talked, the interaction seemingly effortless. My nerves returned now as I flicked on my flashlight and walked into the saloon.

It was still, nothing out of place from what I remembered during my last visit, but the atmosphere was somehow ominous.

"What do you think it was like back then?" I asked, a desperate need to fill the silence overcoming me as I flicked my beam to the mirror and almost jolted at my own reflection.

"What? Hooper's Mill or the saloon?"

I shrugged. "Either, I guess."

"I think the saloon was a place where people came to kick back after a hard day's work," Jack replied. "I think there was a lot of drinking, jokes about women and the female anatomy, and potentially a lot of theft because people can't seem to stop themselves when they covet wealth."

That was an interesting way to look at it. "You don't want to be rich?"

Jack shrugged, noncommittal. "I want to be comfortable. I don't think I need to be rich to be comfortable. Don't get me wrong, being poor isn't fun. I don't want to struggle and worry. I don't think I need to be rich, though."

"Good answer."

Jack smirked as he shifted his beam to the hallway, where I had felt eyes watching me the previous day. I held my breath for a second, convinced I'd see something evil springing to life, but the area looked empty.

"What about you?" Jack asked. "Do you want to be rich?"

"Money doesn't mean a lot to me," I replied. "As long as I have enough for a new pair of Converse every year and my basic needs are met, I'm good. I've learned to live lean."

When Jack didn't immediately respond, I turned and found him staring. "What?"

"I don't want to ask questions you're uncomfortable with ... ."

"But?"

"But you were obviously devastated by your parents' deaths," Jack said. "I know it changed your life in obvious ways, but I have to wonder if you're living the life you dreamed about before they died. I mean ... is this what you always wanted?"

That was a profound question given where we were standing and what we were doing. "Are you asking me what I want to be when I grow up?" I laced the question with teasing, but I was on edge.

"No. You're grown up. I know I give you flak about being young, but you're an adult. You do a few kooky things, but that's hardly the end of the world. I'm asking you what the girl who had two living parents wanted. What did that Charlie Rhodes want?"

I swallowed hard as I fought back tears. No one had ever asked me that. "I don't know."

"I don't think that's true."

"Maybe it's not true," I hedged. "But that seems like a different person."

"I know you probably won't believe it, but I get that. I was a different person when I joined the Marines. I had an ideal in mind. I thought I was going to save the world, and had an even bigger ego then than I do now ... if you can believe that."

I forced a smile. "I don't believe that's possible."

Jack returned the grin. "It boggles the mind, doesn't it? Anyway, I know about becoming a different person. It happened to me at a young age, too. So, what did that girl want?"

"To go to prom with some boy with stupid hair. Justin Fitzgerald. That was his name. When he asked me I thought nothing would ever get better. Then my parents died three days before the prom and he asked someone else before even talking to me and finding out what I wanted.

"Don't get me wrong, I wasn't going to prom no matter what after the accident," I continued. "I couldn't even fathom the idea. The fact that he just walked away and had another date within a few hours – and that's what everyone wanted to talk to me about – taught me a very valuable lesson."

"And what's that?"

"That I should only rely on myself."

"That's not true," Jack argued. "I would never say that distancing yourself from idiots who didn't understand what you were going through is a bad idea, but there are people out there worth knowing. Some of them are even worth relying on."

"Yeah, but if I rely on them and then they die … ."

"You'll be alone again," Jack finished. "That's how it was for you, wasn't it? You were alone."

"I did it all on my own," I confirmed, turning so I didn't have to see the sympathy in Jack's eyes. It somehow made things worse. "I had no aunts and uncles … or grandparents … or even family friends. It was just me."

"And that's too much for any eighteen-year-old kid to deal with on her own," Jack said. "I'm sorry for all of it. You have no idea. But you still haven't answered the question. What did you want to be before it happened? How did you see your life going?"

I shrugged. "I guess I wanted to be a writer, although I was planning on taking an array of classes when I got to college. Instead I had to take a semester off, adjust my college plans because I couldn't afford my original choice, and go from there. I couldn't play around, so I thought long and hard during the six months I was trying to hold on to my parents' house … and failed."

"And you decided to go into this field?" Jack raised an eyebrow. "May I ask why?"

"I've always had an interest in the paranormal." I did my best to sound truthful. That wasn't exactly a lie, after all. I was interested. I simply kept the reason why I was interested to myself. "I did a little research and found people were actually making a living at this. It meant a nomadic life, but I didn't have a home anymore so it didn't really matter, and I focused on this one goal."

"And you made it to the top," Jack noted. "The Legacy Foundation is the place everyone in this field wants to work."

"I know. I'm lucky."

"You're not lucky. You worked hard. You're dedicated. You've earned this."

"I'm also annoying, right?" I was desperate to turn the conversation to something lighter.

"You have your moments when I want to throttle you," Jack acknowledged. "You deserve to be here, though. You need to stop questioning that and go with your gut."

"That's not what you said a few hours ago."

"I was wrong," Jack said. "But I wasn't wrong about coming out here. I don't want you getting a big head because you think I'm conceding that point. I'm not. I was wrong about trying to get you on my side before you even saw the video. That wasn't fair to you."

"But the video is amazing."

"To you. I don't see the same thing you see ... and that's okay. I still shouldn't have tried to bully you into seeing things my way."

I felt a bit goofy given his heavy comments, so I shrugged. "It's okay."

"I'm still sorry." Jack took a step closer so we were practically on top of each other, his eyes seeking as he studied my face. "You know, this is one of those jobs where you could carry a notebook and plot the great American novel on the side while you're working. You could even write some paranormal thrillers, and I bet they would sell well. You don't have to give up on the old dream."

My ears buzzed thanks to Jack's proximity. I heard him loud and clear, though. "Thank you."

"It's okay." Jack awkwardly patted the top of my head. "This will get easier. It'll feel right at some point."

"What will?" I thought he was referring to us, and that caused my heart to jolt. "What's going to feel right?"

"Working with the group. Giving your opinion without backing down. It'll come normally eventually."

"Oh, that."

Jack chuckled. "What did you think I was referring to?"

I felt caught. "It really doesn't matter."

"Tell me."

There's no way I was going to tell him. Thankfully I didn't have to think of a way to divert his attention, because Laura picked that moment to scream at the top of her lungs.

"Jack!"

"What the ... ?"

Jack and I raced to the front of the saloon, spilling onto the street together. Laura, her face a mask of fury, actually made a lewd gesture when she saw us.

"What were you two doing?" Laura's tone was accusatory.

"We were looking for the Chupacabra," I replied. "Why are you screaming?"

"Yes, Laura, why are you screaming?" Jack pressed. "Do you think that's wise in the middle of nowhere?"

Laura looked ashamed. "I didn't mean to scream. When I couldn't find you guys at the fire I thought something must have happened."

"Like what?"

"Like … ."

"Like maybe the beast got you, too," Zach answered, moving up behind Laura in a protective stance. "Once we realized Chris was gone and came looking for you to be sure he hadn't simply rejoined you … and then we found you gone … we thought it might be like a bad horror movie."

"We were actually considering trying to run, but we don't have keys to the rental," Laura added. "I had visions of Jason Voorhees running through my head."

"There's no lake," I said automatically. "Jason wouldn't hang out here, because there's no lake."

"Yes, that's what we should be worried about," Laura said dryly. "My horror movie knowledge isn't up to snuff. Someone flog me now."

"We can do that later if you want," Zach flirted.

"Shut up," Jack snapped, drawing everyone's attention to him. "Where is Chris?"

"Why do you think we were looking for you?" Laura shot back. "It's certainly not because we wanted to watch you fawn all over Charlie."

Fawn all over Charlie? Was she kidding? She sounded jealous, which was ridiculous. "Chris was with you," I reminded her. "How did you lose him?"

"How do you think?" Laura was on the defensive and there was no way she would back down now. "We got distracted, and Chris ran off because it's what he does. We didn't even realize he was gone at first."

"Then, when we came up for air, we thought he probably went back to you guys," Zach added. "We didn't get really worried until we saw the fire was abandoned."

"It wasn't abandoned," Jack said. "We decided to look around to see if we could find anything. We assumed Chris was with you. I still don't understand how you lost him."

I tugged on Jack's arm to get his attention. "They went off in a corner and got hot and heavy. They didn't notice when Chris took off."

"Thank you, Charlie." Jack's tongue practically dripped with sarcasm. "I never would've figured that out on my own."

"You asked."

"Yes, but ... you know what? Never mind." Jack shook himself to regain control. "We need to break apart and find Chris. Where were you guys when you last saw him?"

Laura pointed toward the hotel. "We were out back over there."

Jack was grim. "Then that's where we'll start."

"Great." Laura made a face as she fell into step beside him. "This is so not how I envisioned this night going."

Jack wasn't in the mood for her games. "You'd better hope we find him, Laura."

"Or what?"

"Or you won't like what happens."

Laura was incensed. "Is that a threat?"

"It's a promise."

"I'm sure we'll find him," Zach offered, matching my pace. "He couldn't have gone far. He's probably just watching things with that equipment he's carrying around."

"That's a distinct possibility," Jack said. "Hopefully we'll find him quickly."

WE DIDN'T FIND him quickly.

In fact, we didn't find him at all.

By two in the morning Jack was ready to give up the search. Chris had seemingly disappeared into the night, leaving no trace behind, and Jack's shoulders were heavy with the burden he carried.

"We need to call the authorities." Jack drank half a bottle of water before continuing. "We need to get dogs out here and more bodies to conduct a more thorough search."

I felt helpless … and somehow to blame. "I'm sorry."

"You didn't do this, Charlie."

"I should've listened to you. It was a bad idea. That's what you said. You practically begged me to agree with you, but I didn't. This is on me."

Jack grabbed my shoulders and forced me to look at him. "It's not on you. It's on me. I'm head of security. I should've done better by him. Right now we need help."

I swallowed hard and nodded. "So what do we do?"

"I'll call Bernard and get him to enlist the authorities," Jack replied. "They should be out here shortly after dawn."

"Dawn? That's hours away."

"That's the best I can do, Charlie."

I knew it was true, but it didn't sit well. "I really am sorry."

"Let it go." Jack released my shoulders. "This is on me."

He said the words, but I didn't believe them. I should've known better. It was far too late to fix it now.

22
TWENTY-TWO

*J*ack forced me to remain close once the call was made. I didn't try to wander away. He kept one eye on my every movement, so it wasn't an option anyway. I had no interest in heightening his anxiety, so I didn't put up a fight when he dragged me with him from one end of the town to the other.

Once we saw the police cruisers pulling into town, Jack left me in front of the saloon with a whispered admonishment to stay put before heading in their direction.

"He's wound a little tight this morning, huh?" Laura slipped into the spot Jack vacated and sat next to me, resting her back against the saloon wall as she watched him work. "He's going to have a complete and total freakout if we can't find Chris."

"I don't think he's the only one."

"Why? Are you going to freak out, too?" Laura arched an eyebrow, seemingly intrigued.

I bit back a hot retort and forced myself to remain calm. "I'm talking about Millie ... and Hannah ... and Myron. Don't you think they're going to freak out?"

Laura shrugged, noncommittal. "I hadn't given it much thought. I guess you're right. If Chris is dead ...."

Her cavalier attitude toward our boss, a man who had been nothing but warm and kind, grated. "He's been gone only a few hours. We don't know he's dead."

"We don't know he's alive either."

"Just ... can't you go someplace else and spout your nonsense?" I challenged.

"What crawled up your butt and died?"

"You." I pushed myself to a standing position and shook my head, frustration and weariness threatening to overtake me. At this point I'd been awake almost twenty-four hours and the strain was starting to show. "I don't want Chris to be dead."

Laura balked. "I don't want him to be dead either."

"No, but you seem to be emitting a certain amount of glee over the situation," I pointed out. "You might want to ask yourself why."

"I'm not gleeful."

"No?" I scratched at an invisible itch on my cheek as I regarded her. Now wasn't the time to pick a fight, yet I couldn't seem to stop myself. "Where were you, Laura? Why was Chris alone in the first place?"

"Where were you?" Laura shot back, her face flushing with color as she hopped up. "Where were you when he was wandering around by himself? I'll tell you where you were. You were mooning over Jack, because that's what you spend all your time doing."

I wanted to do the chick thing and smack her, but managed to refrain. "I was hardly mooning over Jack."

"Oh, don't kid yourself," Laura shot back. "We've all seen it. You follow him from one place to the other, one adventure to the other, and you can't stop staring. It's a little pathetic. Do you really think Jack is going to give you what you want?"

"And what do I want?"

"Him," Laura replied without hesitation. "It's written all over your face when you look at him. He knows it. I see it when he looks at you. He thinks it's cute ... like you're a little kid with your first crush. He'll never return your feelings."

I felt exposed. Actually, I felt far more than that. I was annoyed, flustered, frustrated, angry and ripped open for everyone to stare at. Laura thought she knew everything, saw everything. She didn't know or see anything, though. "I don't know what you think you see … but I don't have a crush on Jack."

"I wish I believed that, at least for your sake, but I don't." Laura adopted a faux sympathetic tone. "He's only sticking so close to you because you're the new team member and he's afraid you'll get into trouble. He doesn't really care about you."

Laura meant the words to be a dig. I didn't want to give her power over me, but the statement hurt all the same. Instead of letting her see it, I ran my tongue over my teeth and took a step back. "This is not the type of conversation we should be having when we're looking for a missing person. Chris disappeared on your watch because you were too hot for Zach to pay your boss any attention.

"This isn't on Jack," I continued. "This is on you. Don't even think of trying to blame Jack."

"He's head of security," Laura argued. "He should've been watching Chris instead of you. In fact, you shouldn't have been out here in the first place. You had no legitimate reason to be on this trip and you know it."

I refused to engage in a screaming match with the police so close. I barely managed to hold onto my temper. "I get what you're doing. I've seen it before. You're the type of person who never takes personal responsibility. If that makes you feel better, well, great. I guess that's good for you, but it doesn't work on the rest of us. It won't work when Millie finds out.

"I happen to know that you were too wrapped up in your personal crap to pay attention to what Chris was doing," I continued. "I see what your attack really is. It's a way to cover your guilt."

Anger flashed through Laura's eyes. "I have nothing to feel guilty about."

"Yeah, keep telling yourself that."

Jack was working with the sheriff's deputies, so I took advantage of the rising sun and crossed the street. I needed distance from Laura

– her accusations regarding Jack set my teeth on edge – and I couldn't get it if we were sharing space in the middle of Hooper's Mill.

I took up position in front of the hotel and stared up, mentally moving through rooms until I focused on a specific window on the second floor. I was fairly certain that was the room I stood in and looked out while lost in my vision. The room where I ultimately wouldn't be alone – something evil moving in on me even as Jack stalked the streets searching for me while screaming my name.

I willed myself to return to the vision so I could learn more, pressing my eyes shut as I opened my mind. Why was I here? Why was I in that room? Who would move in on me? How did Jack know I was in danger? Were we here looking for Chris? Was something else going on? How did the Chupacabra fit into all of this?

I had a hundred questions and no answers.

"What are you doing?"

Jack surprised me when he moved to my side. I sensed him a split-second before he spoke.

"Thinking." It wasn't a lie. I couldn't do anything but think right now. "What are you doing? What did the cops say?"

"They're calling for reinforcements and starting a search," Jack replied grimly. "They warned us not to go anywhere. That's not sitting well with Laura – she's over there trying to talk them out of their decision – but it makes sense to me."

"They think we did something to him, don't they?"

"I don't believe that's true," Jack hedged. "I obviously can't see inside their heads, but from a strictly law enforcement perspective it wouldn't make much sense for us to drive out here, set up camp, do something to our boss and then call them."

"We're looking for the Chupacabra," I reminded him. "That might bolster our case."

"In theory," Jack conceded. "But if we really wanted to bolster our case we'd have an exsanguinated body out here for them to discover."

He looked tired when I risked a glance in his direction. Tired and … sick to his stomach. Worry over Chris was eating him alive, but he was trying to be strong for my benefit. I mentally compared him to a warrior, one who fought to the death for honor and loyalty, and then shook my head at my ridiculousness. "How do you know they won't find a body out there?" I asked. "We couldn't really look because it was dark. Now it will be easier to see if he's out there.

"I'm not saying I want Chris to be dead," I continued. "That's the last thing I want. If someone is trying to send us a message, though ..."

"Then killing him would be the way to do it," Jack finished, pressing his hand to his forehead. "This is unbelievable. It can't be happening."

My heart went out to him. "This isn't your fault. You can't blame yourself. I know Laura is spouting off at the mouth, but you didn't do this."

"Is that what she's been saying?" Jack didn't look especially surprised. "I wondered what you guys were talking about."

"She said a lot of stupid things," I groused, tugging a frustrated hand through my hair. "As long as she doesn't have to blame herself for any of this she's more than happy to point the finger at others."

Jack narrowed his eyes to dangerous slits. "What did she say to you?"

I realized my mistake too late to take it back. The last thing Jack needed was to split his focus. "It doesn't matter. It was simply Laura being Laura."

Jack didn't look convinced. "Whatever she said, ignore her. For now, the cops want us out of the way. We have to sit over there and wait for them to arrive and question us." He pointed to the makeshift camp in front of the saloon. "I wanted to help them search, but they absolutely refused."

"They don't want you accidentally tainting a potential crime scene," I mused. "I hope they don't find something out there."

"You and me both." Jack held out his arm and ushered me toward the spot where we pitched our camp. "Why don't you try to take a nap?" he suggested. "We're going to be here for a little bit."

"I doubt very much I'll be able to sleep."

"Try anyway."

"Fine."

I honestly thought sleep was out of my grasp. I was wrong.

I WOKE WITH A start when a man cleared his throat, finding my cheek pressed against Jack's thigh as he rested on the ground and tried to remain still so he wouldn't wake me.

"What … ?" I rubbed the corner of my mouth, frowning when I felt a bit of drool crusted there. "Did I fall asleep?"

"You snored like a locomotive," Laura shot back, her expression grim.

Jack managed a small smile, but I knew it was only for my benefit. "You slept for an hour. It wasn't long. You needed it."

"Did I really snore?" I was mortified.

"And drooled," Laura snarked. "It wasn't attractive at all."

"Ignore her," Jack ordered, shaking his head. "It was fine. You needed the sleep. You were much better off than the rest of us. I think you even dreamed. You were whispering or something in your sleep. I couldn't make it out."

"I think she was having a sex dream," Laura said pointedly. "Can you guess who it was about?"

If Jack understood the challenge in Laura's voice he didn't show it. Instead he merely rolled his eyes and helped me to a sitting position. "Don't give her a hard time, Laura."

"Fine," Laura gritted out. "I won't give her a hard time. I happen to think her little crush on you is cute, even though it won't go anywhere and she'll end up with a broken heart."

I pressed my lips together to keep from lashing out and rubbed my cheek in an effort to cut down on the burn. Jack's eyes were sympathetic. "I … ."

"Ignore her," Jack prodded. "She's just trying to get a rise out of you. Don't let her."

"I am not trying to get a rise out of her," Laura argued.

"That's what you live for, Laura," Jack said. "It's beyond pathetic."

"You're beyond pathetic," Laura shot back.

Someone cleared his throat again and I recognized the sound that woke me. When I lifted my eyes, I found a sheriff's deputy with a notebook in his hand standing on the other side of Jack. He didn't look happy.

"This is Deputy Pierson," Jack supplied, returning to the business at hand. "I believe he has an update for us."

"I don't have much of an update," Pierson countered, his gaze landing on me. I couldn't tell what he was thinking, but his expression didn't reflect friendliness, or hope, for that matter. "We've searched the area and can't find any sign of Chris Biggs. He seems to have disappeared into thin air."

"That's good, right?" Laura rested her hands on her knees. "If you haven't found him, that means he's not dead."

Pierson's expression remained flat. "Is there a reason we should believe he's dead?"

Jack shook his head, annoyance evident. "No. She just likes to talk to hear herself talk."

"That's rich considering who you just let drool on you," Laura shot back.

Jack ignored her. "Like I told you before, we have no reason to believe Chris is dead. We also have no reason to believe that he wandered off on his own. He was looking forward to camping here last night. He had a bunch of expensive equipment with him."

"Maybe he ran off with the equipment," Pierson suggested. "Have you considered that?"

"Not in the least," Jack replied, unruffled. "His family owns the Legacy Foundation. He's rich. He doesn't need to steal equipment and sell it."

"What about ransom?" Pierson asked. "If someone took him, would his family pay ransom?"

"Yes, but I've been in touch with them, and they haven't received a ransom call."

"So he just disappeared in the night and you have no idea how it happened?" Pierson was understandably dubious as his eyes bounced from face to face. "And where were you again when all this happened?"

"We were technically with him, but we got distracted," Zach volunteered. He'd been largely silent since Chris went missing. I had a feeling he was worried he wouldn't get paid now that the guy who signed his contract was no longer around. "He was there one minute and gone the next."

"And how did you get distracted?" Pierson asked.

"Oh, well ... ." Zach trailed off, embarrassed.

"We were making out," Laura answered blandly. "We were behind the hotel and decided to make out while Chris was screwing around with his night-vision scope. The next thing we knew he was gone. We assumed he'd headed back to the fire – which is where Jack and Charlie were – but he wasn't here when we got back."

"And you two were at the fire?" Pierson turned his attention to me. "Were you making out, too?"

"What? No?" I was horribly embarrassed by the question.

Laura snorted. "She has a crush on him, but he doesn't return the feelings. They weren't making out."

Jack scorched Laura with a dark look. "I think we can answer our questions. Thanks."

Laura made a face. "I just meant ... ."

Jack cut her off with a headshake. "No one cares what you meant. For the record, Deputy Pierson, we spent about an hour or so talking ... just shooting the breeze ... and then we decided to look around.

"We each grabbed a flashlight and went into the saloon first," he continued. "We were in there only five minutes when we heard Laura screeching. We came out, asked her what happened, and then immediately started searching for Chris."

"So you were at the fire for most of the night?" Pierson rubbed his chin as Jack nodded. "You would've seen something if Mr. Biggs returned to the main street, right?"

Jack nodded again.

"Well, I don't know what to tell you. We've got dogs coming out here," Pierson said. "We'll look until we find him. You've got my word on that."

"I'd like to help," Jack volunteered. "I have military training. I know how to run a search grid."

Pierson held up a hand to silence him. "It's a nice offer, but we can't accept it. While I don't personally think you're involved, we can't rule you out. You should go back to your hotel and wait there."

Jack opened his mouth to argue, but Pierson shook his head to quiet him.

"There's nothing you can do here," Pierson said. "There's nothing we can let you do. You need to head back to town. Leave your things, because they're part of a crime scene now. Go get some rest. I'll touch base in a few hours."

"I guess that's all we can do, huh?" Jack didn't look thrilled at the prospect. "Well ... I guess that's it. Let's head back to the hotel and talk to the others. I have a feeling this won't go over well."

I had a feeling he was right.

23
TWENTY-THREE

The ride back to the hotel was done in silence. Jack focused on the road and kept whatever thoughts plagued him to himself. Laura and Zach sat in the backseat, not whispering or speaking but making flirty eyes at one another as if we weren't in the middle of a potential tragedy. The simple fact that they bothered doing it given the circumstances irritated the crap out of me.

I stuck close to Jack as we walked into the hotel. Millie and Hannah sat in the lobby, faces grim and drawn. They rushed toward him when they caught sight of us.

"Any word?" Hannah looked tired, as if she'd been woken in the middle of the night and hadn't returned to sleep. I figured that was exactly what happened. I'd never seen the woman look anything less than put together and perfect. Now she looked like a wreck.

"No." Jack gave Hannah a reassuring pat on the shoulder. "They're calling for search dogs at Hooper's Mill. They're still looking. They haven't given up."

"Why are you here then?" Millie challenged. She looked frazzled, as if she was one smart comment away from smiting the town … and everyone in it. "Shouldn't you be out looking for him?"

"They won't allow it."

"Why? You're military. You'd be helpful."

"I'm not a cop." Jack was worn to the bone, but he remained strong for Millie and Hannah's benefit. More importantly, he remained reasonable. "They don't want me roiling up their scene. They don't want me trying to hide evidence."

Millie was flummoxed. "What evidence?"

"They think we might've had something to do with Chris' disappearance," I supplied. "We're suspects, so we can hardly help with the search. They segregated us the second they arrived and kept us in the middle of town so they could watch us."

"Well, that's ridiculous," Millie sputtered. "Why would you do something to Chris and then call them for help?"

"To cover our tracks," Jack replied. "The deputy in charge said he doesn't believe we're suspects, but he can't in good conscience have us out there."

"Are they acting as if they're looking for a body?" Hannah asked, her lower lip quivering.

Jack shrugged. "I don't know. They're just looking in general right now. The longer we go without knowing where Chris is, though, the more likely it is they'll believe we did something to him."

"What about the Chupacabra?" Bernard asked, sliding into the room. I had no idea where he'd been standing, but it was obvious he was listening. "Do they think the Chupacabra got him?"

Instead of scowling at the question, which he would've done under normal circumstances, Jack flashed a helpless look. "We didn't see anything that even remotely resembled a Chupacabra."

"You didn't believe in it from the beginning," Millie pointed out. "You might not see it if it was right in front of you, because you tend to be situationally blind when the mood strikes."

"Charlie and I were in front of the saloon almost the entire time," Jack said. "We would've seen something if it was there."

"Except you were too busy looking at one another to watch for anything else," Laura supplied.

Jack wheeled on her, his hands clenched into fists at his sides and his eyes wild. "Do not even think about putting this off on us. Just because I didn't come down on you in front of Deputy Pierson doesn't mean I won't do it now.

"Charlie and I were sitting by the fire," he continued. "We were talking and minding our own business. You and Zach went off with Chris. You were supposed to be watching each other. You fell down on the job."

Sensing potential disaster given the fury in Laura's eyes, I put a hand on Jack's forearm to calm him. "This won't help."

"I don't care if it helps." Jack was beyond reason, lack of sleep causing him to melt down. "They were supposed to be watching each other. They promised. That was the only reason I wasn't worried. That's the only reason I didn't insist on all five of us staying together."

"You can't possibly blame this on us," Zach argued, speaking for the first time since we left Hooper's Mill. "I told you that staying there overnight was a bad idea. I told you that from the beginning. No one listened to me."

"If you thought it was such a bad idea, why did you agree to go?" I challenged.

"Because … ." Zach broke off, working his jaw.

"Because you wanted to get into Laura's pants," I finished. "You obviously weren't worried enough to forego the possibility of sex."

"We didn't have sex," Laura snapped. "We just sort of … made out. It's not our fault we lost track of Chris. He tends to have a mind of his own when it comes to these things."

"Don't you dare blame him," Hannah hissed. "How can you possibly even consider blaming him?"

"Because he wandered away," Laura spat.

"Except he didn't," I said. "He might've wandered a few feet away, but ultimately he was taken. Whether it was by the Chupacabra or a human, I don't know, but I lean more toward a human. If the Chupacabra was involved, it would've dropped him. It didn't bother hiding Morrison's body."

"We don't know the Chupacabra is even real," Jack pointed out. "We have no idea what happened to Chris. I side with Charlie on this one. I have to believe a human did this. An animal would've killed him where he stood. We would've found him … or at least seen signs of him. Something else is going on here."

"Oh, of course you agree with Charlie," Laura seethed. "You always agree with Charlie these days. It's ridiculous … and annoying … and pathetic … and so freaking annoying!"

"You're freaking annoying," Jack shot back, the muscle in his jaw furiously working. "You should have been watching him!"

"Okay." I knew things were about to spiral out of control and felt the need to step in. "This is getting us nowhere. We need to stop."

Jack murdered me with a look. "Don't tell me what to do."

I had a choice. I could back down and let him rage or I could force him to see reason. Both were dangerous prospects. "I'm not telling you what to do." I chose my words carefully. "I am asking you not to do this. There's a difference."

"How do you figure?"

"Because you're exhausted. I know, because I'm exhausted, too, and I got an hour of sleep. You're running on fumes. You need some rest."

Jack tugged on his hair. "I can't rest knowing Chris is out there. I know the cops think this is either a hoax or we're covering up for ourselves. Right now, I think they believe it's a hoax. The longer he's gone, the less chance he has of survival."

"You can't change his fate right now," I pointed out. "The cops have control. Going back out there and getting yourself arrested won't help Chris. We need to wait until they get back to us.

"Until then, you need rest," I continued. "You need to be at full strength when word comes. If they're not going to continue the search – which is entirely possible if they think we're perpetuating a hoax – then we need to go back out there ourselves and start another search.

"You're going to need your strength for that," I prodded. "You're a strong guy, Jack, but you're running on fumes."

Jack stared at me for a long beat, blinking as he considered the statement. "Fine," he said finally. "I'll take a few hours down. You need to do the same."

"That's exactly what I have in mind."

Jack offered up one more glare for Laura and Zach's benefit before pointing himself toward the stairs. "I'll be back. If the cops call or show up, wake me."

"We're on it," Bernard said. "We'll find him."

I followed Jack up the stairs, halting when I saw his door was open because a maid was inside cleaning.

"I think this is supposed to be a message of sorts," Jack said. "I shouldn't sleep."

"It's not a message. It's simply an inconvenience." I grabbed him by the shoulders and shoved him toward my room. "You can sleep in here with me."

Jack's expression was hard to read when he snagged my gaze. "Excuse me?"

"Just sleep," I stressed. "We both need it. At least this way I'll know you're actually resting so I can close my eyes, too."

"Last time we slept next to one another it didn't go well."

There was no need to remind me of that embarrassing experience. It was seared in my brain. We went to sleep in the same tent, in separate sleeping bags, but woke tangled together, somehow cuddling in our sleep. It was a mortifying memory.

"Don't get full of yourself," I chided. "That was an accident. I don't need a reminder that you're not interested in me that way. It's embarrassing for both of us, but we need sleep. My room is already clean. We can sleep – fully clothed – for a few hours. No one will be the wiser."

Jack ran his tongue over his teeth, internally debating. "Fine. Keep your hands to yourself, though." He left me gaping as he strode into my room, not bothering to glance my way again until he kicked off his boots and climbed onto the bed. "Are you coming?"

I glared as I shut the door and removed my shoes. "Maybe you should take your own advice," I grumbled under my breath. "Maybe you should be the one to keep your hands to yourself."

"That's an interesting option," Jack said, resting his forearm over his eyes as he yawned. "I think you're the one we need to worry about.

I'm used to it. Women can't control themselves when they get around me."

"Oh, you're so full of yourself."

Jack's lips quirked. "Go to sleep, Charlie. You were right about the rest, but we don't have a lot of time. I'm really worried Chris is either already dead or on someone else's timetable. I don't like either option."

"We'll find him." Strangely enough, I was certain that was true. "Now ... go to sleep."

"What do you think I'm trying to do? You need to shut your trap for it to happen."

"Yeah, yeah."

I thought sleep would elude me. I was so tense I figured I'd pretend to sleep so Jack wouldn't be bothered. Much like at Hooper's Mill, though, I dropped straight into sleep ... and woke in another dreamscape.

"**WHAT ARE WE** doing here?"

Jack's gaze was intense as he studied the dream version of Hooper's Mill.

"I don't know." I didn't bother to hide my frustration. "I was hoping for a dream-free nap."

"I once read a study that said dream sleep is more restful than non-dream sleep," Jack offered. "Maybe that's good for both of us."

"Or maybe this is going to be an annoying trip and my subconscious is going to try to give me clues that I won't be able to decipher. Did you ever consider that?"

"No." Jack smiled as he glanced around. "Are we supposed to look for Chris here?"

That was a good question. "I don't know. I don't know why we're here at all. In fact ... ." A flash of something in the upstairs window of the hotel caught my attention. I saw movement behind the curtains – curtains that didn't exist in the real world because they'd fallen into tattered shreds long ago – and I was certain that someone was watching me.

"Jack, I know you're not really here and that my subconscious keeps manifesting you for some reason I don't fully understand, but I need to tell you something."

Jack, his attention directed toward a set of prints on the ground, merely grunted in acknowledgement.

"If I go missing, don't come looking for me."

Jack snapped his head in my direction, surprise evident on his curious face. "What do you mean?"

"I keep having this flash," I explained. I saw no reason to lie. This wasn't really happening. I believed my mind kept manufacturing a clone of Jack to act as the voice of reason in my busy imagination.

"Flash?" Jack arched an eyebrow. "What kind of flash?"

"I think it's something that's going to happen in the future," I replied. "I know that sounds weird, but … I don't know what else it could be."

"It doesn't sound weird at all," Jack said dryly. "I hear crap like that every single day."

"Hear it but don't believe it."

"You say tomato … ."

I smiled despite myself. "Anyway, in the flash I'm up in that room." I pointed so he would know. "I'm not alone. Someone is there with me."

"Someone bad?"

I swallowed hard and nodded. "That's the feeling I get."

"And what does that have to do with me?"

"I see you in the vision," I replied. "You're on the street, yelling for me. You're on the street and seem desperate to find me. A storm is brewing and lightning is flashing and … you're yelling."

"And?"

"And I believe that if you go to that room looking for me, something really bad will happen."

When Jack didn't immediately respond, I risked a glance at him.

"You expect me to sit back and do nothing while you're up in that room in danger?"

"I don't know what will happen to me and I know you don't have any control over what the real Jack will do, but I need him to stay safe. I think something really bad will happen if he goes to that room," I explained. "If I'm meant to die up there ... ."

"You're not going to die," Jack growled, his vehemence taking me by surprise. "I won't let that happen."

"I know." I patted his arm, hoping to offer comfort. "But if I do it's not your fault. I need you to know that. I'm going to do my best not to end up in that room, but if I do ... I know you'll do everything in your power to find me. It's more important to keep yourself safe. It's more important to find Chris."

"It's not more important."

"It feels more important."

"Then you're an idiot." Jack shook his head as he stared at the window. "What direction does the person move when they come for you?"

I gestured with my hand. "As we're looking, I'm on the right but toward the middle of the window, and the shadow comes in from the left."

"Like someone is in the next room or entering from the hallway?"

"As if someone is suddenly there. I don't know how to explain it."

We lapsed into silence, both of us lost in our own little worlds. Jack was the first to break it ... which was a marked change from our interactions in the real world.

"I won't leave you, Charlie. I know you've come to expect that because of what happened with your parents, but I won't do it."

"I don't think you'll have a choice."

"There's always a choice."

"Not this time." I forced a smile for his benefit. "It's okay. I've come to the conclusion – after years and years of self-doubt – that you can't beat fate. What's supposed to happen happens no matter what."

"Really?" Jack was dubious. "I've come to the conclusion that I won't let anything happen to you. I guess we'll have to see who is right, huh?"

"I guess."

"May the smarter person – that would be me in this case – win."

I giggled, the sound taking me by surprise. "Even my dream version of you is bossy."

"Yes, well, that's how I roll."

I WOKE WITH A START, bolting to a sitting position and letting my gaze travel toward a slumbering Jack. He rested on his side, his face serene in sleep.

I was about to rejoin him, hopefully this time without an odd dream conversation, when I heard a distinctive clicking sound at the door.

The movement was small and subtle, but I didn't miss the way the handle moved. Back and forth, back and forth, as if someone was testing it.

My mind was still muddled with sleep, but I understood something very clearly: Someone was trying to get inside my room.

24
TWENTY-FOUR

I stared at the door, my heart rate picking up a notch. The hair on the back of my neck stood on end as my blood turned cold and I stared at the handle.

It was silent for so long I thought there was a possibility I imagined it.

Then the door handle moved again.

Back and forth.

Back and forth.

The room was quiet other than the air conditioner in the window, but the machine was loud enough to supply white noise – which I liked – and the occasional whine that broke the monotony of the droning sound. It also managed to cover the small "clicking" noise of the twisting door handle. I only knew it was happening because I saw the movement.

I remained on my back, my hands resting on my stomach, and watched. Jack's breathing was even as he slumbered next to me. He needed the sleep. The next twenty-four hours would be brutal. Whether he was to blame or not, he would emotionally flog himself until he was broken down.

The best scenario would be discovering Chris somehow wandered off and got lost. The odds of that were unlikely – especially the more time elapsed – but I wasn't ruling it out. Perhaps that was naïve, but I still had hope.

The worst-case scenario involved Chris already being dead. Whether by human or creature design, our lovable, yet absent-minded leader could've been so distracted by what he was doing that someone – or something, for that matter – approached him from behind and took him out with minimal effort. Chris would fight for his life if he saw the enemy coming. If he didn't, he'd go down quickly.

The far more likely scenario – at least in my book because no body had been found – involved Chris being taken and held somewhere. If someone wanted him dead, or to send a message, he or she would've left the body where it was easily discoverable. If the Chupacabra killed him, it would've sucked his blood and left his body behind. Even if another creature arrived to drag him away – and I had my doubts anything big enough to do that lived in the desert surrounding Hooper's Mill – we would've seen marks in the sand. That indicated someone took Chris for another purpose. What that reason was, though, I had no idea.

The handle turned again, causing me to carefully pull myself to a sitting position. Someone was on the other side of the door. It wasn't the maid. She had a key. It wasn't a member of my team. They would knock – some of them would yell – and they wouldn't keep trying after figuring out the door was locked. No, this was someone else.

I cast a look to Jack. He looked almost angelic in sleep. Er, well, he was actually too macho to look angelic. He did look like a beautiful piece of artwork, though. The lines of his face as he slumbered made him look even more handsome. I didn't want to wake him, but I didn't see a way out of it.

Then something occurred to me. I tilted my head to the side as I focused on the door. I didn't need to get out of bed to deal with who was out there. I merely needed to use the abilities I worked so hard to keep secret from those surrounding me.

I chewed my bottom lip as I narrowed my eyes and conjured a picture of the ugly artwork from the hallway into my head. It hung on the wall across the way, right next to Jack's door, and featured a cow skull, bar and some sort of weird machine in a field of corn. The colors were muted and the tone of the painting was depressing. It didn't need to be pretty to serve my purpose.

I squeezed my eyes shut, letting the power build in my chest before releasing it. There was a "whoosh" I knew only I could feel, and then I heard the distinctive sound of someone grunting as the painting whacked into him or her. There was a mild scuffle and then something hit the ground – probably the painting – and footsteps signified a hasty retreat.

"What was that?" Jack jerked to a sitting position, his eyes blurry as he swiped at his hair to move it away from his face. My plan to race to the door and peer outside evaporated as quickly as his dreams.

"Something fell in the hallway." I kept my tone calm and even. "I'm not sure what."

"Oh." Jack didn't look especially alarmed. I considered telling him I thought someone was trying to break into the room, but he'd be furious I didn't wake him, and I wasn't in the mood for an argument. "Okay."

Jack rubbed his cheek as he tried to get his bearings. "What time is it?"

"Almost three."

"Three?" Jack did the math in his head. "I slept for five hours."

"You needed the sleep."

"But we're losing the day. We need to get back out to Hooper's Mill. Surely they've found something by now."

"If they did, they haven't been in contact with us." I turned my head to meet his gaze. "You still look tired."

"You don't." Jack looked me up and down. "You look well rested."

"I slept at Hooper's Mill this morning, too." Plus, I didn't have nearly the amount of guilt radiating through me, although I kept that observation to myself. "I've had more sleep than you."

"Not much." Jack dragged a hand through his hair as he stared at the bedspread. "I'm not good at stuff like this."

I had no idea what he was referring to. "Stuff like what?"

"This." Jack gestured toward the bed and for a moment I thought he was going to say something about our obvious chemistry or the emotions that kept running roughshod over my heart when he was around. I thought he was going to say he felt the same way.

Then he ruined it. He always ruined it.

"I'm not good at letting people boss me around and take over," he supplied. "I didn't want to listen when you said I needed sleep, but I feel better now. Thank you for that."

"Oh, right." I tried to tamp down my disappointment. It wasn't his fault I was developing a crush on him. In fact, I didn't think it was my fault either. I was pretty sure it was Millie's fault for putting the idea in my head and Laura's fault for being a jealous pain in the ass. "It's nothing, Jack. You needed the sleep. We both did."

"Yeah, but you made sure I got it, and … thank you."

It was hard for him to get the words out. I recognized that, and for some reason I felt a giddy jolt course through me at the sheepish look on his face. He really was thankful. That was something, right?

"You're welcome."

Jack smiled, the expression lighting up his dour face. He grabbed my hand – an instinctive move that he clearly didn't plan – and gave it a good squeeze. The simple action was enough to make the energy in the room crackle as we stared into each other's eyes.

I swear it felt as if my heart was in my throat. I thought there was a very real chance I'd pass out. Jack's feelings were harder to ascertain, but I was certain he felt something. He didn't lean closer, but he didn't pull back. Our faces were close; a few inches either way could change everything.

Perhaps Jack sensed it, and that was why he released my hand. His cheeks seemed pinker than normal, but he maintained an air of cool confidence that made me believe he didn't feel the same jolt I did when we touched.

"I need a shower," Jack volunteered after a beat. "You, too."

"Is that your subtle way of saying I stink?"

Jack snickered. "No, but it will make you feel better. Once that's done we should meet with everyone in the dining room. We have some decisions to make."

"Okay." I rolled off the bed and stared at him across the expanse. There was something rueful about his expression that I couldn't quite identify. "Is something wrong?"

"There's a lot wrong," Jack replied. "As for the rest ... ." He helplessly held up his hands and shrugged. "We can only deal with so much at a time. Let's handle showers and dinner. Once we know more about Chris and what happened we can deal with the rest."

I had no idea what "the rest" entailed, but I merely nodded. "Okay."

"Good." Jack moved to the door, wrapping his hand around the handle before twisting it. "Thank you again for making me sleep."

"Thank you for not snoring so I could sleep."

Jack chuckled, the sound warm and comforting. "I'm glad I could be of service." He pulled open the door, his lips still curved in a smile, but the mirth on his face fled as quickly as it appeared.

"What?" I asked, sensing trouble.

"I think more happened in this hallway than a falling painting," he replied grimly, causing me to stare over the corner of the bed and cringe when I saw the item resting on the other side of the door.

"What is that?"

"It's a coyote head," Jack gritted out. "It's ... um ... fresh."

Uh-oh. That couldn't be good, right?

DEPUTY PIERSON arrived within the hour, and he didn't look happy about the latest development. He instructed one of his officers to take photos of the coyote head – which had been rather crudely separated from the animal's body – and then arranged for its removal.

The maid quickly got to work and cleaned the threshold, but I could still picture the head, staring, and the knowledge was enough to cause me to shudder.

"You didn't hear anything?" Pierson's gaze was probing as he stared at me.

"I told you we didn't." Jack's eyes flashed with anger.

"What's going on?" Laura asked, appearing in the hallway. "I thought I heard voices."

"Someone put a severed coyote head outside Charlie's door," Jack replied.

"Really?" Laura arched an eyebrow. "Why?"

"It's a message of sorts," Pierson replied. "People around these parts use coyote heads as warnings."

"They do?" I rubbed my hand over my damp hair. Jack insisted I take a shower during the cleanup effort, and even though it was uncomfortable knowing the cops were working in the hallway, I felt better after the fact. He was freshly showered, too, although he didn't look nearly as refreshed as I felt.

"They do," Pierson confirmed. "It's something of a tradition around here, an omen, if you will."

"Is it supposed to scare us away?"

"Yes."

"Well, that won't work." I slid a look to Jack and found him staring at the floor where the coyote head rested an hour before. "Right?"

"What?" Jack stirred and nodded. "No, it won't. We're not leaving without Chris. If they want us to go, they need to return him ... alive. If he's dead, I'll bring the full force of the federal government down on this place until we know who did it and why."

Pierson's eyebrows flew up his forehead. "How do you expect to do that?"

"The Legacy Foundation works closely with the federal government. Chris is the foundation head's nephew," Jack replied, not missing a beat. "If I know Myron, he's already on his way here ... and he won't come alone."

"I had no idea this guy was such a bigwig," Pierson said.

"Would that have changed anything?" I was legitimately curious. "Would you have searched harder for him if you knew?"

Pierson straightened. "Ma'am, we scoured that entire area. We had dogs. They alerted on Mr. Biggs' scent outside the hotel, but they lost him inside. We put the full effort of our office – and that of the county – into finding him. He's just not there."

"Well, since we know that's not possible, something else must have happened," Jack challenged. "He's out there. At least he was out there. Someone must have taken him."

"The only tire tracks belong to your vehicles," Pierson argued. "We checked the treads."

"Then you're missing something." Jack was adamant.

"He's not out there. I'm sorry."

"What about what happened here?" Jack pressed. "Someone put a warning outside of Charlie's room. That can't be a coincidence."

"How do you know she didn't do it herself for attention?" Pierson asked.

"That does sound just like her," Laura offered, smiling sweetly.

Jack ignored Laura and glared at Pierson. "Because I was with her. I already told you that."

"And what were you doing?"

"What *were* you doing?" Laura asked, her eyes filling with something I couldn't quite identify. "Why were you in here with her?"

"Because the maid was cleaning my room when we came up, and I was exhausted," Jack replied, refusing to let Laura rile him. "We both went to sleep. We were in here together, and she most certainly didn't get up, kill a coyote, behead it, plant it outside her door and then let me discover it when I was leaving."

"You napped in here with her?" Laura was incensed. "On the same bed?"

"No, I made her sleep on the floor, Laura," Jack drawled. "Yes, we slept on the same bed. It's not a big deal."

I knew he didn't mean the words as an insult, but I couldn't help internally lament them all the same. He could at least add that it was difficult for him to stop himself from rolling on top of me and kissing me senseless. What? That's not shallow, considering the circumstances. I can worry about Chris and myself at the same time. I'm nothing if not an efficient multi-tasker.

"So you were in here the entire time?" Pierson asked, ignoring the interpersonal work drama.

"We were," Jack confirmed. "Something woke us. I'm fairly certain it was the painting hitting the floor."

"Yes, I noticed that." Pierson's expression was thoughtful as he stared at the painting. Someone had returned it to its place on the wall. "So, by your theory, someone was trying to send a message to Miss Rhodes. Why do you think she was the focus of the threat?"

"I don't know," Jack replied. "Maybe someone saw us come in here together. Maybe I was the focus of the threat."

That seemed unlikely, but I didn't want to raise Pierson's suspicions regarding the painting. Everyone was laboring under the assumption that whoever was in the hallway bumped into the painting and dislodged it. I didn't want them questioning that too hard, because it would raise inevitable questions.

"I don't know what to tell you," Pierson said. "Most of the department believes you're doing this as some sort of publicity stunt."

"What do you mean?" Laura asked.

"He means that they think we're doing it to boost attention so Chris can pop up in a few hours and say he was stalked by the Chupacabra or something," I supplied. "That's what they assume. They think the coyote head is part of it, too."

"That's ridiculous," Laura snapped. "Chris is out there and he needs help."

"We can't do anything right now." Pierson was firm. "If Mr. Biggs remains missing after another twenty-four hours ... ."

"If he's still missing in twenty-four hours it will be too late," Jack growled. "You know what? Fine. We don't need you. I followed the rules and called the police. I'm done doing things your way."

"What is that supposed to mean?" Pierson asked.

"It means we'll find him ourselves," Jack replied. "We're not waiting around for twenty-four hours. Laura is right. Chris is out there. Charlie most certainly didn't plant that coyote head, which means that we're being watched. I'm not going to sit around and wait for something to happen. I'm taking the fight to whoever did this."

"And how are you going to do that?"

"Don't worry about it," Jack replied, folding his arms over his chest. "I'll take it from here. Have a nice day, deputy."

And just like that, Deputy Pierson was dismissed and we were on our own. Things were about to get serious.

25

TWENTY-FIVE

*J*ack didn't say another word to Pierson, ignoring him as we descended the stairs and met the rest of the group in the lobby.

"You can't go off half-cocked," Pierson argued. "We already looked. He's not out there."

"I believe he said you could leave," I offered, doing my best to appear bold and brash even though my insides turned to liquid at the idea of talking to a police officer with anything less than the utmost respect. "If you're not going to help, you're simply in our way."

"Your way?" Pierson's eyebrows hopped. "Your way to do what?"

"Find our friend."

"He's not out there."

"That doesn't mean we're not going to look."

Jack gestured toward the door, and even though I could tell Millie wanted answers right away she wisely fell into step with us and exited the hotel.

"We'll get dinner and then we have some plans to make," Jack announced. "I'll fill everyone in over the meal."

I risked a glance at Pierson and found him standing in front of the hotel, a dark look on his face. He wasn't happy, but there was little he could do.

"Don't do anything stupid," Pierson called out.

"Don't worry," Jack shot back. "I have no intention of doing anything stupid."

He didn't speak again until we were back at the restaurant, barbecue and drink orders placed, and everyone's full attention on him.

"We're in a tough spot," Jack announced, licking his lips. I could tell he was trying to organize his words before speaking. "Chris went missing in a very short amount of time. I don't know how it happened, but I think it's important to put all the information we have out there so we can come up with a plan."

"And the police aren't going to be part of that plan?" Hannah asked, keeping her voice low. She looked distraught, but she was the sort of person who managed to hold it together under incredible stress. I admired her for it – mostly because I was the type to fly off the handle and then hate myself after the fact.

"The police are working under the assumption that this is a publicity stunt," Jack replied. "They think we're trying to bolster our claims that the Chupacabra is to blame for Wendell Morrison's death by allowing Chris to voluntarily go missing.

"They believe he's going to pop up safe and sound in the next few hours with wild tales of animal shenanigans," he continued. "They also think what happened outside of Charlie's room is part of that plan."

"What happened outside Charlie's room?" Bernard asked, confused. "Did we miss something?"

"I thought everyone knew." Jack rubbed his chin as he related the story, truncating it as much as possible and refusing to focus on the fact that he was sleeping in my room when it happened. I didn't miss the dour expression on Laura's face as he talked, but she wisely didn't interject her opinion. "So, that's where we're at."

"And what's the plan?" Millie asked. She was a strong woman under normal circumstances, but Chris' disappearance was clearly affecting her. I knew she loved him. She didn't have children of her own, and from what I could tell, all her maternal instincts were focused on Chris. She wasn't married to his uncle any longer, but Chris was still family. She'd be devastated if we didn't find him alive.

"I'm going back to Hooper's Mill after dinner and I'm not coming back without Chris," Jack answered simply.

"That's your plan?" Millie arched an eyebrow, sarcasm practically dripping from her tongue. "You think you're going to go out there and will yourself to find him? Jack, I have faith in your abilities, but I don't think you're being rational."

"And I don't think we have much choice in the matter." Jack was calm, but I could practically feel the irritation radiating off him. "We need to talk about what we know and then we're going to talk about what we can realistically accomplish. First, we know that Chris couldn't have been gone long before Laura alerted us that he was missing."

Jack turned his dark eyes to Laura. "I need you to run through exactly what happened once you left Charlie and me."

"I've already told you," Laura protested. "The story isn't going to change."

"Yes, but I need more details." Jack refused to back down. "Where did you go when you left us? How much time did you spend in that spot? What was Chris specifically doing during that time?"

"Oh." Laura bobbed her head. "I see what you mean. Okay. Let me think a second. I want to get this right."

I sipped my iced tea and glanced at Jack. His profile was strong, the sleep had done him wonders, but I sensed an air of weakness, too. He was so worried that he wouldn't find Chris that I wondered if it was possible for him to turn it into a self-fulfilling prophecy.

"Okay, so we crossed the street and were in front of the hotel for a bit," Laura started, her mind clearly busy as she struggled to keep things straight. "It was dark, but we had flashlights and the night-vision scope. I wanted to go inside the hotel, but Zach told me that was a bad idea."

"Why?" I asked. "What did you think you would find in the hotel?"

Laura shrugged. "I don't know. I just like it. It's one of the few buildings in Hooper's Mill that doesn't creep me out."

I could see that.

"Go on," Jack prodded.

"Zach thought it was a bad idea to go into the buildings after dark even though we had flashlights," Laura explained. "The floor is weak in some places. He didn't want to risk anyone falling through."

Speaking of Zach, he was conspicuously missing from dinner. Of course, if I were in his position I wouldn't want to hang around with us either. He looked bad for losing Chris – especially because of what he was doing when our lovable boss disappeared – and he probably didn't want to risk Millie's wrath. Heck, for all I knew, Millie might've already unleashed her wrath and frightened him away. I made a mental note to ask her about it later.

"So we walked around the front of the buildings for about ten minutes," Laura continued. "Chris was still with us. He was using the scope and chattering away. He was excited. It was his idea to go to the back of the buildings."

"Why?" Jack was intent as he watched Laura tell her tale.

"Because he thought that the fire might scare away the Chupacabra. We could hear you and Charlie talking – although what you possibly have to talk to her about is beyond me – and Chris was convinced that your voices would keep the Chupacabra away, so he wanted to go behind the buildings.

"Zach and I agreed, because ... well, because it was darker back there and we thought it might hide us," she said. "The area behind the buildings is different. I don't know if you've been back there."

"I have, but tell me what you saw anyway," Jack instructed.

"There are a lot of low hills back there, like moguls on a ski slope more than anything," Laura said. "There are a lot of them – and even some discarded crates."

"Crates?" That was interesting. "Are the crates new?"

"Newish," Laura answered. "I don't think they've been out there for more than a few weeks. The weather hasn't had time to beat them down yet."

AMANDA M. LEE

"Who would be moving crates out there?"

"It could be Sully or Morrison," Jack replied. "It could also be kids looking for something to cart around their beer. Kegs are heavy, so maybe the crates play into that. Maybe they're putting cups and ice in the crates, and instead of cleaning up their messes they toss the crates behind the buildings instead."

That hadn't even occurred to me. "What about the hills? The rest of the area is pretty flat."

"I looked at the hills, and I'll guess it's simply a case of discarded items from a century ago being overrun by weeds and the rest of nature," Jack said. "I've seen it happen with landfills. Over time, Mother Nature reclaims what's hers. If someone wanted to excavate under those small elevations, they'd probably find wagon wheels ... pieces of furniture ... and old boxes and supplies."

"Chris was fascinated with them," Laura said. "He kept going on and on about history and all that other stupid stuff he loves."

"It's not stupid," Hannah hissed, coming to life. "He likes history. I do, too. Just because you don't doesn't make it stupid."

"Of course not." Millie offered Hannah a soothing pat on the hand. "Don't listen to Laura. We all know she's a whiny complainer who doesn't care about anyone but herself. She's not worth your time."

Laura balked. "Hey! I'm as worried about Chris as the rest of you."

"Obviously not," Millie said dryly. "You're more worried about yourself and whatever it is you think Jack is doing. Yeah, I've seen the way you've been looking at him. You need to get over yourself. If I had to guess, you're ticked off because he slept in Charlie's room.

"I'd be lying if I said I wasn't curious about that, too," she continued. "I'll bet it's for different reasons – jealousy on your part, being a busybody on mine – but it's not important given what's going on. Right now we have bigger concerns. My nephew is out there. He's missing. We need to find him. He's the most important thing."

"I don't care about Jack and his stupid older brother routine with the newbie," Laura spat.

"You care enough to try to convince yourself that's what's going on," Millie countered. "Now ... stuff that part of the talk. Once Chris is safe I'll debate that theory with you until the end of time. You know I love a good fight. It's not important now."

"She's right." Jack didn't look bothered by the debate, but I was having trouble reading him given his rigid determination. In some ways he was closed off, almost brittle. In others he was open and keen to share information. It was an interesting dichotomy. "What happened then, Laura?"

"Nothing really," Laura replied. "Chris took out his scope and sat on top of one of the hills. He focused on the tree line that was about ... oh, I don't know ... a good five hundred yards away. Then he just shut up and watched and pretty much ignored us."

"He gets hyper-focused on stuff like that," Millie mused. "Where did you go?"

As if sensing Millie's potential fury, Laura scrambled to cover her bases. "Not far. We went down about three buildings so we could have some privacy. We could still see Chris. If he got in trouble we knew we could hear him. Then we just kind of ... spent some time together."

"Yes, I think we can all imagine what you were doing," Bernard said pointedly. He sat on Millie's left, and although he didn't touch her I could tell he was offering her solace just by being close. Their relationship was definitely something I wanted to question her about, but I put it away for the time being.

"How long were you separated from Chris before you realized he was gone?" Jack asked.

"It couldn't have been very long."

"How long?"

"About fifteen minutes. Maybe twenty, I guess. It couldn't possibly have been longer than that."

"So, in twenty minutes' time Chris disappeared," Jack said, as he stared at the ceiling. "That's about what I was figuring."

"What are you thinking?" Bernard asked.

"I'm thinking that I don't care what the cops say," Jack replied. "He's still out there."

"But where?" Millie asked. "How could he be out there without you finding him?"

"Because I think there's a part of Hooper's Mill that only certain people know how to find."

"Like hidden rooms or something?" I asked, intrigued.

Jack nodded. "Think about it. It was a boom town. People were expected to gather up a bunch of silver and carry it to a town that probably had a decent number of reprobates running around. That would become cumbersome."

"So you think there's a vault or something," Millie mused. "That makes sense."

"It does," Jack agreed. "I think that Hooper's Mill has a few secrets left, and I'm determined to find them."

"But how do you know?" Hannah asked. "I mean ... how do you know he wasn't tossed into a vehicle and driven away from Hooper's Mill? He could be anywhere."

"No, he can't," Jack said. "Hannah, I know you're worried, but Chris couldn't have been removed from Hooper's Mill. Charlie and I were in the street the entire time he was out there with his night-vision scope.

"We would've seen a vehicle approach," he continued. "For the sake of argument, even if they didn't use their lights – which would be virtually impossible given the rough terrain they'd have to go over to avoid the roads – and even if they somehow figured a way to get close to Hooper's Mill without their lights, there's no way they would've been able to get close without us hearing them."

"They also couldn't carry Chris out," I added. "He's not big but he's solid. They couldn't risk carrying him away from the buildings, because we were already looking for him within seconds of finding out he was missing."

"Exactly." Jack wagged a finger in my face. "That's another good point. There's simply no way Chris could've been carried or driven away from Hooper's Mill without us noticing. He's still there."

"That doesn't mean he's still alive." Hannah was understandably morose. "He might already be dead."

"He might," Jack conceded. "I don't want to give you false hope. He could be dead. But I don't believe that."

"Why?"

"There's no benefit to killing him and hiding the body," Jack replied. "If people want to frighten us away from Hooper's Mill – which seems to be exactly what they want if the coyote head is taken into account – killing Chris is the wrong way to go, because I'll have federal agents all over that property until we get answers."

"Kidnapping Chris doesn't seem the way to go either," Hannah pointed out. "It only draws attention to Hooper's Mill."

"True, but I'm starting to wonder if the person who took Chris did it because he thought it would scare us away," Jack said. "He might not understand exactly who he's dealing with."

"We're going to show him, though, aren't we?" Millie's eyes sparked with determination. "What's your plan?"

"I'm taking a group back to the town, because I don't want it sitting empty for too long," Jack said. "You're calling Myron and getting us some federal help as soon as possible."

"Why am I calling Myron?" Millie challenged.

"You know why."

Millie opened her mouth to argue and then snapped it shut. She nodded curtly, resigned. "Okay. I'll make him move heaven and earth to get us help before the night is out."

"And I'm taking Bernard with me to watch the town," Jack said. "We're not going to allow anyone in or out of there."

"And me, too," I added.

"Not you." Jack shook his head. "You're staying here with everyone else."

"But why?"

"Because I'm not risking anyone else being taken."

"You're taking Bernard with you."

"Yes, but he's trained for certain things." Jack averted his eyes, and I knew exactly what he refused to utter.

"And he has a penis," I pointed out. "That's what you're really saying."

"I'm not arguing with you," Jack warned. "You're staying here."

"No, I'm not."

"Yes, you are."

"I'm not, and you can't make me."

"I'm your boss, and I can make you."

"Then I quit." Even uttering the words caused my stomach to twist, but I was determined to see this through. Now more than ever, I knew it was important for me to go back to Hooper's Mill. There was something there to find, and they would need me to find it. "I'll figure out my own way to get there. I'll take a cab if I have to."

"You're not going." Jack was on his feet, his nostrils flared. "I'm laying down the law."

Somehow I remained calm, although it was something of a miracle. "Do you want to bet?"

Jack didn't react well to the challenge. "You're staying here. That's the end of it."

"I guess we'll just have to see, huh?"

26
TWENTY-SIX

"Don't even think of separating from me."

Jack was a growling mess by the time we hit Hooper's Mill. We argued long and hard at the hotel, going at it like a long-married couple heading for divorce (and maybe prison given how tempestuous things got), but ultimately he relented and allowed me to tag along.

I wasn't the only one who bullied her way onto the search party.

"Stop barking at her," Millie ordered, her expression fierce as she planted her hands on her hips. "I know you're trying to be all alpha and protective, but talking to her like she's two won't help matters."

Jack stared at Millie for several moments, his expression dark and twisted. "Don't you think about separating from me either."

Instead of shrinking back, Millie merely snorted and rolled her eyes. "Boy, given the mood I'm in, I dare whoever is behind this to try and grab me. In fact, I'm looking forward to it."

"Stop saying things like that," Jack hissed, rummaging through a duffel bag until he came up with several flashlights. "You'll give me an ulcer if you keep saying things like that."

"I'm not leaving this place without Chris." Millie's eyes fired with determination. "It's not going to happen ... so that means a showdown with whoever is doing this is in the cards."

"There will be no showdown," Jack argued. "This is a search-and-rescue operation. We're not here for a showdown."

"You say potato." Millie made a deranged face as she handed me one of the flashlights. "Are you ready to get down and dirty?"

That seemed like a loaded question. "I'm ready to find Chris," I replied, testing the flashlight before continuing. "I think we should start on that side of the street." I pointed toward the side anchored by the hotel.

Jack narrowed his eyes. "Why do you say that?"

"Because Chris disappeared behind those buildings, and it makes the most sense to me," I replied, refusing to let his tone irritate me to the point where I snapped. "If we work under the assumption that we're trying to find a hidden vault or room somewhere, I think it makes the most sense for it to be located by the hotel."

Jack rubbed his thumb between his eyebrows. "I don't disagree. I'd like to hear your ideas first."

"Think about it," I prodded. "Richard Hooper owned the town and set things up for himself above all else. He lived at the hotel. It said so in the documents we got from the clerk's office."

"I forgot about that." Jack nodded. "Great point."

"I'm full of good points," I said. "Hooper owned the hotel. He probably wanted to keep his money close. If someone studied this town long and hard – someone like Wendell Morrison – he might have figured that out, too."

"And maybe he was spending most of his time searching the hotel because he realized that the silver – if there was any – was probably secreted away in Hooper's hidden room," Jack surmised. "Look at that building, though." He gestured for emphasis. "It's surrounded on both sides. That doesn't leave many options for hidden rooms. It must be hidden in plain sight."

"That means the room is built into the design and has a hidden entrance," Bernard said. "If the entrance is built correctly, we could be looking right at it and not see it."

I wasn't so much worried about that as I was worried about hidden surprises inside the room. I figured I could use my magic to sense the location. Doing it without anyone noticing would be tricky, but I would figure it out. It wasn't finding the room that caused me the most concern. No, it was walking inside and facing what happened to Chris that caused me to involuntarily shudder. What would happen if we found the room and realized we weren't alone?

I flicked my gaze to the hotel, licking my lips as I internally debated. "We can't simply focus on the hotel."

"You just said the opposite," Jack argued.

"I know, but hear me out." I held up my hands. "Hooper owned the whole town. The buildings all run together. We've been in the hotel multiple times now and haven't seen anything.

"What if the secret room is between two of the buildings?" I continued. "Like over there, for example." I gestured toward the building with a sagging roof on the left. "I only looked inside briefly, but I think that was the claims office."

"So what?" Jack followed my finger with his gaze. "Why is that important?"

"I get what she's saying." Bernard bobbed his head, his enthusiasm ramping up.

"It's great that you understand, but how about sharing with the class?" Millie suggested, temper flaring.

"The claims office is where people would file permits to mine," Bernard explained. "It's also where they would bring silver to be weighed and sold."

"So?"

"So you wouldn't want to be wandering around town with hunks of silver if you could help it," Jack said. "They're saying it would make the most sense for the room to be between the hotel and the claims office so thieves wouldn't be tempted to jump miners on the street."

"Exactly." I pressed my lips together and forced what I hoped resembled a smile. "I don't think we should ignore everything else, but I do think it might be prudent to start in there."

"Prudent?" Jack cocked a dubious eyebrow. "I don't think you even know what that word means."

"I know what it means. That doesn't mean I believe it applies to me, but I know what it means."

"Ha, ha." Jack flicked a spot between my eyebrows, the action playful even as his face sobered. "Okay. That makes sense. We'll start at the claims office."

"No. We need to split up, with two of us going into the claims office and two of us going into the hotel," I corrected.

Jack balked. "We are not splitting up."

"We have to." I refused to back down. Chris' life might depend on how fast we acted. I couldn't shake the feeling that we were running out of time. "We need to cover two floors in each building. We need to knock on walls and be able to listen on the other side. That's how we'll find the room."

"If it even exists," Jack countered. "We're running on a theory."

"It's a good theory."

Jack made a disgusted sound in the back of his throat. "I think it's a bad idea."

"And I think she's right and we have no choice," Millie said. "If Chris is close, he might be in dire straits. He could be tied up. He could have a head injury, for all we know. I mean, how else did whoever took him manage to get him away from Laura and Zach without them hearing a commotion? It would make sense for them to knock Chris out."

"I get what you're saying, but this makes me nervous," Jack said. "I want to find Chris, but I'm not going to do it by sacrificing one of you."

"No one is going to be sacrificed," I said. "We all have radios and we'll stay in constant contact."

"Fine." Jack scratched at the back of his neck, the skin red and angry from frequent attacks of guilt and worry. He would rub it raw before everything was said and done. "Charlie will come with me to the claims office. Bernard will go with Millie to the hotel."

"No." Bernard vehemently shook his head, taking everyone by

surprise. "I saw the claims office the first day we were here. It's a mess. It's not safe for Charlie. You and I need to handle that building, Jack. Besides, it looks as if a storm is going to roll in, and that could make that place even more dangerous if the rain gets inside."

"We can't let the women go on their own," Jack argued.

"The women?" I made a disgusted face. "Really? You can't let 'the women' go off on their own? What kind of Neanderthal are you?"

"The kind who wants to keep you safe," Jack answered without hesitation. "I don't like the idea of you two wandering off alone."

"And yet Millie and I have been in the hotel alone together already," I reminded him. "The sun is still out. Yeah, it looks as if that might not last long if those storm clouds are any indication, but it still won't be pitch black even if it storms. No one will move on us if we're in teams, especially while it's still light out. If we haven't found the room by the time the sun sets, we can come up with another plan. Until then we're wasting time."

Jack wasn't convinced. "Charlie . . . ."

"She makes sense, Jack," Millie interjected. "We'll be close and have our radios on at all times."

"We'll be careful," I added. "You have to trust me eventually."

"I trust you a great deal," Jack replied.

The words warmed me to my core. "Thank you."

"I trust that you're loyal, brave and giving."

My cheeks burned under the praise.

"I also trust that you act before you think, you talk before you think and you jump in with both feet rather than testing to see if sharks are in the water," Jack added. He grabbed my shoulders and forced me to meet his gaze. "Don't make me regret this."

"I won't." I meant it. I had no intention of making him regret any of this. "We'll find Chris. This is our best shot."

"I know. Just make sure we don't lose you in the process, okay? That's not a trade I'm willing to make."

. . .

MILLIE AND I HEADED straight for the hotel. I lingered by the front door long enough to offer a reassuring wave to Jack before disappearing inside. I headed straight for the shared wall, furrowing my brow as I studied the ragged wood.

"I don't see how a door can be hidden there," Millie offered after watching me run my hands over the dilapidated wood for a few minutes. "There are no hinges or seams."

"No, but that doesn't mean there's not a door somewhere around here," I said, shifting my attention to the back of the lobby. "Like behind the staircase."

Millie followed my gaze. "Oh, I get what you're saying. It would make more sense for Hooper to hide the door in a place people would be less likely to wander."

"Exactly." I gripped my flashlight tighter as I headed in that direction, biting off a sigh when Jack's voice came over the radio.

"Are you two okay?"

I looked to Millie and gave her a silent order to answer while I focused on slowly running my light beam over the wall behind the staircase.

"We're here and we're fine," Millie said. "Charlie is searching the area underneath the staircase right now."

"That's probably smart," Jack said. "Do me a favor and knock on the wall so I can listen to determine if it's hollow. This place is a total wreck, and I doubt very much anyone has been walking around here. It's almost dangerous with how weak the floor is in some places."

"I've got it." Millie left me to continue my search and walked about ten feet away. "I'm between the front door and the staircase. Give it a listen."

"Got it."

Millie rested the radio on the floor and then rapped on the wall. She listened intently until someone knocked on the other side, repeating the process three times before reclaiming the radio.

"That sounds as if there's nothing between your wall and mine," she said.

"I think so, too," Jack agreed. "The room isn't here. Charlie has a good idea about it being behind the stairs. Make sure you watch her. If you find the room call us right away. Don't go looking inside on your own."

"I heard that," I grumbled. "Make sure you watch me, Millie."

Millie grinned at my annoyance, the simple act lightening the mood. "I'll watch her, Jack. We're not far away. Remember that."

"You feel far away," Jack said as a rumble of thunder rolled. "We're going to spend another ten or twenty minutes checking every wall over here. After that we'll be over to help you. I think this storm is going to be a doozy, so keep your eyes open."

"Got it."

Millie fastened the radio to her belt and watched me run my hands over a specific spot for what felt like the fifth time. "Do you feel anything?"

"I don't know." I reached further. "Come here. I could be imagining it, but I almost believe there's a seam."

"Really?" Millie scurried over, placing her fingers where I indicated and widening her eyes as she traced the spot. "It's the size of a small door."

"You feel it, too?" For the first time since arriving a burst of hope rushed through me. "It's odd, right?"

"It is." Millie drew her eyebrows together as she lifted her flashlight and worked around the seam. "It's clearly here, yet … there aren't any hinges."

"No handle either," I noted. "I still think it's something."

"I think you're right."

"Stay there and watch. I'm going to see if I can find something by the counter over there to use as a tool."

"Okay." Millie kept her fingers busy tracing the seam as I picked my way through a pile of debris in the corner. There didn't look to be anything useful, but I wasn't ready to give up. "While you're looking, why don't you tell me about your nap with Jack?" Millie suggested.

I glanced over my shoulder and found her grinning. The simple act of finding something irregular on the wall clearly had her feeling better, too. "It was innocent," I replied, turning back to my search.

"The maid was cleaning Jack's room and he needed some sleep. I worried he was going to fall over or something because he was so tired. There was nothing to it."

"The sad thing is that I can't decide if you're trying to convince me of that or yourself. I hope it's me. If you're trying to convince yourself, you're even dumber than I thought."

"Excuse me?"

"Oh, Charlie, it wasn't meant as an insult," Millie said.

"It sounded like one."

"That's because you're emotionally worked up where Jack is concerned. You like him. The sooner you admit it, the better it will be for everybody."

"I most certainly do not like him. I mean ... he's a good security chief. He's a nice enough guy. I like him as a friend. But I don't like him any other way."

That was mostly the truth.

"I think you're trying to convince yourself of that, and it's a little annoying," Millie said. "I don't have time to mess with it now, but we're going to have a very long talk about you ignoring very blatant signs as soon as we find Chris."

Signs? Something about the way she said the word niggled at the back of my brain. "What signs?"

Millie didn't immediately answer. Apparently she decided to play coy.

"What signs?" I repeated, straightening. When I turned my attention to where Millie stood only moments before, she was gone. There was a gaping hole in the wall right behind the staircase. I could see only part of it from my vantage point, but it was clear that Millie found our door. "Seriously? I can't believe you found it."

I hurried over to poke my head inside, hoping beyond hope that I was about to find Millie and Chris in the middle of a well-deserved reunion. Instead, I found a dark room with zero lighting and no sign of either of my friends.

"Millie?"

No answer.

"Chris?"

Still nothing.

I reached for the radio affixed to my belt, my heart thudding, and pressed the button. I felt mildly numb as thunder roared hard enough to shake the building. "We found a door. Millie is missing. I … I have to go look for her now."

My delivery was flat, but it took everything I had to force out the words. My inner danger alarm pinged with nonstop warnings and my ears buzzed as if I was about to pass out. I knew turning back wasn't an option.

"What?" Jack's tone was incredulous. "You lost Millie?"

"We found a door. It's right behind the staircase. I … it's dark."

"You stay right where you are," Jack ordered. "We're on our way."

"I can't wait." I swallowed hard. "I have to look."

"You don't have to look." I could practically see Jack's panicked expression in my mind. "You wait right there for me. Do you hear me? You wait!"

"I can't. I have to go now. Whatever happens, Jack, don't think it's your fault. This is how it has to be."

"Charlie!"

My mind drifted to the vision, and I swallowed hard. Jack was here. I was here. The storm was here. Everything I saw in my head was about to converge.

"This is always how it was meant to be."

I said the words and then released the radio button. I briefly pressed my eyes shut, chastising myself for being an absolute idiot. Then I stepped inside the room and embraced what I was certain was my fate.

Every road was meant to lead here, after all.

27
TWENTY-SEVEN

$\mathcal{J}$ gave my eyes a moment to adjust to the gloom before stepping completely inside the room. My heart pounded, the thunder rolled and my knees felt weak as I slipped inside. It was small. That's the only thing I registered before the door swung shut behind me, plunging me into absolute darkness.

I reached for my belt, looking for the flashlight I thought I'd secured there as I tried to keep from panicking. It was gone, and it was only then that I realized I left it sitting on the floor next to the spot where I'd been looking for a tool to pry open the hidden door.

"Welcome to the party."

I jolted at the new voice, my blood running cold. I turned slowly, deliberately, and stared into the stale and murky darkness where the door used to be. "Zach?"

A flashlight switched on, illuminating a chilling face. Zach, his smile smug, offered me a haughty look.

"You figured it out, Charlie," Zach said in mock congratulations. "I'm so proud of you."

His tone told me pride wasn't the emotion rolling through him. I could feel what was coiling beneath his shiny veneer, and it most certainly wasn't pride. It was something I got a rare glimpse of a few times before, something he managed to shutter quickly. He didn't bother hiding it this time, though. That probably didn't bode well for me, because all I sensed was abject evil.

"I guess I should've realized it was you." I was proud I managed to speak without my voice shaking. "It only makes sense."

"Really? I thought I played the game with superb intellect."

"And I think you're not nearly as smart as you think you are," I shot back. "Where is Millie?"

"She's ... around."

"And Chris? Is he still alive?"

"My, my, my. You're full of questions, aren't you? I always knew you were a curious sort. Do you want to see your friends?"

"Is that a trick question?"

"No, but I don't really care how you answer," Zach said. "Move that way, please."

His voice was so pleasant it set my teeth on edge. I tracked the flashlight beam and realized there was a set of stairs in the room. They were back in the corner, extremely narrow and frightening to look at, but I had no doubt he expected me to climb them.

"And when we get up there ... what happens?"

"I guess you'll have to wait to find out."

"And what if I don't do what you ask?"

"You don't have a lot of options here, Charlie." Zach adopted a pragmatic tone. "If you want to be difficult I can kill you here. Do you want to die before you have all your precious answers?"

I licked my lips as I debated how to respond. Jack was coming. He'd be looking for us. He knew we were searching for a door behind the staircase, so that's where he would start looking. A cursory glance toward the door told me the hinges were only visible from this side. Jack would have to tear through the wall to get to us. I had no doubt he would – and would most likely succeed – but it would take time.

It was time we most likely didn't have.

"Fine." I stepped toward the stairs. "If Millie and Chris are hurt ..."

"You'll do what?" Zach was back to being haughty. "What exactly are you going to do, little girl? You don't have the power here. Quit pretending you do."

I understood why he felt that way. But there were a few things he didn't know. "You'd be surprised what I'm capable of."

"Oh, you've left me surprised on more than one occasion, Charlie. But I don't think it's for the reasons you think."

"I guess we'll have to wait and see, huh?"

"I guess we will."

I rested my hand on the knotty bannister. It was so weak it threatened to give way before I even started my ascent. "We have other people with us. You know that, right?"

"Yes, your precious Jack is with you," Zach said. "He's been with you since the start. Every single time I tried to isolate you, Jack has been there. Except for this time. You really shouldn't have separated from him, Charlie."

"And you really shouldn't underestimate me."

"You're the least of my worries." Zach took me by surprise when he groped at my waist. At first I thought he was trying to get a free feel. Then I realized he was confiscating the radio. "I don't think you'll be needing this." He stared at it disdainfully for a moment and then hurled it to the floor. "Jack won't be able to save you this time."

"I also wouldn't underestimate Jack. Of course, I don't need him to save me."

"Bold talk."

"I guess I'll have to follow it up with some action."

"That will be interesting." Zach's eyes were keen as they locked with mine. "You should see your face. Your expression is priceless. You had no idea it was me."

"That's not entirely true," I argued. "I knew there was something wrong with you. That story you told about the Chupacabra, it was a complete fabrication, wasn't it?"

"I was simply playing to my audience."

"You knew the body wasn't Dominic Sully the whole time. You had to play it cool. Did you steal his identification to buy yourself time?"

"Do you want to chat or get this over with?" Zach challenged. "I'm sick of chatting. That seems to be the only thing you do."

"You're not the first person to tell me that," I grumbled, tightening my grip on the railing. I could hear the storm raging outside, although it felt as if I was listening from a great distance. The inner sanctum of the hotel was well constructed and protected.

"Move, Charlie." Zach poked his finger into my ribs. "You won't like it if I have to move you."

"You won't like it regardless," I snapped. "You have no idea what's coming your way."

Zach snorted. "I like your fighting spirit."

"You won't in a second."

I started climbing, keeping one hand on the bannister as I gathered my magic. It took everything I had to keep from letting it loose before it was time. I managed to keep it together until I hit the top of the stairs, and then I cast a dark glance over my shoulder and locked gazes with Zach. "You can't win."

"It's funny, but I was just going to tell you the same thing."

"Yes, but you don't have all the information."

"And what information is that?"

"That I'm done playing around." I released the magic, bolting upward as it punched behind me. After gathering it for so long, pouring so much energy into the corral, it was like letting a herd of horses break free to stampede the town. Zach widened his eyes at the brief flash of light accompanying the power and then let loose a howl as the magic shoved him over the railing. He seemed to fall forever, and then I heard a sick thud when he hit the ground. I paused at the top long enough to listen, for the first time hoping my magic managed to do real harm to a person.

Zach groaned somewhere in the darkness. He was back on the first floor, I could tell that by the way the sound bounced around the room, but he wasn't dead. "What was that? I ... what was that?"

"Retribution."

I turned my back to him and felt for an opening at the top of the stairs, finally discovering a handle and pushing it. I expected to pop into the room on the second floor – the one from my vision – but instead I found myself in another small room. This one was dark save for a battery-operated lantern hanging from a hook on the wall. I was curious and confused, but not alone.

"Millie?" Relief coursed through me as I saw her resting on the floor with her back against the wall, Chris' head in her lap. She looked angry, blood running down the side of her face as she glared. "Are you okay?"

"They got you, too?" Millie was furious. "I'm sorry. I wanted to warn you, but he hit me before I could."

"Don't worry about him." I pressed my hand to Chris' forehead. He was far too warm. "We need to get him out of here."

"Yeah, but … ." Millie gave me an odd look. "What do you think is happening here?"

That was an interesting question. "What do you think is happening here?"

"This isn't over," Millie supplied.

"Of course not. But Chris has a fever. He might have internal injuries, for all we know. At least he's alive. We need to find a way out of this room. Jack should be downstairs. I called him on the radio before … well, before I got sucked into the same trap you did."

"But … ."

"But what?"

A shadow moved from the corner, giving way to a set of extensively detailed cowboy boots. I opened my mouth to issue a warning … or maybe even scream … but it was too late. Our new guest was already speaking.

"But what about me?"

I swiveled quickly, prepared to put up a fight. That inclination all but evaporated when I recognized the woman standing above me. "Naomi?" She'd been hidden in the shadows when I entered. I couldn't see her. Of course, to be fair, I didn't search very hard. I thought Zach was working alone. That was a stupid assumption.

"You're certainly quick today, huh?" Millie shot me a dumbfounded look. "Did you really think I'd be sitting here doing nothing if I were alone?"

I hadn't considered that. "Oh, well ... ." I pressed my lips together as I straightened, regaining my footing and positioning myself so I was between my friends and Naomi. For her part, the daughter of the rancher looked both frightened and annoyed. It was an interesting combination. "So ... what's up?"

"Oh, geez." Millie slapped her hand to her forehead. "I can't believe you're our saving grace."

I was having trouble wrapping my head around that, too. "I guess I'm behind, huh?"

Millie made a sarcastic face. "I guess so."

I absently rubbed my cheek to give myself a moment before focusing my full attention on Naomi. "And how are you involved in this ... cluster of crap?"

"How do you think?" Naomi drawled. "I want the silver."

"The long lost silver supposedly hidden somewhere in Hooper's Mill, right?"

Naomi let loose with a "well, duh" look. "What else?"

"But you're rich." I hated to point it out, but she apparently didn't realize it. "Why would you need a few lumps of silver when you're rich?"

"I'm not rich."

"I've seen your ranch. You're rich."

"No, you've seen the ranch where I live but have no way to sustain," Naomi clarified. "Do you have any idea how much money is owed on that ranch?"

"I believe you mentioned it, although you weren't nearly as aggravated at the time. Still ... why would you think the little bit of silver that's supposed to be here could help?"

"Because it's a lot more than a little bit of silver. It's millions of dollars' worth of silver and gold."

That sounded a bit fantastical. "You think there's more than a million dollars' worth of silver and gold here?"

"I know there is. My father did a ton of research. He was the leading expert on Hooper's Mill for a reason. Why do you think he wanted the property so badly?"

"Because his ancestor was one of the original owners."

"And he got swindled."

"Or he simply sold out because he saw the writing on the wall," I countered. "I think it probably became clear at a certain point that Hooper's Mill wouldn't survive. It was a boom town."

"And that means a lot of silver and gold moved through it."

"What gold? I've yet to hear anyone mention gold."

"My father said there was a great deal of gold moving through the town. He would know. He spent years researching the town's history. That's why he wanted it so badly."

"I get that, but I don't believe it." I chose my words carefully. "Why would Richard Hooper leave piles of gold and silver behind?"

"He had no way to transport it. He was going to come back, but he ran out of time."

"See, that's just it ... he didn't run out of time," I said. "He lived for another couple decades or so after he left Hooper's Mill. Why would he ignore that treasure?"

"No, he died a few months after," Naomi corrected. "My father told me."

"And yet a search we ran earlier in the week says that's not the case. He moved to a different state. He lived there for years. He had plenty of opportunity to return. He simply chose not to. That doesn't make sense if he really had a fortune hidden here."

"No ... my father told me."

"And by your own admission when I met you the first time – and essentially the second time, too – you said your father seemed to believe alternative facts when it came to the history of Hooper's Mill," I pointed out. "You said you learned differently on your own."

"I did. I learned that my father knew something no one else did."

"Right." She was clearly gone in the head a bit. There could be no other explanation. "So ... what? You and your father came out here searching for the silver and gold together?"

"We did that for years," Naomi confirmed. "We made a grid. We searched high and low. We never found anything. We didn't even find the door you walked through on the main floor. Speaking of that ... ." She broke off, wrinkling her nose. "Where's Zach?"

"I knocked him down the stairs. I think he's still alive, but I didn't wait around long enough to ask him any questions. You could go check on him if you're worried."

Naomi snorted, legitimately amused. "I'm good. If he's alive, he'll keep. If he's dead, there's nothing I can do about it, so why work myself into a lather?"

"Good question. I don't have an answer. Go back to your father, though. Did you kill him?"

"I didn't." Naomi shook her head. She didn't appear offended by the question. "That was Zach."

"And how did you and Zach hook up?"

"We went to high school together. We were friends back then. We met up again as adults and things changed a bit. We became involved."

"He listened to your father ranting and raving about Hooper's Mill and got it in his head to come looking for the silver himself," I surmised. "He wanted to get his hands on the loot before your father could."

"Yes, but it took a lot longer than he thought," Naomi said. "At first we came out looking once a week. We thought for sure we'd find the stockpile within a few days. But days turned into weeks. Then weeks turned into years."

"And it never occurred to you that the story was a myth?"

"No. Legends and myths all have some basis in fact."

"Tell that to the Loch Ness Monster," Millie muttered.

I flicked a gaze toward her and Chris, worry crowding my stomach thanks to our boss's pale features. I had to move this along. "So you and Zach were determined to get the silver for yourselves. Something must have changed."

"We were working separate from my father," Naomi explained. "I worked with my father, too. I didn't want him to get suspicious. I hoped we could find the money and take off without him knowing,

start a new life that didn't involve him complaining about the mortgages and how he might lose the ranch."

"But something else happened, didn't it? Dominic Sully stopped
talking about buying Hooper's Mill and actually moved on it. You
realized you were running out of time."

"I did. Zach and I upped our game. We started coming out here
five times a week."

"And dropping earrings, huh?"

"That is my earring," Naomi conceded. "If you have it on you, I'd
like it back. It's a family heirloom. I didn't even know I dropped it
until I returned home one day and realized it was gone. I had no idea
where to look for it ... so thank you."

"It's back at the hotel."

"I guess I'll have to pick it up there."

"Is that what you were trying to do this afternoon?" I asked, something occurring to me. "Were you looking for the earring? Is that why
you tried to get into my room?"

"That was also Zach. I'm too smart to be seen at that hotel. I mean
... you had no idea I was involved, and I'll bet you didn't completely
trust Zach. I wanted to keep my name out of things."

"Your father is dead," I reminded her. "How did that happen?"

"He discovered Zach and me out here one afternoon," Naomi
replied, her tone blasé. "He knew what we were doing. He claimed I
betrayed him, kicked up a fuss. He tried to hit Zach, but Zach
eluded him.

"Zach wasn't trying to kill him really," she continued. "Dad
wouldn't stop ranting and raving. My father had a knife and he
threatened to get it. Zach hit him over the head to shut him up.
Unfortunately, he realized too late that my father could have him
thrown in jail for that."

"And that's how you decided to make it look like the Chupacabra
was responsible."

Naomi shrugged. "It seemed as good a culprit as any. We looked up
the marks on the internet, and Zach copied them to the best of his
abilities. It was all we could think to do."

"But what about the exsanguination? How did you get the blood out of him?"

"You'll have to ask Zach about that. I didn't want any details. I just know it involved medical hoses and some sort of weird little pump. It was gross, and I've chosen not to dwell on it."

I couldn't blame her. I wouldn't want details on that either. "Still, this entire plan is a mess. How do you think you're going to get away with it?"

"It's not all that difficult," Naomi answered. "You're here looking for the Chupacabra. I think it's time to introduce you to it."

My stomach twisted at the maniacal look on her face. "How do you think you're going to manage that? We outnumber you."

"Yes, but this equalizes everything, doesn't it?" Naomi shook the gun for emphasis. "Now, who wants to die first?"

That was a question I wasn't ready to answer. We were out of time.

28

TWENTY-EIGHT

"So you're just going to shoot us and call it a day?"

I had no idea how I managed to remain calm despite the gun in Naomi's hand. I should have been panicking. I should have been crying or begging for my life. I should have at least been trying to reason with her.

Instead I was still. I was somehow detached even as the walls shook from the thunder and the rain thudded against the roof. I was tired of this ... of *all* of this. She had no idea who she was messing with, and I wasn't opposed to letting her find out if it meant protecting Millie and Chris.

"That's the plan," Naomi said brightly. "If you have another idea I'm happy to listen to it."

"I'm curious about how you think you'll get away with it." I opted to go on the offensive. "A gunshot isn't something you can simply gloss over. Your father was struck on the head and then Zach did ... something ... to make it look as if it was a Chupacabra attack.

"While questions are still being bandied about regarding his death, it was much easier for the medical examiner to write off one death as unexplained and possibly caused by a predator animal," I continued. "It won't be that easy when you add another three."

"Five," Naomi corrected. "I can't very well let your other two friends call for help, can I?"

Yup. She was definitely deranged. There was no other way to describe her flat affect.

"And how do you think you're going to get the jump on Jack? He's a trained military operative. He was like a crazy Navy SEAL or something." That was a blatant lie but she didn't need to know that.

"And mighty fine to look at, huh?" Naomi's eyes sparkled. "I've been considering trading Zach in for a newer model. What do you think? If I pitch my plan to Jack, will he help me find the silver and run away with me?"

"Not a chance," Millie hissed.

"Because of this one?" Naomi waved the gun in my face. "I couldn't decide if they were together when they stopped at my house to question me. There was a certain … vibe … between them.

"When Zach came back this afternoon and said he couldn't get in Charlie's room because Jack was sleeping in there with her – and he said something weird about a painting flying off the wall and attacking him, but I chalked that up to too much sun – I couldn't help but wonder," she continued. "Will Jack avenge your death?"

I shrugged. "Jack will do his job. That's what he does."

"That wasn't really an answer."

"It's the only answer I have," I said. "I'm more curious how you think you're going to manage to take everyone out now that Zach is out of commission. I mean … you've got three of us here and two people outside. Jack is trained. How are you going to get Zach out of here if he's hurt?"

"What makes you think I'm taking Zach with me?"

The way she asked the question chilled me to the bone. "You're going to kill Zach, too?"

"It makes sense since he's been running around with your group. Why take him with me if I don't have to?"

"He was still alive when I last saw him. Hurt, but still alive."

"That can be fixed."

She was unbelievably sick. Her eyes were vacant. I should've realized the two times I talked to her, yet I missed it both times. How? I fancied myself someone who reads people well. I read Zach perfectly, for crying out loud. Sure, I didn't understand exactly how evil he was, but I read him and knew to stay away.

With Naomi, I didn't recognize the evil coursing through her. I couldn't help but wonder if it was because I saw a grieving daughter when I looked at her – something I identified with – and didn't care to look any deeper. Had I at least tried we probably wouldn't be in this predicament.

"So you're going to shoot all of us and then what?"

Naomi's face was blank. "What do you mean?"

"No one is going to believe we were all killed by the Chupacabra … especially if we're full of bullets."

"I don't care about that," Naomi said. "I only care about finding the silver and running. I should be across the border before anyone discovers your bodies. I just need a few days. With all of you here … I'll get that."

"You won't." I felt bolder as I squared my shoulders. "We have people at the hotel."

"So I'll take care of them when they get here. It's only two women … and I owe one of them for making out with my boyfriend anyway."

"It's not only two women," I argued. "The only reason they stayed behind is because they're waiting for federal agents. The head of the Legacy Foundation – who just happens to be Chris' uncle – sent help. They're waiting to show the agents the way out here."

For the first time since I stumbled into the room, Naomi looked legitimately afraid. "You're making that up."

I shook my head. "It's true. They'll be here in a few hours."

"But … no!" Naomi pressed the heel of her hand to her forehead as she struggled to maintain control. "That can't be. I had it all planned out!"

For a brief moment I thought she would see reason and let us go. I would've let her flee to protect Millie and Chris. Local authorities or the feds could've picked her up later. I wouldn't have cared.

The way Naomi's expression twisted, however, told me she was leaning toward making things worse. She wasn't going to let reason get in the way of her plan. She was going to kill us. She thought that was her lone way out. That meant I had to stop her because I was the only one who could.

"You're lying." Naomi screeched as she shifted the gun in my direction. I reacted the only way I knew how – with magic.

"Son of a … !" I ducked my head and gathered my powers, focusing on the piece of wood in the corner and throwing it in Naomi's direction. Hard.

The woman sputtered as it hit her, smacking her face so hard that blood instantly appeared at the corner of her mouth. She looked dazed, confusion etched on her pretty features. She didn't relinquish the gun, though.

"What happened?" Naomi asked, her voice thick.

"I have no idea what you're talking about," I replied, flexing my fingers and using my powers to lift the board a second time. I knew this blow would take her down. "But you're not going to make it to Mexico. I can promise you that."

The board slammed into the back of Naomi's head, pitching her forward. I kept my eye on the gun so I could catch it, making sure it didn't fall to the ground and inadvertently go off.

I watched with dispassionate eyes as Naomi collapsed to the floor. She used her face as landing gear, which probably meant a broken nose, and the sound echoed when she bounced against the wood planks. I couldn't feel too bad about it. Sometimes karma does come through in the end.

I stared for a long moment and then shook myself out of my reverie, turning toward Millie and Chris with a purpose. "How is he?" I knelt next to them and pressed my fingers to Chris' neck. His pulse was rapid and thready. "Do you know what's wrong with him? Did they hit him on the head?"

"He's got a knot on the back of his head," Millie replied, her eyes lasers as they connected with mine. "I think he'll be okay as long as we get him help."

AMANDA M. LEE

I moved to stand. "Jack and Bernard are out there. I'll find a way out of this room and bring them to you."

"Yeah. That sounds good." Millie's expression was thoughtful. "Just one thing."

"And what's that?" I averted my gaze as I stared at anything but Millie's face.

"What did you just do?"

"I have no idea what you're talking about," I lied, wiping my palms on the front of my jeans. "I'll get help."

"But … ." Millie's expression was hard to read. She didn't look disgusted – or even fearful – as much as intrigued. We couldn't get into this now, and I was hopeful she would let it go in favor of fussing over Chris. If she let it go now, there was a chance she'd later think she imagined it.

"I'll find Jack."

I grabbed the lantern from the hook and ran it parallel to the wall, letting loose a low whistle when I managed to find an ancient door handle. I turned it, gave a hard tug, and heaved a relieved sigh when the door opened.

I was so thankful for light – even that which accompanied a storm – that I could do nothing but smile. We were going to make it after all. "Good. This is good. I'll leave the door open so I won't have any trouble finding my way back."

Millie arched a challenging eyebrow. "Can't you just use whatever magic you have to find your way back?"

Crap! She wasn't going to let it go. I should've seen that coming. "I think you're tired," I replied calmly. "You probably think you saw things you really didn't."

"Yeah, that's not what happened, Charlie."

I ignored her, moving the lantern to a spot on the floor to her right. "Wait here. I'll get help."

"Fine." Millie trailed her fingers through Chris' hair. "Hurry. I want him checked out by a doctor as soon as possible. He only opened his eyes long enough to see it was me and then blacked out again. I don't like it. He's too still. I want him back on his feet … like pronto."

248

"We both want that." I forced a smile before moving into the adjacent room, widening my eyes when I realized where I was. It was the bedroom where I'd found the earring. That made sense, of course. If Naomi and Zach discovered the hidden staircase, they would've spent a lot of time moving inside – looking for doors and hidden crevices – as they searched for their precious silver.

I moved to the window, my eyes widening at the torrent of rain. Zach mentioned something about storms being rare but fierce in the area on the day we met him, but I hadn't given it much thought. The street was practically flooded, and it was going to make getting help here all the more difficult.

I craned my neck looking for a hint of Jack or Bernard. The street was empty, signifying that both men were probably on the main floor. All I had to do was walk down the stairs and find them.

Then the unthinkable happened.

Jack appeared out of nowhere, racing to the center of the street and staring at the building façade. His eyes moved to mine, even though I was certain that he couldn't possibly see me in the darkness.

"Charlie!"

My stomach twisted as I recognized the scene from my vision. I should've known it wouldn't be that easy. It couldn't possibly be.

"Charlie!" Jack sounded anguished.

I opened my mouth to answer, hoping he'd hear me through the glass, and then I remembered the second part of my vision.

By the time I swiveled it was already too late. The shadow was moving ... and it was moving fast.

IT ONLY TOOK A moment to register the fact that Zach was about to throw himself on me. Somehow he'd made it up the steps and was coming after me.

I didn't think. I reacted. The magic inside of me spurted out, grabbing the flimsy armoire from the wall – it was really more a humiliated hunk of junk more than anything else at this point – and hurling it at Zach.

I didn't wait to see if it would work, instead hopping over the remnants of what used to be a bed and tearing into the hallway. I didn't know if Jack could hear me, but I bellowed anyway.

"Inside the hotel! Go to the second floor! It's Zach and Naomi!"

I didn't wait to see if Jack would barrel up the steps. Instead I scrambled into the hallway, turning toward the back staircase rather than the front when Zach's arm shot out to grab me.

I raced through the narrow space, launching myself at the dilapidated staircase everyone had said looked as if it was about to fall as I felt Zach's fingers brush against my hair. I stumbled as I attempted to descend without tripping forward, gripping the railing to keep my balance.

"I'm going to kill you," Zach hissed, his breath ragged. "I'm going to rip your heart out of your chest. You've ruined everything!"

"You ruined it yourself," I shot back, pounding down the steps. I heard Jack's voice in the hotel as he yelled my name. He was heading up while I was going down, racing into a dark world where I had no idea what to expect. At least he would find Millie and Chris. That was something, right?

"Come here, you … ." Zach didn't get a chance to finish whatever hateful thing he was about to say because the stair I landed on gave way at that exact moment.

It was like a cascade of dominoes after that. Once the first step went, the rest followed, one step failing right after the other as everything attached to the stairwell railing tumbled. I was no longer running, instead falling into a gloomy darkness. I screamed when I realized what was happening, but there was nothing I could do to stop it.

I fell for what felt like forever, hitting the floor below hard enough to knock the wind out of me. I did my best to protect my face from falling debris, grunting when Zach landed on top of me.

He didn't move, which was a blessing, but I was in so much pain I couldn't muster the strength to push him off my back. My head felt as if a cloud was invading, pain exploding through my temples. I hit something going down, and my hip throbbed.

Even in my confused state I managed to register movement to my left. Only a sliver of light filtered through the dust and darkness, coming from the second floor and the window at the top of the stairs as the storm continued to barrel down.

I didn't know what to expect. Zach was on top of me, dead or unconscious, I couldn't say. It could be Naomi, I reasoned. She might've regained consciousness and headed in this direction to cut me off. If it was her, I didn't have the strength to fight her off a second time.

The being that moved into the light, though, wasn't human. I registered four feet – more like paws really – and red eyes as I struggled to hold onto consciousness. My mouth dropped open when I saw ridges on the creature's back, and I cringed when it emitted a high-pitched screech.

The Chupacabra.

It couldn't be, and yet … it was.

"Holy smokes!"

I didn't know what else to say as darkness overwhelmed my mind. The last thing I heard were claws clacking against wood … and then I knew Jack was close because I felt him before he made a sound.

"Charlie!"

Jack was here, which meant I was safe. That simple knowledge allowed me to let go and embrace utter blackness.

"WAKE UP! YOU WAKE up right now!"

Jack's voice traveled a long distance to pierce through the haze surrounding my brain. I struggled to open my eyes, and when I did, I found myself resting on Jack's lap as he cradled me. The events of the past hour ran through my head at a fantastic rate as I attempted to make my tongue work.

"There you are," Jack choked, smoothing my hair. "I thought maybe you weren't going to wake up."

I had no idea what to say, so I went with the obvious. "I saw the Chupacabra."

Jack didn't look bothered by the statement. "Is that what you're calling Zach? He's dead, by the way. He broke his neck on the way down. I was worried you'd done the same."

"Not Zach." Still, it was a relief to know he was gone. "I saw it. It was here. It ... looked at me."

"Okay." Jack stroked the back of my head. "Okay. I believe you."

I wasn't sure he spoke the truth, but I was in too much pain to argue. "My back hurts."

"I'll bet everything is going to hurt once you're not in shock. You took a long, hard fall. What were you thinking going down the back steps?"

"He cut me off from the front. Plus ... I didn't want to lead him back to Millie and Chris. Are they okay?"

"Bernard is with them. Help is on the way. The roads are going to be rough because of the storm, but Myron will find a way to get here."

"That's good."

I was so tired that keeping my eyes open was becoming a terrific struggle. "Jack, I really did see the Chupacabra. It was right in this room. I swear it."

"Okay, honey. It's okay."

"It was here. I think this room is its den."

"I'm sure you're right."

Now he was just placating me. "It was Zach and Naomi all along. I didn't see it."

"None of us did. How could you expect to see that?"

"I knew there was something wrong with Zach."

"I think that was obvious to all of us."

"Naomi fooled me." I swallowed hard, my throat dry. "I saw myself when I looked at her. I didn't see anything else."

"You're not to blame. It's okay. Everyone is going to be okay. I need you to hold on until the paramedics get here. Bernard called. They're on their way."

"That's good. I think I'm going to pass out again."

"I really wish you wouldn't," Jack argued. "For once, I think it would be smart for you to keep talking. Can do that for me?"

"Probably not."

"We can talk about the Chupacabra."

Well, that was an interesting offer. "It had ridges on its back and red eyes. It made a screeching sound."

Jack stilled. "That wasn't you?"

"What?"

"That screeching sound wasn't you?"

I shook my head. "It was the Chupacabra. It left when I heard your voice."

"Well … hmm."

"You still don't believe, do you?"

"I don't know. I believe in you. Tell me about the Chupacabra and we'll see what I believe when you're done. How does that sound?"

Because he needed it, I did as he asked. It was the least I could do.

29

TWENTY-NINE

I woke in the hospital shortly before midnight. I'd managed to hang on until Jack heard sirens, but after that it was too much for me. I had no idea how I managed to get from the back room of the hotel into the ambulance, but apparently I did … and I was still alive.

I flicked my eyes to the monitor next to the bed. It was quiet. I didn't know much about vitals, but mine looked great. They were hopping without making the display angry, so that had to be good. At least that's what I told myself.

I shifted in the bed, jolting when I saw Jack sitting in a nearby chair watching me. The lights were dimmed, and I almost missed him save for his glittering eyes.

"Welcome back."

"Thanks." My voice was raspy and I was ravenously thirsty as I tried to struggle to a sitting position.

Jack hopped to his feet, propping a pillow behind my back as I settled. "Do you want some water?"

I nodded, grateful, and watched him pour a glass from the pitcher on the nightstand. He popped a straw in it and held the glass to my face.

"Slowly," he prodded. "Don't make yourself sick."

I was so dry his admonishment went largely ignored, and I gulped the entire glass before stopping to gasp. Jack wordlessly filled it again, and this time I drank slowly. Finally, when I was satiated, Jack returned the glass to the nightstand.

"What happened?"

Jack cocked an eyebrow. "You don't remember?"

"I remember," I replied. "I mean after. You said Zach was dead. What about Naomi?"

"She's alive, although she's got a concussion," Jack answered. "I can't believe you got the jump on her and smacked her in the head with a board. That was brave ... and a bit stupid."

I ignored the dig as I focused on the other part. Is that what Millie told him? I guess I shouldn't have been surprised. It wasn't as if she could tell them the truth. Still, she protected me. I wasn't sure what to make of it. "I was running on instinct."

"Well, you're alive, so I'd say your instincts served you well." Jack picked at the nubs on my blanket. "Naomi admitted everything to the police. She blamed all the terrible stuff – her father's murder, the attack on Chris, the dead coyote outside your hotel room – on Zach, but she'll be going away for life anyway."

"She said the same thing to me. I can't decide if I believe it or not. I do think Naomi was smart enough to steer clear of the hotel. I think that means the coyote is definitely on Zach."

"Naomi said he tried to get into your room another time. It was the night you came home drunk."

"Why? That was before I found the earring."

"I have no idea, but I don't like the scenarios I've been coming up with," Jack said. "It doesn't matter now. He's dead."

"How is Laura taking it?"

"How does Laura take anything? She's angry and blaming everyone else."

"Well ... she's probably just embarrassed," I said after a moment. "I know I'd be jealous if I made out with a sociopath. Still, Naomi's story doesn't make much sense. Zach was making out with Laura when

Chris went missing. She has to be the one who went after him. Do we know how that happened?"

"No, but that's a very good point. I hadn't thought of that. I'll make sure to point it out to the cops."

"And what about Chris?"

"He's dehydrated and has a concussion of his own," Jack replied. "They drugged him so he'd remain docile. The doctors are flushing his system. He's expected to make a full recovery, but it's doubtful he'll wake up before morning. Hannah is with him."

"And Myron? Did he ever show up?"

"He did. He's with Millie."

That was surprising. "What about Bernard?"

Jack smirked. "I believe they're sharing nursing duties. Millie has a hand fracture, but is otherwise fine. By the way, whatever you think you know about Bernard and Millie, forget it. That's their business."

"Okay." I'd let it go ... for now. "Did Naomi tell her story about the silver and gold?"

"Yes, and the cops think she's completely full of crap. There was never any gold in that area to their knowledge, and whatever silver was found wouldn't be nearly the windfall that Naomi seemed to think."

"Part of me feels bad for her," I admitted. "Her father raised her on lies and she couldn't quite seem to break away from them. She thought he was telling the truth, and that's ultimately what got him killed."

"Yeah, well, Hannah talked to the medical examiner while we were waiting on news about you guys," Jack explained. "The medical examiner mentioned that they noticed the blow to Morrison's head, but they thought it was because he fell while being attacked. They're going back over their notes again."

"And how did Zach get all the blood out of Morrison?"

"I have no idea, and I don't care to find out."

He wasn't the only one. "So ... that's it, right? The mystery is solved. Morrison was killed and the Chupacabra is real."

Jack shifted on his chair. "I thought maybe you might have thought better about what you said to me right before you passed out," he hedged. "You took your own blow to the head, after all."

Of course he would hope for that. He didn't want me to suffer from a bout of crazy after the day we had. But I was more certain than ever that what I saw was real.

"It was really there, Jack."

Jack blinked several times before responding. "Then I believe you."

"Really?" I couldn't help being dubious. "Since when do you believe in things like that?"

"Since you put your life on the line to save us all. I think you deserve a little faith."

"That's quite possibly the nicest thing you've ever said to me."

Jack smirked. "Don't let it go to your head." He exhaled heavily as he stretched out his legs and got more comfortable on the chair. "It's late. You need your rest. We're hopefully packing up and getting out of here tomorrow. It all depends on what Chris' doctors say. You should sleep now."

"What about you? Are you going back to the hotel?"

"No. I'm watching our hero to make sure she's safe."

The simple statement warmed my heart even as it made me feel like a bit of a goof. "I'm no longer in danger."

"And yet I can't forget the feeling I had while racing through the street of a western ghost town to find you. In fact … ." Jack broke off, his expression unreadable.

"What?"

"It's weird, but while I was out there I had a tremendous case of déjà vu," he said. "It was like I was remembering something from a dream."

My heart skipped a beat. It wasn't possible, was it? "What?"

"I don't know. I think it was a conversation between you and me. It's hard for me to wrap my head around. I swear you told me that if you went missing that you would be in the room where Zach attacked you.

"By the way, I have no idea how you tipped over that armoire and shoved it against him, but that was a good move because it slowed him down," he continued. "You made a lot of good moves today. Millie said you knocked Zach down the stairs, hit Naomi in the head with a board and somehow managed to smack Zach around with an armoire. I'd say you had a full day."

He was glossing over the dream as if it were simply an odd occurrence. I knew better. "Well ... I'm nothing if not resourceful."

"There is that." Jack's grin was weary. "You really need your sleep, Charlie. I'm tired, too. If you're a good girl and get your rest I promise to make sure you get something other than barbecue before we leave tomorrow."

Oddly enough, that was the best offer I'd had all day. "Olive Garden?"

Jack snorted. "I think I can manage that ... or at least something similar."

"You're on." I slouched lower on my pillow and let my eyes drift shut. "I really did see the Chupacabra, Jack. I swear it."

"Then I think you'll be Chris' favorite person when he wakes up. Make sure I'm there when you tell him."

"Sounds good." I rolled to my side and hugged the pillow. "Jack?"

"Ugh. You can't be quiet even when you have a head injury, can you?"

"You said I was the hero. Heroes get to talk as much as they want."

"Fair enough."

"I just wanted to say something."

"I'm listening." Jack sounded as tired as I felt, but he kept his eyes open.

"I knew you would find me. I think that's why I wasn't afraid."

"I'm worried that you weren't afraid, because you've got a head like a rock. But I'll take the other option right now, because it makes me feel better," Jack said. "Now ... sleep."

"Okay." I pressed my eyes shut. "I still knew you'd find me ... and the Chupacabra is definitely real."

"Oh, geez! Someone shoot me now."

"Not until after I've had my Olive Garden."

"Deal."